Sarah Meyrick studied Classics at Cambridge and Social Anthropology at Oxford, which gave her a fascination for the stories people tell and the worlds they inhabit. She has worked variously as a journalist, editor and PR professional. Alongside her day job, she is Director of the Bloxham Festival of Faith and Literature. Her first novel – *Knowing Anna* (also published by Marylebone House) – was long listed for Not the Booker Prize 2016. Sarah lives in Oxfordshire with her husband. For more information, see www.sarahmeyrick.co.uk.

The Restless Wave

SARAH MEYRICK

First published in Great Britain in 2019

Marylebone House
36 Causton Street
London SW1P 4ST
www.marylebonehousebooks.co.uk

British Library Cataloguing-in-Publication Data
A catalogue record for this book is available from the British Library

ISBN 978–1–910674–54–3
eBook ISBN 978–1–910674–55–0

Typeset by Fakenham Prepress Solutions, Fakenham, Norfolk NR21 8NL
First printed in Great Britain by Ashford Colour Press
Subsequently digitally printed in Great Britain

eBook by Fakenham Prepress Solutions, Fakenham, Norfolk NR21 8NL

Produced on paper from sustainable forests

In memory of two family members who took part in the extraordinary feat that was D-Day:
Surgeon Commander Jack Carlton, Royal Navy
(1907–1979)
Major John Hanson-Lawson, Sherwood Rangers Yeomanry
(1914–1978)

Prologue
6 June 1944

Afterwards, it is hard to recall the departure with any sense of continuity. Edward can only conjure a kaleidoscope of crystal-clear but disconnected images. The swarming army of armoured ants, all heading for embarkation points along the south coast. The small boy in short trousers who grins from ear to ear and holds up his hand in a Churchillian V-sign, before being dragged away by his harried mother. The precipitous plummet in morale, when they hear that the operation has been put off for twenty-four hours because of the weather. The news sends Fairbairn into a fearful temper, and he smokes cigarette after cigarette with barely a pause for breath.

The crossing, in contrast, is all too vivid. At first, everyone is simply awed into silence by the sight of the Channel, alive, infested with vessels of every description. Supply ships, destroyers, torpedo boats, assault craft, flotillas, stretching as far as the eye can see. Thousands and thousands of craft of all classes, all intent on the same purpose. Somewhere in the distance, he hears the plaintive sound of the bagpipes. 'The Road to the Isles' floats eerily across the water. Four years after the humiliation at Dunkirk, the British are sailing back to France, the torch-bearers of liberation. It is an honour to be part of this great enterprise. An exodus of mighty Israelites crossing the Red Sea for the promised land. A surge of sap rises in Edward's heart; he thinks of King Henry V on the eve of Agincourt. 'Once more unto the breach, dear friends, once more . . .' If ever there's a time to 'stiffen the sinews, summon up the blood', this is it. He has to stop himself crying out loud, 'God for Harry, England, and Saint George!'

But then the Rhino craft, loaded to the gunnels with jeeps, lorries, ambulances and men, begins to pitch and roll in the choppy sea. Pulled by a freighter, the barge is built of steel pontoons and as un-streamlined as it is possible to be. The weather may have improved sufficiently for the operation to go ahead, but they are still tossed about like flotsam on the tide. They are drenched in spray; Edward's open prayer book is soaked. The surface of the craft becomes slick with seawater and vomit. He launches into an impromptu rendition of the old Navy hymn:

> Eternal Father, strong to save,
> Whose arm hath bound the restless wave.
> Who bidd'st the mighty ocean deep
> Its own appointed limits keep . . .

Men in life jackets and steel helmets crowd around him and join in, tentatively at first, and then with more confidence. By the time they reach the chorus, they are almost bellowing it out:

> Oh, hear us when we cry to thee,
> For those in peril on the sea!

The craft lurches on the swell. The acrid smell of sick and diesel catches at the back of his throat, yet Edward is utterly, unnaturally calm. It is the hour for which he was born. He thinks of his father and, inevitably, Kipling's poem comes into his head.

> If you can keep your head when all about you
> Are losing theirs and blaming it on you,
> If you can trust yourself when all men doubt you,
> But make allowance for their doubting too . . .

He is a small boy, sitting on his father's lap. "'Yours is the Earth and everything that's in it'," reads Papa. Then all at once, it is as if the earth and everything in it has exploded. Overhead, they

2

hear their bombers pounding the coastline. Alongside, there is gunfire from battleships, destroyers and cruisers. Then, a sudden uncanny silence, an orchestrated pause to allow the troops to land. In the few seconds' respite, it is as if all Edward's senses are on overdrive. He notes that the sun is coming up. That on the headland, the gorse is a blaze of yellow. He can just make out a church tower in the middle distance. Has he seen this on the map? He wonders if Monsieur le Curé is at his morning prayers, yet even as he forms the thought, he remembers that it is barely dawn. A seagull flies across the front of the boat, oblivious of the mighty armada below.

And then, a hailstorm of enemy machine-gun fire rains down on them. All hell breaks loose as the Germans unleash the full force of their artillery, rockets and mortars. A shell clips the very edge of the landing craft and the barge lurches into a sandbar and sticks fast. They have come to rest some distance from the shore and the chances of a dry landing are evaporating. Looking down to assess the depth of the water, Edward sees bodies – one, three, five, ten – bobbing up and down in the water. 'Oh, hear us when we cry to thee for those in peril on the sea.' One khaki figure, carried on a current, strikes the metal side with some force and, as the body bounces away into the whorling water, Edward notices that it is a headless torso. *If you can keep your head, keep your head, keep your head,* he thinks. *Poor bastard! 'Earth to earth, ashes to ashes, dust to dust: in sure and certain hope of the resurrection to eternal life, through our Lord Jesus Christ.'*

He hears Johnson in noisy argument with the CO; it is clear that they are significantly adrift from their target. Then they are unloading, disgorging men and equipment along the seashore. The doors open and a mob of soldiers topple into the sea and are soaked. Edward keeps his balance, but only just; he is wet, and his uniform stiffens horribly into cardboard as he staggers through the waves. Utter chaos ensues as they run, then crawl, up the shore, heavy with equipment. The beach is already jammed with men and vehicles. Mines explode; there is a sharp smell of gunpowder, fluorescent flashes of fire. Bullets buzz around his head like angry bees, the noise ringing in his ears to the exclusion of all else. He sees Fairbairn stumble, Stevens fall. Yet there is nothing to do, nothing to do but go forward, forward, forward, dragging himself in the direction of the rendezvous.

1
Nell, April 2016

Nell was struggling to keep her cool. When she met Mike Emory for the first time last month, she suspected he was a bore, but today he seemed to be speaking pure gobbledegook.

'The fact of the matter is, Nell, that we need a paradigm shift here. If you don't take your IT provision to the next level and pronto, Ofsted will be down on you like a ton of bricks. The question is, is your current system fit for purpose going forward?' He looked round the room for support. 'Before we get granular, can I suggest a bit of blue-sky thinking here? Why don't we run a few ideas up the flagpole?'

The nods of agreement from her colleagues made Nell wonder fleetingly if she was missing something. Perhaps she wasn't taking the school's IT needs seriously enough. Certainly Fiona, her deputy, seemed very impressed by Mike. Now he was suggesting that his company would offer a game-changing tailor-made solution designed to deliver optimal performance.

'We're all about giving one hundred and ten per cent, Nell,' he said. 'We see ourselves as change agents. Results-driven. As I always say, if it's not working for you, it's not working for us. Value-added is our middle name, Nell.'

If he used her name gratuitously once more, she'd scream. Which would be embarrassing in front of two colleagues and Kevin Letts, the school governor who'd been co-opted on to the IT subcommittee on the grounds that he worked at Curry's. She was gripping the pencil in her hand so tightly that her fingertips had turned white, and she was in danger of starting to chew the end. Something she never did, and an absolute no-no in her classroom.

She cleared her throat and stood up, smoothing her skirt. 'I do apologize, Mike. I really need to be somewhere else. You'll have to excuse me. I'll leave you in Fiona's capable hands. I'd be happy to look at your proposal when there's a bit more detail to discuss, but you should know that our budgets are very tight indeed. We're having to make difficult decisions about our spending.'

Mike leapt up to shake her hand. 'Of course, Nell, of course. Busy woman! We can touch base again when we've got our ducks in a row. I'll action that and ping you an email.'

Nell made her way to her office via the staffroom, where she made a cup of tea. What a crashing waste of time. Where did people learn to speak like that? Was there some sort of training in business-speak cliché or did you just absorb it by osmosis if you hung about in the wrong crowd? Perhaps there should be a degree course in jargon, along with golf studies and all the other ridiculous non-subjects you could study these days.

'Somewhere else' was only a slight bending of the truth. She still had a heap of paperwork to go through before the end of the day. Or perhaps that should be 'close of play'? Diane, the school secretary, had left a neat pile on her desk, covered with luminous sticky notes, colour-coded according to an esoteric system of priority Nell was yet to understand. And no doubt emails galore would have been 'pinging' into her inbox since she last checked it at lunchtime. She wondered idly if there was a market for some kind of cliché bingo game. She pictured colourful cards, jaunty graphics and boxes to tick when anyone 'pushed an envelope' or 'thought outside the box'.

Kevin was quiet, she thought. *He looked like a startled rabbit.* It was hard to get parent governors at St Sebastian's and it had taken months of encouragement to persuade him to put himself forward. Mind you, when Mike was in full flow, there wasn't much space for anyone else to contribute. *Blame the chair*, she thought. *Note to self: I should have managed him better. That's what I'm here for.*

Actually, that wasn't what she was here for. She was here because she had wanted to be a teacher for almost as long as she could remember. She was heart-and-soul committed to the children in her care; she, if anyone, knew what a difference a good teacher could make. IT might be important – essential these days, obviously – but it was only a tool to deliver the things that really mattered. Like learning and discipline and life chances, along with a healthy dose of fun and kindness.

And in a catchment area like St Seb's, which served one of the most deprived areas of Oxford, of the country even, school could inject the one bit of stability and calm during the day. Some order into the chaos of a childhood lived in deprivation and poverty. It might be a bit of a hobby horse – OK, an obsession – but she was convinced children thrived on routine and structure and knowing what was what. The satisfaction, the emotional rewards of teaching were enormous. On a good day she felt she had the keys to a magic kingdom in her hands. On a bad one, she feared she would drown under the weight of the insatiable demands of government targets and the intractable problems of the children in her charge.

She was here now, in this particular office, because the head, Rob Thomas, had gone off on long-term sick leave due to stress halfway through last term, the day after Ofsted placed St Seb's in Special Measures. As deputy head, she'd been asked to step up and was now acting head. Anyone outside the system might see that as a golden opportunity for the understudy to shine. Anyone inside the system knew that 'poisoned chalice' was a better description. The reality was that her workload had doubled – at least – overnight. She'd managed to offload some of her responsibilities as deputy to Fiona, but she was still in the classroom for half the time. Of course, she loved the teaching – it was her lifeblood – but she was sinking under the pressures of acting headship. It was now obvious that the pre-inspection School Evaluation Form had been horribly out of kilter with the reality. A bit of digging had thrown up serious questions about the way the welcome injection of Pupil Premium funding had been spent and she was the one left clearing up the mess.

She'd hoped that Rob would be back for the summer term, but she heard this morning that he'd been signed off for another month. Nell was going to be the one facing constant HMI visits to check on progress. There was every indication that they were going to be fast-tracked into becoming an academy, a move to which at least half the staff and who knows how many parents were adamantly opposed. Surely they were going to have to call in reinforcements now? Pull in a supply teacher to help plug the gap?

Nell sighed as she waited for her laptop to wake up. Why was it so *slow*? Underinvestment in IT, no doubt. ('A poor worker blames her tools,' tutted her mother with a shake of her head.) But how did you decide between spending tens of thousands of pounds on IT or repairing that leaky roof on the Year 6 temporary classrooms, which as their name suggests were never meant to be permanent anyway, or taking on extra learning support staff? Particularly when Rachel Wilkes reported increasing numbers of children arriving in Reception barely able to respond to their own name, let alone knowing any of their phonemes. Half of them still needed help getting dressed, which meant PE lessons were a bit of a joke, and a good number couldn't sit still for more than about three minutes at a time. *I'll give you paradigm shift*, she thought.

Oh God! She was tired and it wasn't even the first day of term. Today had been an INSET day. The children arrived back tomorrow. Usually, her heart would be singing at the thought of all those bright faces. Now she just felt weary. She hadn't been sleeping well; she really must have an early night. At least the term started on a Thursday, so they would be eased in with a two-day week. Settling the children back to work after the holidays, even a short one like the Easter break, was always an effort. Some of the more vulnerable kids really struggled with routine after the anarchy of home. It would help if she had had a real break over Easter, rather than spending most of it

8

on the School Improvement Plan. Ah well. Best-laid plans. At last, the laptop fired into action. Nell opened her inbox and set to work.

By Friday night she was feeling both better and worse. The first day of term had started well; she arrived at school at 7 a.m. feeling much more positive after a good night's sleep. She met Fiona on the doorstep.

'Sorry to bail out on you last night,' she said, with a wry smile. 'Blessed paperwork.'

'Blessed Mike, more like,' said Fiona. 'To be fair, he calmed down a bit after you'd gone. I think he was trying to impress you.'

'Well, he called that one wrong! But look, we'll talk again when you're further on. And thanks . . . I do appreciate it.'

Once the children arrived, Nell was relieved to feel the familiar lift to her spirits. The sun was shining and the kids were smiling. The job was demanding, but manageable. And by the end of the day, staff and children were back in the swing of things. She watched them file into the hall for assembly, consulted her notes and made sure she could pick out the three new children, whom she wanted to welcome. She took pride in knowing every one of the 315 pupils by name. She allowed herself a brief moment of satisfaction that this was *her* school, for the moment at least. By hook or by crook she would do well by these children, whatever it took.

Nell's optimism lasted until approximately 3.20 the next afternoon when a familiar figure barged her way past Diane and into Nell's office. Kelly Meacher was vast, shapeless and filled the room. She brought with her the smell of cigarette smoke, cheap perfume and body odour. Her hair – poorly dyed with two inches of roots showing – was pulled off her face in a tight ponytail. Her fleshy arm wobbled as she shook her fist at Nell.

'Ms Meacher, what seems to be the problem? Would you like to sit down?' Nell kept her voice as calm as she could. It was always an effort not to treat angry parents like naughty children.

9

'No, I fucking wouldn't!'

'*Please*. How can I help?' *How indeed?* thought Nell. Kelly Meacher had four children at St Sebastian's, the youngest of whom joined Reception yesterday. There was at least one more child at home, and it looked as if she might be pregnant again, but you could never be quite sure until she turned up in the playground with a pram. Somehow, though as far as Nell knew she lived on benefits, Kelly had a new pram for each baby.

'You bloody teachers! You disrespect my kids, just because I live up the Binks Estate!'

'I'm sorry?' said Nell. 'Is this something to do with Kar–ian? Mrs Wilkes seems to think she's settling in well.'

'There you go! *Carrie-Anne!* That's not how you say 'er name, is it?'

'Isn't it? I'm sorry, I didn't—'

'I know you bloody didn't! And nor did that cow Mizz Wilkes, neither. It's *Kardashian*, innit? What do you think the fucking dash in the middle's for?'

Nell struggled to keep a straight face. The older Meacher children were called Kraig, Kyle and Krystal. Kardashian was a new one on her, although the celebrity surname was familiar. 'Oh! I thought it was a hyphen,' she said. Kelly threw her a murderous look. Did she think Nell was being sarcastic? Nell stood up, to signal the end of the conversation. 'I appreciate you putting us straight on that, Ms Meacher,' she said briskly. 'I'll make sure Mrs Wilkes knows. And in the meantime, please accept my apologies for the misunderstanding.'

Kelly glowered at her. She looked as if she was about to say something more, but perhaps thinking better of it, she turned and left the room. A faint whiff of sweat and righteous anger lingered and Nell opened the window before collapsing into her chair with relief. She'd give herself a moment to recover before going in search of Rachel.

By the time Nell arrived home that night, the episode with Kelly Meacher was beginning to feel slightly less entertaining. It didn't help that she'd fought to find a parking space and had to carry a big box of files halfway down the road to her flat. When she unlocked the door into the shared hall, it was late and she was hungry and fed up. It was no picnic, being a teacher, let alone acting head of a school in Special Measures, and she could really do without aggressive parents. Her first head when she was an NQT always said that there was no such thing as difficult kids, only difficult mums and dads. He had a point.

She climbed the stairs and opened her own door. 'Honey, I'm home!' she called out before she could stop herself. *Must stop doing that*, she thought. What had started out as a silly joke between herself and Mark had become a defence mechanism. Although she told herself it was sensible – better, surely, that no one guessed she was on her own, and therefore vulnerable, though who knew whether anyone in the flats was fooled – she suspected the daily lie was not exactly helping her to move on. And since last week's shock, she'd decided that moving on could not be delayed another moment.

She opened the fridge and reached for the cold bottle of Pinot Grigio that was her Friday treat. Even at her most miserable, she refused to drink on a school night, but Friday gave her the green light. She poured herself a large glass, enjoying the welcome sight of the cold pale green wine in her favourite wine glass. Music on, while she found something for supper. Adele, perhaps. Always balm for the broken-hearted. And comfort food: fresh pasta, maybe, with Parmesan and an avocado and rocket salad. Ice cream for pudding. She'd done her usual big pre-term shop, which meant the freezer was full of possibilities.

It was eleven months and a day since he had left. The date was indelibly marked in her brain because Mark chose her fortieth birthday to inform her that, on reflection, he didn't see a future with her and, actually, he didn't want children, thank you very much, couldn't really see himself as a father. No matter that they'd talked about marriage and family on and off over the past four and a half years. No matter that hitting forty was a milestone for many people, and a bit of a watershed if you happened to be a woman and childless. No matter that he broke the news over dinner at Luigi's, presumably because he was counting on her being far too controlled to make a scene in public. He knew, he *knew* that she wanted children. She'd never made a secret of it. Fuck's sake, why did he think she worked with kids all day long? And now she'd lost the chance.

She really had been getting over it. From the outset – well, not quite the outset; there was the delicious, unexpected moment when she found herself pouring a glass of red wine all over his new shirt in the bistro – she had refused to give in to self-pity. She told herself that he was a loser and didn't deserve her. She would throw herself into work, push herself harder than ever. Not allow herself to dwell on what might have been. And it was almost working. She could contemplate her forty-first birthday with something approaching equanimity. She'd be busy at school that day, anyway; she'd take a cake in to share at break-time, but there'd be no need to make a particular song and dance about it.

But in the holidays . . . She drained the pasta, stirred in some fresh pesto and took another swig of wine. In the holidays she'd only been doing what she always did. She took the bus into the city and went to the Ashmolean because that was one of her beginning-of-the-holidays treats. Her friend Fran had cried off at the last minute – a childcare crisis, but she did have two under-fives – which was a great shame because Nell was looking forward to a good catch-up, but she didn't see why that should stop her seeing the Andy Warhol exhibition. And she'd been enjoying herself: there were more than a hundred works on display and, as well as the more iconic, familiar material, a lot of the items on show were less well known and revealed a whole new side to the artist's character.

Then all of a sudden, she saw them. Mark – and a petite woman with long, blonde hair. His new girlfriend, presumably. Fran's partner, Pete, still played Sunday league football with Mark, so she'd heard he was seeing someone. The two had their backs to her, which gave Nell a moment to watch unobserved. Mark's arm was lightly draped over the woman's shoulder. He leaned in to tell her something. *Bloody cheek,* she thought. *To bring her here! When Mark isn't even interested in art and only ever came because it was* my *thing!* At that moment, the woman laughed and turned slightly towards him, so Nell could see her face. *Pretty*, she thought. *And young. Much younger than me.* And then she saw, unmistakably, a bump. The woman reached out for Mark's hand and guided it to her pregnant belly. Perhaps the baby had kicked and they were sharing the moment.

Nell turned her back and walked out of the exhibition, down the stairs and out into Beaumont Street, where it had started to rain, and she retched into a gutter. She wiped her face on the back of her hand and set off on foot, blindly at first, and then up the High Street, down the Cowley Road and all the way home. She arrived home an hour or so later, wet through and shivering, had a hot bath and went straight to bed, where she stayed for the best part of twenty-four hours. Later she checked Facebook – till now she'd been so good about keeping her distance, she'd signed up to Facebook's 'take a break' settings and everything – and discovered that the woman was called Ellie. And that she and Mark had announced their engagement on Valentine's Day.

A fortnight later, she was still shaken. *Bastard Mark, whose new girlfriend – or should I say fiancée – even almost has my name. Bastard, bastard Mark, who couldn't really see himself as a father*, she thought as she finished her second glass. *And more fool me for putting up with him as long as I did.*

She switched on her laptop and logged on to Facebook. She knew what she needed to know now, so she would finally 'unfriend' bloody Mark and block all updates. That way she didn't have to have anything more to do with him. Ever. It was Friday night and she'd forget about Kelly Meacher and Ofsted and the spreadsheets she was supposed to be working on. She'd see what Fran was up to this weekend. See if anyone else was planning to do the Park Run tomorrow; she really ought to as she'd skipped the gym tonight. She might check the cinema listings. She'd have to work some of Saturday and all day Sunday, probably, but she would take some time out too. She'd got better things to do with her life than waste time thinking about what might have been.

2
Edward, June 1915

It must have been the hiss of the snake that woke him.

One minute he is deep in sleep, and the next, wide awake, his heart thudding uncomfortably in his chest. Hot and sleepy, it takes a moment or two for his brain to catch up. In the nightmares that are to plague him into adulthood, there is always a disorientating jumble of images: a swish of movement, a forked silver tongue, an arched neck that transforms into a sinister hood as the cobra spreads its neck ribs sideways.

And then – nothing. The snake vanishes, leaving only a sliver of fear. Edward is alone in his bedroom, taking his afternoon rest under the mosquito net. He knows he must stay in bed until Ayah comes to wake him or risk her wrath. The shutters are drawn against the midsummer heat, but it is still so suffocatingly hot that his hair is sticking to his forehead. He knows that even turning over in search of a cooler spot on his pillow will make him hotter still. Just as he is wondering if he conjured the snake out of his dreams, he hears a scream.

When his father comes home that evening, he finds Edward red-eyed and hovering on the verge of fresh tears. A tightness in the corners of his father's mouth signals Papa's displeasure.

'Come, come, son,' he admonishes him, with scarcely concealed impatience. 'You know these things happen. Mercifully it was only the *dome*. A new sweeper is easily found. Abdul, at least, was at the bazaar.'

Edward realizes with a shock that, for Papa, the events of the afternoon mean inconvenience, not tragedy. Losing his *khansama*, on whom the entire household depends, would have been a greater nuisance. But he cannot get out of his head the sound of Ayah's terror, the sickening image of the livid purple stain spreading like spilt ink up the sweeper's arm towards his neck. The man gasped for air, his legs twitching like a dying insect, while Edward stood rooted to the spot in the doorway.

'No, no, no, *Baba* Edward!' Ayah, catching sight of him in a pause for breath from her keening, shooed him back inside the bungalow. '*Jow!* Away inside, *ekdum!*'

Now, he experiences a fresh wave of relief that Ayah is unharmed. Though she wept and wailed, she couldn't go too close to the sweeper, because the *dome* was untouchable. Another frightening thought: if Edward had raised the alarm when he saw the cobra, rather than lying in bed awaiting Ayah, could he have saved the sweeper's life? He was being obedient, but was his behaviour cowardly?

He opens his mouth to consult his father on this point when he notices Papa's expression is dark. The muscles on his face are twitching with irritation. 'Edward, you must learn a sense of proportion. It is one thing to mourn the loss of your dear Mama and your brother, but the death of a native servant is quite another. It is of little consequence.'

Papa clears his throat. 'A soldier must be brave at all times. Cultivate the habit of courage. Never forget that we are here to set an example. Now, it's time you were ready for bed. I am going to dine with the Armstrongs.'

Papa calls for Abdul to see to his bath before drinks at the club and dinner with his commanding officer. Colonel Armstrong is a big man with a loud voice and a tremendous handlebar moustache. He sports a dashing patch over the left eye that he lost in battle. Papa, who fought alongside him in the Second Boer War, assures Edward that the Colonel was awfully brave. The eyepatch takes nothing away from the Colonel's splendour in his red and gold uniform, especially when mounted on his fine black horse, Star. Edward covets the Colonel's ceremonial sword.

Despite his commanding presence, Colonel Armstrong has a twinkle in his remaining eye and carries an endless supply of peppermints in his pocket, which he is always happy to share. His company has seen Edward through many a long afternoon on the clubhouse verandah watching his father play polo. 'Splendid shot!' bellows the Colonel, swelling with vicarious pride in his adjutant's prowess. 'Mark and learn, dear boy, mark and learn,' he tells Edward. 'Your turn before too long.'

'Yes, sir,' says Edward, never letting on that he finds polo noisy and violent. He quite enjoys his early morning riding lessons with his father's *syce*, but only last week he overheard Iqbal telling Papa in tones of disgust that Baloo was a pony for a missy-*baba*, that Sahib should be looking for a livelier mount for his son. Edward loves Baloo precisely because he is so docile. Fortunately, Papa merely laughed.

'You mean *you* want a livelier pony, Iqbal,' he said, slapping the *syce* on the back. 'Master Edward is only seven. Baloo will suffice for now.'

Mrs Armstrong, the Colonel's wife, is altogether more frightening. While the Colonel is smiley, Mrs Armstrong has darting beady eyes and a perpetual frown. She is brisk and bossy and is always telling people what to do. When she calls her servants, her voice turns into an ugly shriek. Mama used to call her the model Memsahib. Edward doesn't think this was a compliment.

When Mama and baby Arthur were taken ill three years ago, Edward and Ayah were sent to stay with the Armstrongs. Edward can just remember hovering on the threshold of his mother's bedroom – no closer in case he caught their fever – while Mama raised a feeble hand in farewell. He recalls a hazy blur of white, a glimpse of her nightgown behind the mosquito net. She already looked like a ghost. He remembers thinking it was unfair that Arthur was allowed to stay in the cradle at her bedside.

The Colonel's house was much grander than his adjutant's bungalow and full of corridors, and Edward, at four, found it confusing. He was looking for the nursery when he mistakenly opened the door into Mrs Armstrong's bedroom. She was at her toilette and whereas Mama might have beckoned him in, Mrs Armstrong dismissed him with an irritable flap of her hand, as if he were a fly. 'Shoo, child! Shoo!' she cried. 'Back to your ayah at once!'

To make matters worse, the Armstrongs had two large and alarming dogs, and three large and alarming children. Violet, Raymond and Iris were all older than him and, like their mother, tended to issue orders in superior voices. When they grew bored with him, he was unceremoniously banished to the nursery.

Three wretched days later, Mrs Armstrong called Edward from his bed early in the morning with the news that his father was in the dining room. Assuming rescue was at hand, Edward hurtled down the stairs, two at a time, almost tumbling head over heels in his haste. But Papa looked all wrong. White-faced and unshaven, yet still standing as straight as if he were on parade, he made no move towards him. Edward pulled himself up short. A heavy silence hovered in the room, the hush broken only by the ticking of the grandfather clock. Then Papa cleared his throat and told him that Mama and Arthur were dead.

'My dear Randolph, you must leave the boy and his ayah with us,' said Mrs Armstrong. 'You have more than enough to do until after the funeral.'

Edward silently implored his father to resist. He longed to be at home, with his beloved collection of toy elephants. But Papa half bowed, thanked Mrs Armstrong for her kindness and withdrew stiffly from the room, abandoning Edward to her mercy. She called for Ayah to give him his breakfast, adding that she must speak to the children.

Whatever Mrs Armstrong said had the uncomfortable effect of turning Iris, closest to his age at seven, into his constant companion. Iris had firm ideas about mourning and insisted on draping him in thick black clothes from the dressing-up box. She also told him a disgusting story about a family dog that went missing for two days before being found dead in a ditch, swarming with maggots.

'That's why your mother and the baby must be buried at once,' Iris informed him bossily. 'Otherwise they'll be all

18

maggoty, too.' Already hot and bothered by his heavy mourning costume, Edward felt himself sway. He was either going to faint or be sick, possibly both.

'Oh do buck up, child!' cried Mrs Armstrong, bustling into the room with a vase of lilies in her hands. 'Iris, dear, go and find his ayah, a glass of water and the smelling salts.'

Now his father reappears in Edward's bedroom, no longer wearing his uniform, but just as dashing in white tie, a starched turned-up collar and tails.

'That's more like it!' he says, observing with approval that Edward has washed his face and swallowed any remaining tears. Like his father, Edward has bathed. He is sitting on the floor in his pyjamas, absorbed in a game involving his elephants. The heaviest – a cast-iron ramp walker with articulated legs – is trampling on a crude red-and-green wooden snake Edward bought in the bazaar with his pocket money. The other elephants are egging him on, making loud trumpety noises through their trunks. The snake, made of soft balsa wood and really too big in proportion to the elephants, is beginning to look quite bashed about.

Papa sighs. 'Perhaps you would be better off at Home,' he says. 'But while we're at war . . . well, it's simply not practical. There are greater claims on the fleet. Now, say your prayers and go to sleep. Lessons tomorrow.'

'Goodnight, Papa.'

Before he falls asleep, Edward thinks about Home. He has always known the day will come when he will be sent to England. Violet, Raymond and Iris are at school in somewhere called Bournemouth, where their grandparents live. Mrs Armstrong took them there last year and was away so long that Edward almost forgot what she looked like. 'While the cat's away . . .' chuckled the Colonel, with a stagey wink in Edward's direction. *If Mrs Armstrong is a cat*, Edward thinks, *she is the sort that arches its back and hisses.*

Edward has some grainy photographs of his mother's family outside their house in England, taken before she came out to

India. Mama once told him about playing in the snow with her brothers on Christmas Day, but it is still beyond him to imagine Home. Will he be able to take his elephants? Will they like Home? He likes to sleep holding his very favourite, Ebony. Ebony might be plain compared to some of the others that have coloured silk coats, but she is smooth to the touch and fits perfectly in Edward's hand. She was a present from Mama on his fourth birthday. And what will happen to Ayah when he isn't there any more? According to Ayah, the Armstrongs' ayah was sent back to her village when the Armstrong children went Home.

'Ayah?' he calls. 'Are you there?'

'I am here, *Baba* Edward.'

'Sing the *Talli* song, Ayah?' He feels he can ask, because his father is safely out to dinner. Papa considers Edward too old for nursery rhymes now he is seven.

'Oh, *Baba* Edward, what would the Sahib say?'

'Please, Ayah!'

And Ayah takes him in her arms and rocks him as she sings.

> *Talli, talli badja baba*
> *Ucha rotit schat banaya.*
> *Tora mummy kido.*
> *Tora daddy kido.*
> *Jo or baki hai.*
> *Burya ayah kido.*

> Clap hands, baby,
> They make good bread in the market.
> Give some to your mummy.
> Give some to your daddy.
> What is left over
> Give to your old ayah.

3
Hope, January 1945

Hope was hiding. Because it was January, it was very cold. Cold enough to see your breath. She was wearing two of everything she could lay her hands on: two pairs of long grey socks, two pairs of underpants and a second grey jersey over her own. She thought the extra one was probably Faith's, and Faith would be cross when she found out, but Hope didn't care. Faith was usually cross with her anyway because Prudence usually was, and Faith always copied Prudence. She'd also taken the blankets from her bed, just in case she had to stay in the stable all night. She'd made herself a sort of nest in the hayloft, but she was beginning to wonder if that was such a bright idea because the blankets were scratchy. Nonetheless, they were an extra layer against the hay, which was scratchier still. Hope suffered from eczema and she could feel the inside of her arms beginning to itch already.

Below her, Duchess stamped her feet against the cold and blew a noisy raspberry. The sound she produced was so like a fart it made Hope snigger. If Richard was here, he wouldn't be able to contain his mirth, but then he wasn't yet five. And William liked to copy Richard, so he would get the giggles too. Even Grace, who was big enough for school so should really know better, was as bad as the boys about things like that. They were such babies.

Hearing Duchess moving about made Hope glad she'd clambered up the ladder into the hayloft. She adored Duchess, but Alf – who worked on the farm and wasn't quite right in the head – told her that Duchess weighed at least a ton and she should steer well clear. Not get under Duchess's hefty hooves.

21

Hope was scornful; Duchess loved her and would never do anything to harm her. It may be that Alf didn't understand this because he was simple. She'd never admit it to the others, but she was a bit frightened of him, actually; one eye was higher than the other and he looked at you sort of sideways, and she couldn't always make out what he was saying because his words came out funny.

Dot and Ruby, the land girls, rolled their eyes and laughed at Alf when he was out of earshot. One of them, she wasn't sure which – they were just Dot-and-Ruby – did quite a good impression of him. But Hope overheard Aunt Mabel tell Mama that Alf was a godsend. Dot-and-Ruby were all very well, but they were city girls and flighty, she said. Alf was as strong as an ox and Uncle Lionel would never manage the farm without him, especially now the Cousins had gone. 'Not that they had to,' she added, shaking her head in disbelief. 'They could have stayed. What were they thinking?'

Surely Duchess wouldn't have forgotten all the times Hope brushed her down or stroked her mane or sneaked her an apple when no one was looking? Duchess was her *friend*. Her only friend in the world. Hope had whispered any number of secrets in her ears since they'd lived in Apple Tree Cottage and she was quite sure Duchess understood every word.

Without her, Duchess would have been lonely on her own too. It was almost a year since Duke was taken away in a horsebox and, although Duke was frightfully bad-tempered, Hope could tell that Duchess missed him. Hope was still not sure where they took him, either. The grown-ups insisted he was needed on another farm because of the War, but there was something about Aunt Mabel's tone of voice when she said this that Hope distrusted. She wouldn't let herself think too much about the other possible explanations. The Cousins talked Uncle Lionel into buying a tractor before they went away. He was reluctant to start with, but after a few false starts, he now admitted that, come ploughing time, he could turn round a field in half the time. Hope was desperate to ride on the tractor, but she hadn't yet convinced Uncle Lionel to take her. Perhaps she could talk Dot-and-Ruby into it. One of them was learning to plough.

Poor Duke being sent away because of the War, and poor Duchess too! Everything hateful that happened was because of the stupid War. It was because of the War that the grown-ups shushed you up so that they could listen to the boring old news on the wireless. It was because of the War that Cousin Walter's plane was shot down by the Germans and now he was dead. It was because of the War that Cousin Fred was a prisoner of war. It was because of the War that Uncle Lionel never smiled any more, and Aunt Mabel wept while she washed the pots.

And now it was because of the War that Father had come home and they were supposed to be leaving Apple Tree Farm to go and live in Birmingham. Prudence was being annoying about it. She kept talking about 'going home' because she was six when they left Birmingham. As far as Hope was concerned, Apple Tree Farm was home and always would be. It was where the boys were born and it was where they all lived. But Prudence was ten, eleven next month, and she seemed to think that made her almost a grown-up. She was very bossy. All those weeks when Mama was taking the train to Southampton to visit Father in hospital, Prudence took charge, because it was just after the news about Cousin Walter and Aunt Mabel was too unhappy to look after them.

'Be good for Prudence, my darlings,' said Mama, smoothing the sleeves of her best coat when she set off for the station in the mornings. When she came back home in the evenings, she used to go straight to bed without any supper because visiting people in hospital was very tiring and, besides, she was exhausted after the journey. Prudence didn't mind a scrap. She liked telling them all what to do and, while that was all right for the babies, Hope was perfectly capable of looking after herself and doing her chores without Saint Prue reminding her.

Hope was in charge of the chickens. That meant feeding them, refilling their water trough, collecting the eggs and shutting them up at night, so that Mr Fox didn't get his nasty teeth into them. It also meant cleaning out the hen coop once a week and putting in fresh straw. She was less keen on that part because it was smelly, so sometimes she persuaded Grace to help her. Grace was only five and would usually bend to Hope's will. Either way, she always made sure the chickens had clean straw on Sundays because it wasn't fair to expect them to live in their own mess.

Last autumn, she helped Dot-and-Ruby with the apple harvest. It was back-breaking work because it was a bumper year, according to Uncle Lionel, with more fruit than he could ever remember, so they all worked extra hard. Every day after school she and Faith went out into the orchard to help move the ladders and fill the baskets and carry the apples to the barn where the crates were set out, so that the fruit could be sorted before being sent to market. There was a special basket for the misshapen and bruised apples that had to be kept for the pigs, and another for fruit that wouldn't keep long enough to sell, but would be all right for the family, as long as it was peeled and bottled in the next fortnight.

After picking and sorting, it had always been up to Aunt Mabel and Mama to keep back as much unbruised fruit as they thought they would need for the winter months, but last year they were never there when you needed them, so Hope more or less made the decision herself. She kept back seven crates, which she thought was about right, because there were a lot of people to feed, even without the Cousins. You had to take into account Alf and Dot-and-Ruby and now Father was an extra mouth to feed. Every time she thought about that, she got a knot in her stomach because it was very important not to be wasteful in wartime, and if she'd got it wrong, people would be cross with her.

Now it occurred to her for the first time that if they moved to Birmingham they wouldn't be here to eat the apples anyway, so there would be far too many and they'd probably rot. Unless they took them with them to Birmingham, which didn't seem very likely, because apples bruised if you weren't careful. Every piece of fruit you kept back had to be wrapped in old newspaper for storage in the hayloft. She could smell the comforting appley smell from her hiding place. Grace could manage apple-wrapping quite well, with her little fingers, although she sometimes lost concentration and dropped one, and it was difficult not to be annoyed when your back was aching after all the hard work in the orchard. Prudence never helped, because she said someone had to look after the boys.

Hope was also convinced she'd picked more blackberries than anyone else last October, though the annual blackberry championship seemed to have gone by the wayside. You were allowed extra sugar rations at jam-making time and Mama always told them how important the blackberry harvest was to see them through the winter. Two years ago, when she was five, Hope won, but last year Mama said that Faith had pipped her to the post. At first, Hope thought this meant something to do with the pips in the fruit, but it turned out that it just meant Faith had picked more berries than she had. Her older sister seemed to have hands of leather; she didn't seem to notice the thorns on blackberry bushes, when Hope's fingers always ended up pricked and purple. Hope was determined to win again this time, but Mama and Aunt Mabel appeared to have forgotten about jam-making.

'Honestly, Hope, do you really think anyone cares about that any more?' said Prudence irritably when Hope asked her when they were going to make the jam. And when Hope argued back, saying that everyone knew it was important to lay down stores for the winter and that even if Mama didn't care, she, Hope, did, Prudence said, 'Suit yourself!' and stalked out of the room, leaving Hope to make the jam unaided.

She'd done her very best, getting the pan and the water and the sugar and the fruit all ready on the kitchen table. She washed the blackberries and weighed out the sugar, very carefully, so as not to waste any, just as Mama showed her last year. But just when she thought it was all going very well, she looked away for a minute and the mixture boiled over, and she burnt herself and it had really hurt and she had to go and find Dot-and-Ruby to help. Even then, when Dot-or-Ruby had helped her sort out the mess and put baking soda on her arm, and they'd bottled thirteen jars of jam as a surprise for her mother, Mama seemed more irritated than anything else. She said Hope was too young to go making jam on her own and was cross that Mrs Clifton at the village shop had given Hope the extra sugar ration without checking with her, because she might have wasted it.

'But I was so careful!' said Hope, burning with the injustice of it. 'I thought you'd be glad I remembered it was jam time!'

'Yes, dear,' said Mama distractedly. 'Now, where's Prue? It's time those babies were in bed.'

Now Prudence was busy organizing the packing of their possessions into crates for Mama. She'd made Faith write the labels which were tied on each crate. Faith did everything Prudence told her to do, just because she was the oldest. Faith even claimed to remember the rectory in Birmingham, but Hope wasn't at all convinced, because Faith was only five when they left.

Hope supposed there would be school in Birmingham and it was bound to be just as hateful as it was in Dorset. Prudence refused to answer any questions about school, which only went to show she almost certainly didn't remember as much as she pretended. Hope certainly wouldn't miss Lidstone Parva Church School and Miss Giles who loathed her. School was detestable. She was always getting into trouble and she didn't have any friends. The other children in the infants class were an indistinguishable blur of torturers and bullies.

She had hoped it might be easier this year, as she had Grace to look after, but after the first two weeks Grace said she didn't want to sit next to her in class any more, because she'd made friends with a girl with red pigtails, an evacuee called Vera. It wasn't just Vera: she had a little gang of friends. Everyone always loved Grace because she had a baby face and a halo of blonde curls. 'My angel,' said Mama, and now they all called her

Amazing Grace. All the way home, Grace chattered on about Iris and Joyce and Lizzie and Kenneth, leaving Hope more bewildered and lonely than ever.

Hope didn't believe Mama or Aunt Mabel would notice if she played truant, and Prudence and Faith were in the Big Class, so she could probably pull the wool over their eyes if she walked to school with them as usual in the morning, then doubled back across the fields once their backs were turned. But Miss Giles would be sure to ask Grace where she was and Grace couldn't tell a fib to save her life.

Hope sighed. Apple Tree Farm had been their home for *ever*. She couldn't imagine why anyone would want to leave. Although, truth to tell, now Father was home, everything was topsy-turvy. He was so tall – and so cross most of the time – that the cottage felt half the size it used to be. He kept banging into the furniture on his crutches and once he knocked his head on a beam and that made him shout a rude word out loud because of his head wound.

For a long time he wore a dressing on his head, which Mama had to change every night. It finally came off at Christmas time, which was supposed to be cause for celebration. Hope wished that he still wore the bandage because he now had an ugly red gash, like a bloodied fork of lightning, right across his temple, and the skin around it was a horrid blotchy purple. One of his eyes was pulled upwards at the outside corner because of the stitches and the stitches looked like little black insects crawling up his face. The worst thing, the very worst, was that the harder you tried not to look, the more your eyes were drawn to the wound.

When Father first came home, poor little William burst into tears every time he saw him. He still sometimes ran away when Father came into the room, and the way he clung to Mama's legs drove Father to distraction. Richard was only a little braver. Hope was doing her best to set an example. The trouble was, Father did tend to roar when provoked. She could hear shouting now, but it was Mama's voice, not his. Someone had noticed that

Hope was missing. The itching on her arms was spreading up her neck to her face and she was very cold. It was very tempting to answer the call, but if she stayed hidden for ever, they couldn't go to Birmingham.

Or could they? Perhaps they would leave her here with Aunt Mabel and Uncle Lionel and Alf and Dot-and-Ruby. She'd be a sort of orphan. Maybe Aunt Mabel would adopt her to make up for the Cousins. She could be a comfort to her aunt and everyone would say, 'Thank heavens for Hope.' There'd still be Duchess, but then there would also be Miss Giles and horrid Lidstone Parva Church School. There was talk of Dot-and-Ruby moving into their cottage when they'd gone, so perhaps Hope could live with them until she was a grown-up. Mind you, she'd heard Dot-and-Ruby talking about after the War and she was pretty sure their plans didn't involve Dorset. They came from London and talked longingly of going out for ices and to the flicks and to dances. Why did everyone insist on leaving Apple Tree? First the Cousins – and look what happened to them – and now her own family and, one day soon, Dot-and-Ruby. With a howl of frustration, Hope buried herself deeper into her makeshift nest and pulled the blankets over her head to shut out the sound of her mother's voice.

4
Nell, April 2016

'Well, you've set the cat among the pigeons,' Fran told her the next morning after the Park Run.

'What do you mean?' Nell was only half listening as she presented her barcode to a volunteer for scanning. She was hoping for a time under twenty-five minutes.

'Your little punctuation note for teachers. On Facebook last night?'

Nell laughed. 'Oh dear! Was I a bit sarcastic?' She tried to remember what exactly she had written. Something about the difference between a hyphen and a dash. She thought she'd been quite witty.

'Why? What's anyone said?'

'Oh, I'm sure it's nothing. It'll blow over,' said Fran.

She could hear concern in Fran's voice. 'What will blow over?'

'I think you've got up a few people's noses. Did you mean to share your thoughts with the world and his wife? It's just . . . it seems to be going viral.'

Nell began to panic. 'Viral? How the hell did that happen? It was *nothing* . . . just letting off a bit of steam on a Friday night. I'd had a crap day and, you know . . . the Mark thing hasn't helped.'

'Look, don't worry about it. I'm sure it'll pass. Do you want to go and find a coffee? Pete will survive with the kids for another half-hour if I text him.'

But Nell thought she'd better get home – and fast. She was beginning to get a bad feeling about this.

Half an hour later the feeling was very bad indeed.

She reread her post. 'Calling all teachers! Please note, new advisory on punctuation. We need to start teaching our little darlings that a dash and a hyphen are NOT the same. In future I will insist that dashes are written precisely 2 mm wide and hyphens only 1 mm. Rulers will be used to check. Am planning to write to our beloved Education Minister and her chums at the DfE proposing this is part of KS2 assessment. This insight is based on experience in school today (gold star for taking my professional development so seriously!) when I found out that the little mark in the name Kar-ian is a DASH not a HYPHEN and must be pronounced, i.e. Kar-dash-ian! How inspired is that? Think of the ink Kar-ian will save not having to write out the missing letters! A teacher friend once told me about a child in Glasgow called Pocahontas McGinty, after the Disney movie. Sadly, Google suggests this is an urban myth. But, come on, let's hear the wackiest names you've come across . . .'

In some ways it wasn't too bad. At least it wouldn't have been, if it had been seen only by her friends, as she intended, but something had gone horribly wrong. The sheer number of comments below made it abundantly clear that she'd broadcast her post to the whole world. Checking back, she remembered she'd changed the settings to 'Public' last month, when she wanted to voice support for the teachers' march on Westminster against forced academization. For some reason – she hadn't been on Facebook much recently, for Mark-related reasons – she never changed the settings back.

She wasn't sure it had quite gone viral – how exactly did you define that anyway? – but clearly the post had been widely shared. She began to count the number of comments and gave up at fifty. How many more people had read it and not commented? Lots of her teacher friends had responded with 'likes' or examples of their own. Between them, they claimed to have two Chardonnays, a Tinkabelle, a Tiara, a Diesel and an Ace in the playground. Her university friend Josh, who taught at Liddells, a prep school for boys in north Oxford, reported having two Tarquins, a Ptolemy, a Cosmo and a Peregrine in his class. A couple of people had mentioned Jamie Oliver and the Beckhams and other celebrities who called their kids daft names, and that seemed to have got a fair few people fired up, for and against. There were quite a few 'What were their parents thinking?' type comments about people called things like 'Joe King' or 'Hazel Nutt'.

Kelly Meacher was less impressed. 'Snotty cow who doz she think she is?'

'Total bitch. You ok hon? Am here for you, you no that, right? xxx,' Shaneece Power, who had children in Years 2 and 4, responded. Last term Nell had had to call the police when Ryan, the older boy, arrived in school with a knife under his coat. Shaneece was still spitting tacks that Ryan had been excluded from school as a result.

'Thats harassment innit you should defnately report her.' This from Leanne Morgan. Her son, Jason, was Kyle's best friend.

'Rite snob if you ask me. Just cos she went to colege and you didnt' and 'Fuckin cheek! Up herself, tipical teacher' were followed by 'What do you expect of a fucking woman?' All posted by names she didn't recognize. She skimmed down the string of comments, all in much the same vein. Two more leapt out at her. 'No wonder St Sebs got slammed by Ofsted. Crap teachers = crap school. Pile of shit.' And, chillingly, 'Where does the stupid cunt live? Someone needs to pay her a little visit.'

Nell felt sick. What had she done? If ever there was an argument for staying offline after a couple of glasses of wine, this was it. And she was usually so careful! She couldn't believe she'd been so stupid. The name thing – well, if anyone knew what it was like to be landed with a stupid name, she did. Not that anyone else knew that. That was one thing, but the whole punctuation thing, the thing about how to write properly, sounded superior and judgemental. Actually, the whole post sounded judgemental. Sneery. Which she probably was. Scratch beneath the surface of her liberal *Guardian*-reading exterior, her so-called social conscience, and she was nothing but a snob. A stuck-up, middle-class snob who was getting her comeuppance.

She refreshed the page a couple of times and more comments trickled in. Half a dozen times she considered responding, but she couldn't think of anything she might say that could possibly make things better. There was no option but to delete the post, change her settings and hope it went away. A storm in a teacup.

Mid-morning on Sunday, she got a text from Susie, a friend from the gym, where Shaneece Power happened to work in Reception. Nell had missed her early morning spinning class for that very reason. 'Thought you'd better know Shaneece on the warpath. Screenshot of your post on her FB page. Loads of comments. Take care. S xx.' Nell came back from buying a carton of milk to find a missed call from Ray Graham, the Chair of Governors at St Seb's. He wanted to see her at 8 a.m. on Monday. It could only be about one thing.

Next morning, after a sleepless night, Nell was at her desk even earlier than usual. She had dressed with care: smart black trousers, new white T-shirt and her favourite red linen jacket for confidence. Not quite her interview suit, but not far off. Her always neat hair was immaculately straightened.

Ray arrived at ten to eight. A thickset man in his late fifties, he was a local builder made good. He'd lived on the Binks all his life and appeared to be related to half the families on the estate. It was most definitely his manor. Having dragged his way up by his bootstraps from unpromising beginnings, he believed that almost anything was possible if you worked hard enough. Although he insisted his own success came about in spite of, rather than because of, his schooling, he was passionate about the importance of education. He'd been a local Labour councillor for years and knew his patch like the back of his hand. He was bluff and uncompromising, prone to occasional noisy outbursts when things didn't go his way. That said, he'd staged a pretty impressive coup on the governing body after the dismal Ofsted inspection report. Although a little wary of him, Nell couldn't help but admire his force of character.

'Have you seen the latest?' he said. 'Not looking good. Dog's breakfast, if you want my opinion.'

He opened his laptop and showed her. Someone – Shaneece, presumably – had set up a Facebook community page for the parents of St Seb's. There was already an official parents' page on the school website, but this was something new. Nell leaned forwards and saw not only a screenshot of her original post but also her own picture. She let out a groan.

'They say it's about providing a platform for the parents of St Seb's,' said Ray. 'A way of getting their voices heard. Standing up for the community. All very well, but I don't like the tone.'

'What are they saying?'

'You don't want to know,' said Ray heavily. 'Put as politely as I can, there's a lot of teacher-bashing. Let's teach our bloody teachers a lesson and so on. And your name's mud. They say you're kicking the school while it's down.'

Nell took a deep breath in an effort to keep her voice from shaking. 'What are we going to do? Can we stop them?'

'I assume you're aware of the school's social media policy?' Ray took a copy of the four-page document out of a buff folder and passed it across the desk to her.

'Of course. I helped draft it.'

'Then you'll understand that I need to suspend you, pending a full investigation.'

Nell felt the blood draining from her face. She put her head in her hands. It was spinning. Surely the policy was first and foremost about safeguarding issues and, thereafter, questions of confidentiality and data protection?

'I'm no expert,' Ray went on, 'but there's a real question here about you bringing the school into disrepute. Not to mention being derogatory about a child. I'll get in touch with the powers that be, get their spin on this. Either way, we'll need to say something to staff, let the parents know. We need to nip it in the bud, before it gets any nastier. With a bit of luck this might calm things down a bit. If people feel we're taking it seriously.'

33

'Calm things *down*?' Nell was trembling with the effort not to burst into tears. She would not, *would* not, cry in front of Ray. 'Are you serious? Won't suspending me just stoke the fire? Blow it up into something even bigger?'

'Might do,' said Ray flatly. 'But I don't think I've got any option. Don't let's make this any more difficult than it has to be. Best if you head home before the mob arrives. I'll be in touch.'

5
Edward, April 1919

For almost the first time since leaving India, Edward is warm. Now that the summer term has begun, the temperature in England is beginning to feel almost like winter in the Punjab.

When he first arrived and couldn't stop shivering, he took himself to the sickbay. He thought perhaps he had contracted fever on the ship. He had been as sick as a dog on the voyage. He wasn't alone – the weather had been particularly stormy and it seemed that most of the passengers were vomiting overboard. Before long, even the effort of going outside was too much. People dispensed with dignity and were sick everywhere. The overflow from the latrines swished all over the middle deck. The smell was quite appalling.

The Bay of Biscay was the worst. Edward lay on his bunk, convinced he was going to die and praying for mercy. When the ship finally pulled into Southampton, he was still wobbly and several pounds lighter than when he'd left home.

The six months that followed were bewildering, to say the least. Nothing Edward had known in India prepared him for either England or school. The endless grey days and crippling cold were quite beyond his imagination. He was convinced he could feel the damp creeping into his bones and green mould spreading through his veins. That was before the snow came and he developed painful chilblains. How could this be Home, always spoken of in such reverential terms?

The terrors of snakebite, malaria and rabies are as nothing compared to the rigours of his English prep school. His father chose Clive House on the grounds that it caters especially for the sons of men serving the British Empire overseas. Boys can stay there all year round if they have no relatives to take charge of them in the holidays. The headmaster – a retired brigadier – is unsparing in his discipline. School routine involves daily cold showers and a great deal of running in the mud on the South Downs.

Even that is trifling set against the terrors of the curriculum, for which he is woefully unprepared. Edward soon discovered that his education in Miss Jenkinson's garrison schoolroom was as full of holes as his thin grey socks. He fares not too badly in Geography, and his English is tolerable, probably because he spent a great deal of his childhood alone with books for company and one of his favourites is his Bartholomew's atlas. He likes Scripture. The rest of his lessons hold fear and bafflement.

Worse, far worse, are the other pupils. His father told him he would be travelling out with two other boys bound for Clive House, making it sound as if that was a good thing. He met Stubbs and Hamilton on the ship. The three boys were in the charge of Miss Myers, Mrs Armstrong's niece, who was returning to England after a season in India.

'Failure of the Fishing Fleet, with first-class honours! Silly cow!' said Stubbs, the moment her back was turned. He was broad shouldered, far taller than Edward, and walked with a swagger. He surveyed the cabin and carelessly lobbed his belongings on to the biggest bed, leaving Edward and Hamilton to share the bunks.

'She's been fishing?' he asked, confused. It seemed unlikely; Miss Myers was pale and slight, and prone to tears.

'No, you ignorant *chokra*!' said Stubbs, giving him a hefty shove. 'Where've you been, you ass? Living under a stone?'

'*You* know,' said Hamilton, with a look of condescension. 'Her people sent her out to find herself a husband. Nothing doing, so she's heading for home again with her tail between her legs. Mind you, Mama says her chances of netting a husband in England are even worse. There are no decent men left after the War.'

36

'Just think, she could have been your stepmother if she'd played her cards right,' said Stubbs nastily. 'But I suppose even your father has standards!' That Papa might remarry had never occurred to Edward. He found the thought disconcerting.

In an instant, it seemed, Stubbs and Hamilton – both a year older than him – had sized him up and found him wanting. They ganged up against him, alternately tormenting and ignoring him.

'Been *fishing* recently, Meadows?' Stubbs sneered at regular intervals, especially if poor Miss Myers was in earshot. 'Caught anything interesting? Crabs perhaps?'

At least at Clive House they are in the year above, so there is some escape. Yet Stubbs, despite being a new boy, has swiftly established himself as King of the Jungle, with Hamilton only too happy to serve as his chief courtier. The view that Meadows is a *goondah*, a berk, and beneath notice, has spread like fever through the school, simply because Stubbs says so. Edward has become adept at melting into the background, making himself to all intents and purposes invisible.

He finds some comfort in the school chapel, which of all unlikely things reminds him of his old life. In India, church parades were a constant. Sunday by Sunday, the regimental band led the troops down the Mall towards St Thomas's as the natives looked on, and Edward felt his heart swell with pride because his father served the British Empire and that meant Edward was part of something splendid.

For all the thousands of miles between them, the chapel at Clive House is curiously similar to St Thomas's, with its dark wooden pews, brass eagle lectern, stained-glass windows and the familiar smell of furniture polish and incense. On the walls hang the same boards commemorating in golden letters the names of men who died in the service of King and country. Sunday services are reassuringly familiar. Edward is more than happy to sit and listen to the village parson, or sometimes the Brigadier, preaching his sermon. The longer the better, because here at least he is safe from Stubbs and his cronies. More than that: the chapel is the one place he ever feels at peace.

Yet things have taken an unexpected turn for the better. He has just spent the most glorious fortnight with his uncle and aunt over Easter. Uncle Hubert is his mother's younger brother, and recently returned from the Front where he served with distinction as a chaplain. He won the Military Cross at the Battle of Passchendaele after running into no-man's-land to help the wounded while under fire from the Germans. He and Aunt Florence are his guardians. Edward was supposed to have spent the Christmas holidays with them, but at the last minute, Uncle Hubert wrote to say he must stay at school because Aunt Florence was unwell.

'My goodness, you are so like your dear mama!' says Aunt Florence when he finally arrives at the rectory. Unexpectedly, she hugs him. 'It's marvellous to meet you at last, Edward. I'm awfully sorry about Christmas. I do hope it won't be too dull for you here.'

Uncle Hubert has a country living near Exeter, and their manservant, Barker, met Edward's train. Stepping down from the pony and trap, Edward takes a huge breath of fresh air. The smell is extraordinary, nothing like the spice of India or the cabbagey air of school, but sharp and clear and clean. He can see the sea, sparkling silver in the distance. The rectory, though large, has a wide door with a brass knocker, and a friendly face. He feels his spirits soar.

'I'm sure it won't be dull, Aunt,' says Edward dutifully. 'It's very kind of you to invite me.'

Aunt Florence looks at him, as if weighing him up, and smiles. 'Hmm,' she says. 'By the look of you, young man, I'd say you need feeding up. Would tea and scones be welcome?'

She steers him indoors, towards the kitchen, sunny and warm and full of the promise of good things to eat. The cook has flushed cheeks and a generous figure wrapped in a floury apron.

'A young man in urgent need of your baking, Mrs Appleton,' says Aunt Florence.

'You come in, Master Edward,' says Mrs Appleton, with a wide smile. She has several teeth missing but there is no doubting her warmth. 'Come on in and sit yourself down. We'll have tea on the table in a minute.'

After tea, Aunt Florence takes him upstairs to his room, which has sloping whitewashed walls and a tiny window through which Edward can't quite glimpse the sea, even standing on a chair. It is sparsely furnished, with little more than a narrow bed covered by a faded patchwork quilt and a chest of drawers with brass handles. In one corner there is a box of toys and books that Aunt Florence explains were once Uncle Hubert's. They have no children of their own. Edward can see *Treasure Island*, *The Adventures of Huckleberry Finn*, *A Study in Scarlet*. There are glass marbles of all sizes, a collection of toy soldiers and a strange device that Uncle Hubert later explains is called a thaumatrope. When you spin it, the thaumatrope magically turns two pictures on strings into one overlapping image. There is a spinning top and, perhaps most excitingly, a wind-up clockwork train.

At the sight of such treasures Edward is rendered speechless. Aunt Florence misreads his silence. 'Nothing very exciting, I'm afraid, and possibly too young for you,' she apologizes. 'Perhaps you'd like to bring some of your own things here for your next visit? We hope you'll be back for the summer holidays.'

'Oh no – I mean it's simply *marvellous*, Aunt!' says Edward, with shining eyes. 'But perhaps I might ask Papa to send my elephants, if you truly don't mind.'

There follow two of the happiest weeks Edward can ever remember. Mrs Appleton fusses around him as his ayah used to, delighting in plying him with hot apple pie or freshly baked bread from the oven. If the weather is fine, she gives him a sandwich wrapped in waxed paper and a bottle of lemonade, which he slings in a haversack along with a book. Uncle Hubert lends him an Ordnance Survey map and teaches him how to read it. It's like an atlas, only better. The symbols soon turn from squiggles into a marvellous code that conceals the secrets of the landscape. He spends his days exploring the lanes and scrambling up and down steep paths to the sea, returning to the rectory exhilarated and scratched and muddy in time for tea. On the single day the rain sets in, he curls up under his quilt with *Treasure Island*. The only books he brought from home were his Bible and a copy of Rudyard Kipling's *Rewards and Faeries*, a gift from his father who is particularly keen on the poem 'If –'. Papa has explained that it sets out the ideals of manhood, and that the poet wrote it for his own son.

When it is time to go back to school, Edward almost weeps with frustration. Two weeks of being fed and cared for but otherwise blissfully left to his own devices are coming to an end and it feels like losing a limb. His aunt has shown him nothing but kindness and seems to understand his need for his own company. His uncle has taken a great deal of trouble to get to know Edward, asking him all about his wanderings and the flora and fauna he has found in the hedgerows. He's promised to teach Edward how to use his precious Kodak Brownie next time he visits so that he can take photographs on his walks.

Edward has observed that Uncle Hubert is scatter-brained and incorrigibly curious about his fellow man. The two qualities are inextricably linked. Uncle Hubert is perpetually late for appointments for the simple reason that he cannot resist falling into conversation with passers-by, from Smith the coalman delivering his load ('such an interesting man'), to Dr Spratt on his village rounds, to Sir Aubrey Forbes, the Master of the Hunt, out exercising his fine chestnut charger.

Every morning over breakfast, Uncle Hubert asks Aunt Florence if she knows what day of the week it is and, better still, what he is supposed to be doing. He presents both questions with the air of a man who cannot possibly be expected to know such esoteric information. And Aunt Florence rattles through a list of appointments, then spends the day reminding him at intervals that it is the hour for lunch or his confirmation class or, once during Edward's stay, long since time he was leading Farmer Davey's coffin into church. Uncle Hubert makes it to the funeral by the skin of his teeth. 'But he was cool as a cucumber in the pulpit,' says a misty-eyed Mrs Appleton afterwards. 'Takes a wonderful funeral, does the Rector.'

'I simply don't understand it,' Uncle Hubert laments afterwards, perplexed. 'My pocket watch is playing tricks on me again. Time has been running away with itself all day.'

'All day, my dear? Don't you mean all week? Or all your life?' says Aunt Florence with a smile.

Now Edward has no alternative but to tear himself away from the loving shelter of the rectory and return to the punishing regime of rules and lessons and the casual cruelty of the other boys. Aunt Florence, he notices, wipes her eyes with a lace handkerchief as she waves him off, pressing one of Mrs Appleton's fruitcakes into his hands. Even Uncle Hubert seems to be clearing his throat more than usual.

'We'll miss having you about the place, dear boy,' he says, a little too heartily. 'But not so long till the summer holidays, eh?'

Only twelve weeks, he tells himself, back at school at the beginning of term. *Only twelve weeks until the holidays.* It is an unfamiliar pleasure to have something to look forward to, and Aunt Florence has promised to write.

Meanwhile, he is steeling himself for his remedial mathematics lesson, a weekly ordeal that he dreads. It is becoming ever more obvious to Edward that Miss Jenkinson is not used to teaching boys, because before the Great War, boys always went Home once they were six. Only the most rudimentary arithmetical skills were deemed necessary to equip a memsahib to run her household. Once her pupils knew how to add and take away, Miss Jenkinson considered her duty done and abandoned the subject with relief. Which means Edward knows nothing of times tables and has utterly failed to master long division. He does not understand fractions and has never before encountered geometry and algebra.

In consequence, he is required to spend an unhappy hour after lessons on Tuesdays with Major Molyneux, whose face was horribly disfigured by burns in the Battle of Amiens. One ear is missing altogether and his mouth is oddly lopsided so that he dribbles when he speaks. His hands shake uncontrollably.

Edward knows he should mind none of this because the Major is a War Hero, but he finds it difficult to meet Major Molyneux's eye and quite impossible to concentrate on the numbers in his presence. Faced with the Major, he slides into a sort of mute paralysis, further infuriating the master, who becomes ever more agitated as the long hour passes. Edward can sense the distress building inside him like water in a steam engine, but has no idea how to avert it.

Today, for the first time, Major Molyneux has instructed him to come not to the form room, where they normally meet, but to his private quarters on the third floor. The staircase is narrow and forbidding and Edward is dragging his heels. Glancing out of a small window on the half-landing, he tries to take comfort from the watery sunshine outside. He reminds himself about the lighter evenings, a delightful novelty after the short days of winter. Perhaps he will take himself off into the woods after his lesson, if there is time before prep. He will reread the letter that arrived this morning.

He touches his pocket for luck. True, it was written and posted in late February, but it is still a letter from his father. Even a long and rather boring description of the annual regimental polo tournament sparks a surge of nostalgia. He fears his own letters to Papa have been somewhat miserable; the ecstatic accounts of his marvellous Easter holidays, posted in Devon, will not yet have reached him. Papa writes of a possible new posting; rumblings on the North Western Frontier mean that the regiment looks certain to move north to Peshawar.

His father ends the letter with the familiar exhortation. 'Remember, my dear Edward, to study hard and to strive for great things, that you may become the man you were born to be and do your duty to our Lord and His Majesty the King. Your affectionate Father, Papa.' Edward sighs. He does not want to let his father down, but Papa has never had to solve equations for Major Molyneux. He pauses at the top of the stairs, screws up his courage and raises his hand to knock at the Major's door.

Edward is still shaking after his encounter with the Major when Lewis, a prefect who also happens to be captain of the First XI cricket team, tells him he is to report to the Headmaster. 'Word to the wise, Meadows, I'd get your skates on,' he says. 'The Brig was looking pretty severe.'

Edward's heart sinks to his boots. How can the Headmaster know already the shameful, unspeakable thing that has just happened in Major Molyneux's rooms? His hand on Edward's head, as he shoved him roughly to his knees. His shout of impatience when Edward fumbled with the Major's buttons. His animal groan when it was all over. What can Edward possibly say in his defence? He turns and heads for the Headmaster's study like a man going to the gallows.

To his surprise, the Brigadier, though hawk-like as always in his black gown, does not seem angry when Edward enters the room. Nor is he alone.

'Uncle Hubert!' Edward says, with delight.

'Edward, dear boy!' Uncle Hubert gives him an awkward, brief hug.

'Meadows, your uncle has grave news for you,' says the Brigadier. 'You must prepare yourself.'

Edward looks up, startled. Does Uncle Hubert know about the Major, too? 'I didn't . . . I mean, I don't know why . . .' he stumbles.

Uncle Hubert waves away his words. 'Edward, dear boy, I have bad news, such bad news. A telegram . . . your dear Papa . . . the Spanish flu . . . I'm so awfully sorry.'

And Edward begins to make sense of the fact that his summons and Uncle Hubert's unexpected appearance have nothing whatsoever to do with Major Molyneux. Uncle Hubert has come to Clive House to tell him that his father has died, a victim of the influenza epidemic sweeping the world and now raging in India.

'But Papa is *never* ill! I had a letter from him this morning!' he blurts out. 'Besides, he won at polo and he has a new posting.' Even as he speaks, he knows he is tilting at windmills. Uncle Hubert shakes his head sadly.

'Bear up, Meadows,' says the Brigadier, not unkindly. 'I suggest you take your uncle for a short tour of the grounds before he has to return home. You may be excused prep tonight.' He shakes hands with Uncle Hubert and ushers them both out of the room.

Edward and Uncle Hubert walk aimlessly. It has begun to drizzle. There seems nothing much to say. Uncle Hubert has no more information and little to offer by way of comfort. He doesn't know if the influenza has claimed the lives of anyone else in the household. There is no news of Ayah or Abdul or Iqbal. The funeral has already taken place, his father buried next to his mother and little Arthur in the churchyard at St Thomas's. Edward's life as he knows it has come to an abrupt end. It is almost as if it never existed.

'What will happen now?' asks Edward. 'To me, I mean? I am . . . I am all alone.' He is struggling to take in the news. He fears he may cry at some point, but for the moment, a sort of numbness is keeping his tears safely at bay. His father, he thinks, would be pleased with the way he is conducting himself. He is showing the courage expected of a soldier.

'My dear boy, you may be an orphan, but your Aunt Florence and I . . . we are your family. The Brigadier has kindly agreed to keep you on until the end of term. It seems the fees are paid. Thereafter . . . well . . . I imagine your father has left provision. If not, there are scholarships and so forth. I'll look into it.'

His uncle looks at his pocket watch and gives a startled cry as he realizes that he is in danger of missing his train home. As he prepares to take his leave, Edward is struck by an urgent thought. 'My *things*,' he says, seizing Uncle Hubert's hand.

'Your things?'

'My books, my elephants. I need my elephants. Can you ask Abdul to send them? Please?'

'My dear boy, I'll do my level best,' says Uncle Hubert, then he is gone.

6
Nell, April 2016

The next few days were hellish. Nell read and reread the social media policy. She was right that there was a strong focus on online safety. Certain sites were blocked on the school network and usage of the internet in school was closely monitored. That much was obvious. More widely, staff were not to form friendships with parents, carers or pupils that could lead to professional relationships being compromised or allegations of impropriety. Safeguarding was such a number one priority these days that it was little wonder she'd remembered that.

There was also a chunk in there about ensuring all the parental permissions were in place for any images or videos of children that went online, but that was a no-brainer. They'd been doing that in schools for years, whenever there was the slimmest chance of anyone getting a camera out. And the policy recommended – but did not insist – that all privacy settings were set to 'friends only'. Well, she knew that.

But Ray was quite right. The policy did indeed say that staff should not conduct themselves in a manner that might lead to valid parental complaints. However many times she went over it – and boy, did she go over and over and *over* it – Kelly Meacher had a valid complaint against her for implicitly questioning her choice of name for her daughter. And she was probably guilty of bringing the school into disrepute, too, although to be fair there was nothing in her post that mentioned St Seb's. She hadn't even named the school as her workplace in her profile; it just said 'teacher'. She couldn't believe it: her beloved St Seb's! She'd poured her life and soul into the school for the last nine years, first as a class teacher and for the last three as deputy head. She'd fought for this community, battled to give these kids the very best experience of learning. She believed in them, every single child. She was a good teacher – and she was on their *side*, for heaven's sake! She thought the parents knew that. The last thing, the very last thing, she ever wanted was to do the school down. ('The road to hell is paved with good intentions,' said her mother.)

On the other hand, she couldn't quite shake off the feeling that Shaneece and her cronies were doing considerably more to damage the reputation of St Seb's with their wretched community page than she ever did. Ray was right; she'd been checking the page and the tone was savage. The accusations against her were becoming wilder: she'd called Kelly Meacher a bitch; she'd hit Ryan Power the day he was caught with the knife. She was unstable. She was sacked by her last school. They wanted her out.

There was also a whole section in the social media policy about the duty of parents, not that she supposed Shaneece or Kelly had read it. Parents and carers were asked to raise concerns or complaints directly with the school rather than posting them on social media sites. And parents should not post malicious or fictitious comments on social media about any member of the school community. Surely that was as clear as daylight? So why was Nell the one being punished by being suspended?

The feeling of injustice was compounded when she discovered that the campaign against her had moved on to Twitter. She heard this from Susie by text: she wasn't on Twitter so couldn't look. Maybe that was a blessing; she wasn't sure that checking Facebook every few minutes was good for her. In fact, she increasingly felt sick and shaky just switching on her laptop. She disabled the Facebook app on her phone so that at least she stopped the slew of vicious comments appearing in her updates.

'Thx for letting me know,' she texted back. 'What are they saying?? Don't want details. Just let me know if I should be concerned for my safety.' That might be a bit paranoid but she'd read about some shocking cases of trolling that included threats of violence, rape even, and she was shaken by that comment on Facebook about paying her a visit. Maybe she was overreacting. But it felt as if she'd inadvertently crossed an invisible line, transgressed a moral code. That there was a ferocious mob out to get her.

Round and round it went in her head, made worse by radio silence from Ray. All she'd had was a curt text at lunchtime on Monday with a press statement that would be given out to the media if any calls came in. The *Oxford Mail* did the Ofsted report to death and she'd given them lots of positive quotes about the School Improvement Plan and everything they were doing to turn St Seb's round. Would the fact that they knew her mean they'd be sympathetic – or that they'd hang her out to dry? And what if the radio and TV came after her? Or if it went national? ('If you can't stand the heat, get out of the kitchen,' tutted her mother.) Not that she could feel any more exposed than she already did. What if they found out where she lived? Would they come banging at her door?

By Wednesday night she was at the end of her tether. Still nothing from Ray. What was happening with the investigation? And what exactly had he told her staff? What was everyone saying about her? She'd had a couple of texts – one from Diane and another from Fiona – but that was it. To be fair, Fiona said they'd all been told not to contact her and, presumably, they were all flat out because she wasn't there, but still . . . Three times she picked up the phone to ring Fran, but on each occasion she stopped before calling. Fran would tell her she was overreacting. Probably say she'd give her eye teeth for a day or two off work with no small kids under her feet. At the very least, she should be using the chance to catch up on paperwork. Trouble was, she just couldn't concentrate.

Finally, she was summoned to a meeting in school on Thursday evening. As well as Ray, the Chair, there was Doug, the Vice Chair, Jane, representing the Diocese because St Seb's was a church school, and John from County Hall. Doug had always been supportive towards her, though her guess was that he was under Ray's thumb. John she knew of old, a great ally of Rob's. Would that make him for or against her? Right now, he was studiously avoiding her eye. Jane – the only other woman in the room and relatively new in the post – she barely knew.

The meeting was everything she feared. Ray was fuming.

'Have you seen this?' He waved a copy of the *Oxford Mail* at her, barely able to contain his temper. 'A full bloody page! Rerunning the whole Special Measures fiasco, line by bloody line. As if we needed reminding!

'And you know we've had a reporter from the *Daily Mail* on to us, as well as the local rag? Apparently *The Sun*'s sniffing about too.' Nell didn't know. She felt her chest tighten.

'One hell of a cock-up, Nell. Just when we don't need it!' He shook his head in disbelief. 'Haven't got time for this Facebook rubbish myself, but honestly! You're the acting bloody head, for God's sake! Shouldn't you be setting an example? I don't know what you were thinking!'

'In that case, can I suggest we go right back to the beginning? Ask Nell to talk us through the chain of events, so that we're all clear exactly what happened?' Jane managed to take the wind out of Ray's sails; he could hardly disagree.

Nell tried to snap into competent teacher mode. As calmly as she could – and if she could hear the tremor in her voice, everyone else probably could, too – she talked about Kelly Meacher's visit to her office, her outburst. The late-night post, for which she took full responsibility. The action she took to shut down the thread the next morning, as soon as she discovered what had happened. Her deliberate refusal to enter a slanging match online, on the grounds that it would do more harm than good. 'Look, I know I've messed up. I'm really sorry,' she said. 'I'll do whatever I can to put this right.'

'You bloody bet you will!' said Ray. 'For God's sake, you knew what you were taking on when you took the helm. You know what we're up against. You've been here long enough, haven't you?'

There was an uncomfortable silence in the room. Doug shuffled his papers. John shook his head wearily.

'Look, Ray,' said Jane, calmly. 'We are where we are. We've got to meet the other parties in this, obviously. But we've got the screenshots. And we now know how it started. I think we've pretty much covered things for now. Unless you've got anything to add, Nell?'

Nell was too shocked by Ray's attitude to speak. Surely the Chair of Governors should be standing up for her? Covering her back, not throwing her to the wolves? Maybe even challenging the fictitious claims being made online about her? Did he not realize the hours she worked, the strain she was under, trying to do a half-decent job in impossible circumstances? ('A chain is as strong as its weakest link,' said her mother's voice, as clear as a bell.) Dumbly, Nell shook her head. Time to go home.

7
Hope, March 1952

Hope was steaming, simply steaming. She had just had another blazing row with Father. How could he calmly announce that they were moving – just like that? Not just moving house, like any normal family, but moving a hundred miles away to Lancashire because he'd got some stupid new job? He was insufferable. And he was so pleased with himself, even if he was trying to disguise his pleasure in piety.

'When God and the good lord Bishop call, I have little option but to obey,' he said at breakfast. '"Then said I, Here am I, Lord. Send me."'

Hope could have screamed. Her father seemed to think it was an honour being invited to take up a new post in a new diocese, at the personal recommendation of the Bishop of Birmingham. Apparently they needed a vicar who understood the motor industry and Father fitted the bill. For all Father knew, the mouldy old bishop was probably trying to get rid of him by sending him to the other end of the country! She didn't even know where Lancashire was and she certainly didn't know anyone who lived there. None of them did! It was so unfair! She had *plans*, not that anyone ever bothered to ask her.

It would be just like when they moved to Birmingham at the end of the War, and that was every bit as hateful as she feared it would be. Another detestable school and another detestable teacher and instead of green fields and apple orchards, street after street of shabby shops and bombed-out houses and potholed roads. Even the *people* looked grey. She hadn't noticed that so much in the countryside, somehow, but in the city it was inescapable. Everyone looked poor and wretched. They had grey faces and ugly utility clothes to match, and to make matters worse, all spoke in a funny accent that Hope struggled to understand.

And that gave the other children a stick to beat her with. They mocked the way she spoke as la-di-da. Somehow no one dared tease Prue – they were scared of her, probably – and Faith and Grace seemed to know without being taught how to change their voices to blend into the background. But Hope couldn't do it. She tried copying Prudence – sticking her chin up in the air and speaking in the ringing tones of their mother – but she lacked the authority to carry it off, and that provoked more mockery still.

It didn't help that she was forever getting lost in Longbridge. Every morning she was faced with the unpalatable choice between walking to school with Miss Prim and Miss Proper (Amazing Grace trailing at their heels) or going it alone and arriving late. While the latter was preferable, missing the bell meant she risked being reprimanded by her teacher and ridiculed by her beastly classmates, who seemed to think there was something funny about the fact that she couldn't find her way. But how did anyone know which turnings to take when the streets were all such a mess?

She missed Duchess so much that she cried herself to sleep for months. She missed the chickens – smelly straw and all – and Dot-and-Ruby and their laughter, and she even missed Alf. She missed lying in the grass under the apple trees at apple-blossom time. And she missed running barefoot in the meadows.

Perhaps the biggest change of all was that Father was there all the time now, ruling with a rod of iron. Unlike other fathers, who did proper jobs that meant going out to work in offices or factories or hospitals, Father was always prowling about the house. It was as if he *lurked*, waiting to catch the children at some misdemeanour or other, with the express purpose of roaring at them. He was a despot. A dictator like Hitler or Mussolini.

51

Stalin, maybe. Yet all the ladies of the parish thought he was too marvellous for words! They fluttered around him like wasps round jam.

As for Mama! Mama seemed to have turned into a . . . well, Hope couldn't think of a word to describe someone who tiptoed around a tyrant the way she did. A doormat, perhaps. She was afraid of his outbursts and constantly on edge. She spent her life trying to avert his rages before they erupted. She treated him like a monster who had to be appeased with offerings. It was all so *feeble*. Hope was never going to kowtow to her husband like that. No, siree! Not that she was planning to have a husband at all if she could help it.

Life had been so much simpler at Apple Tree. Nowadays, it was all household prayers before breakfast – even Gladys, who came in every day to help Mama, was expected to be there – and the daily drill on their Bible verses. They all trooped off to church on Sunday mornings, dressed in their best, in their hats and gloves, and trooped back again after lunch to help with the Sunday school. Prue and Faith helped Father with the Boys' Brigade, poor fools. You wouldn't catch Hope anywhere near them, not that Father had suggested it. She had better things to do with her time.

Surprisingly, considering how dismal she was at every-thing at school, Hope was not actually the worst of the sisters at memorizing the Bible. She'd discovered that as long as she repeated the allocated verse out loud a few times, she could conjure up a picture that helped it stick in her brain. So 'I-will-lift-up-mine-eyes-to-the-hills-whence-cometh-my-help' was easy because she pictured Gladys, transported to Dorset, carrying her bucket and mop down the Purbecks. For 'I-am-the-light-of-the-world: he-that-followeth-me-shall-not-walk-in-darkness,-but-shall-have-the-light-of-life', she re-membered walking home in the Blackout, which was still in force when they first moved to Brum. Once she'd fixed on an image, she could almost invariably rattle off the verse when Father turned his beady eye on her. Sometimes he even said,

'Well done, Hope,' and she could tell he was impressed. Or at the very least surprised, which had its own satisfaction.

Prue never slipped up, but Faith frequently got in a muddle. Like Mama, Faith was definitely frightened of Father and had developed a stutter that only emerged under his gaze. Sometimes she even cried, which wound him up no end. Amazing Grace appeared to sail through on a wing and a prayer — and if she couldn't remember her verse, all she had to do was smile at Father and promise to do better next time.

Prudence, Faith and Grace were all at the Grammar School now, and took the bus to their prissy school with its blazers and ties and summer boaters. Hope — obviously — failed the exam, and now she was stuck at Longbridge Secondary Modern for Girls, where all the dimwits went. Richard and William would be going off to boarding school when they were thirteen, as long as they could get scholarships. Which sounded a lot more fun than Longbridge Sec, but then they were boys, and boys had all the fun.

Actually, after the first beastly year when she was always in the wrong place at the wrong time and totally flummoxed by having to remember a dozen different teachers, Longbridge Sec hadn't been quite as frightful as Hope feared. It helped that the school nurse had insisted she have her eyes tested, and she now wore glasses. They were hideous but at least she could read what was on the blackboard. She still did badly in every subject except Art and Music. She loved painting, splashing about in bold, bright colours, and Mama taught them all the piano, and funnily enough she could read music more easily than words. The black-and-white notes made more sense, somehow, than letters on a page which had a nasty habit of tripping her up.

True, her nickname was still Hopeless, but she had a bit of a turning point when she discovered that she could make her classmates laugh. It probably helped that she wasn't actually scared by any of the teachers — none of them came close to Father in one of his furies, not even Miss Taylor-Brown, the hairy-chinned headmistress – so she willingly took on the role of class clown with little concern for the consequences.

Best of all, she had a proper friend. Betty Phipps was her partner in crime. Betty's mother and two older brothers were killed in the bombing in the city centre in August 1940. They'd gone up to town on the tram to see the animals at the Market Hall, as an end-of-holidays treat, leaving three-year-old Betty behind with her grandma because she had measles. And then Betty's father never came home from Burma, so she stayed on with her grandma, who was a bit soft in the head now, and let Betty do pretty much as she pleased. Lucky so-and-so.

Hope liked Betty because she was as large for her age as Hope was tall. Hope was the tallest by far of the four sisters, and lanky to boot. You certainly couldn't miss Betty: she was broad-shouldered and heavily built and had a purple birthmark on her neck, which didn't bother her a scrap. She talked nineteen to the dozen and laughed like a drain. Nor did she care about school; she was simply marking time till she was fifteen, and regarded lessons as a minor inconvenience.

She'd got it all worked out. She was going to be a hairdresser like her mum – Betty already helped her Auntie Rita in Rita's salon on a Saturday – and you didn't need exams for that. On the way home from school, Betty and Hope often stopped by the salon, which was called Hair Today, very sophisticated. They would pore over all the latest styles in Rita's magazines, because Betty was going to restyle Hope's straw-blonde mop the day they left school. She'd got a bit of time to think about what she wanted, because it was a rule that the Meadows girls kept their uniform pigtails while they were still at school. Hope liked the Italian cut – short and shaggy, but somehow also sculptured – as modelled by Gina Lollobrigida and Sophia Loren, but Rita wasn't convinced Hope had the wave you needed for the fluffy kiss curls. Betty and Rita thought she should go all out for a gamine Audrey Hepburn look. It was very short and layered, an almost masculine cut, with a high-cut shaggy fringe and was called a pixie cut.

Betty latched on to Hope in the second year, and together they had a high old time of it, cocking a snook at Miss Taylor-Brown and her petty rules and regulations. Hope took inspiration from Betty's insouciance. It was such a relief to find someone who wasn't cowed by convention, the way her sisters were, or her mother. Betty's example – her ability to roll with the punches and still come out smiling – offered Hope a glimmer of light at the end of the stuffy tunnel inhabited by her family. Betty would make short shrift of Father, that's for sure. She'd love to see his reaction if she brought Betty home to tea! Not that she ever had, mind you. It was simply beyond her imagination to picture Betty with her sausage-like fingers eating Victoria sponge at the rectory.

But now – now it looked as if she wasn't even going to be here to take over Betty's Saturday job sweeping up for Rita when Betty started her traineeship. She wasn't going to be here when she turned fifteen in April and could legitimately throw her hated school hat into the canal, though she was already preparing herself for a fight with her parents over that, because they'd be bound to insist she stayed on to sit her O levels, for all the good it would do anyone.

Hope looked at her watch. It was Saturday and not yet midday, so Betty would be at Hair Today. *Hair today, gone tomorrow*, she thought crossly, but she'd made up her mind. It was going to be an Audrey Hepburn pixie cut. Hah! Her father would hate it.

8
Nell, April 2016

By the middle of the following week, Nell was beside herself. She'd barely gone out since the meeting, almost a week ago, so great was her fear of seeing anyone from the school community. Her neat and tidy flat, with its minimalist furnishing and soothing clean lines, had turned from sanctuary to prison. She couldn't eat without vomiting and she couldn't sleep either. Today she'd watched two DVDs back to back, before dropping into bed at midnight. After tossing and turning for two hours, she decided to walk the streets. At least at two in the morning she could be fairly confident no one would be about. She pulled on an old sweatshirt, a tatty pair of leggings and her trainers, and let herself out into the silent street.

Spring! she thought, surprised. It was proper spring. Her favourite time of year. Normally. It had been an early Easter, so the summer term started earlier than usual. From her flat, she'd been dimly aware of sudden rain showers lashing at the window, swiftly followed by bursts of sunshine. Typical April weather. But even in the dark she could see the signs of spring. Early summer, even. She usually loved that sense of optimism that fresh green leaves brought. The longer days promising evening drinks by the river, picnics, punting on the Cherwell. *Cherry blossom*, she thought. She would go in search of cherry blossom. The best place in the city was the Woodstock Road, which would be lined with trees in flower. Leafy north Oxford. It was probably a good four miles, but the walk would clear her head. Perhaps the exercise would wear her out and help her sleep.

She set out, a phantom drifting through a city that was a ghost of its usual self. The traffic that usually choked the city's arteries had loosened its grip. The occasional taxi or delivery van sped past, but almost nothing else. Even the all-pervasive cyclists seemed to be asleep. Students all in bed, perhaps, with exams approaching. Up the Cowley Road, its usual colour tucked away behind locked doors and metal grilles. She reached Magdalen Bridge, the crossing place between town and gown. On she went, past the Botanic Garden and Magdalen College and into the heart of ancient Oxford, beloved of *Morse* and *Lewis*. Would someone appear with an axe or hammer in hand? Oh God, should she be listening out for footsteps behind her? She decided she didn't care. At least if a lunatic knocked her over the head, all this would be over. At the very least, she'd have an excuse for feeling so utterly rubbish. She pictured herself lying in a clean hospital bed, her head bandaged. *Then they'd be sorry*, she thought.

She'd go up Parks Road, she decided, avoiding St Giles. She didn't want to go anywhere near the Ashmolean. As she walked past the Natural History Museum she remembered when she taught Year 4 and used to take a trip to the Pitt Rivers. They offered some brilliant workshops there – she particularly loved the one with masks – but inevitably the thing the kids always wanted to see was the shrunken heads, which gave her the collywobbles.

Her own favourite object in the collection had to be the enormous Canadian totem pole, almost as tall as the museum itself. She loved the carvings on it; every time she visited, she spotted something new. There was a bear with a frog in its mouth, and another bear holding a person. A raven with a human being between its wings. She really ought to visit again, she thought. Perhaps without thirty eight- and nine-year-olds next time. She probably liked it because it reminded her of the games she used to play with her brother in the woods. She saw him now – the ringleader, who got everyone else to play the game he wanted. Because she was little, she was always the one who had to be captured or rescued or whatever else he decreed.

But she really didn't mind, because she so wanted to be part of the game, and it meant that they didn't leave her out. Once, they rolled her up in a rug and trussed her up into a sausage with orange bailer twine, and she didn't even mind that, though some of the grown-ups got cross. Presumably because she was halfway to suffocation, she thought now. *Oh, Will*, she thought. *Is this how you felt? Like you were falling down a well?*

Did kids still play Cowboys and Indians, she wondered? She had a feeling it wasn't acceptable any more. Didn't some celebrity get into trouble for having a Cowboy and Indian-themed party a couple of years ago? Just like when Prince Harry went to a fancy-dress party with a swastika on his sleeve. That's right: it was the singer Pixie Lott. (Pixie! Another name to conjure with. She didn't think she'd ever taught a Pixie.) She was accused of being ignorant and disrespectful to Native Americans. No doubt she was vilified on Facebook and Twitter and Instagram and all the rest of it.

Oh *God*. How did it happen, this public lynching of people? Presumably Pixie Lott didn't even think about it beforehand. She probably assumed that dressing up as Tiger Lily was just a bit of harmless fun. Not that Nell wanted to defend racism or sexism or anti-Semitism or anything else, but you had to wonder why it was suddenly OK to attack people so viciously in the name of tolerance. And if you were Pixie Lott, you were going to have tens of thousands of followers and the humiliation would be ten thousand times anything Nell was going through. That said . . . there was a sort of deal you had to accept in exchange for fame, because it was only by courting publicity that you got to be a star in the first place. *Whereas I can't think of anything worse than being famous*, she thought. *I've never wanted to be any kind of public figure. Let alone an Aunt Sally.*

Worst of all, she was coming to the conclusion that perhaps her accusers were right. Maybe she deserved their contempt. After all, if she was such a great teacher, why did Ofsted put St Seb's in Special Measures? She was deputy head before she stepped into Rob's shoes. Surely she should have *known* things weren't right. Never mind that the goalposts kept moving. Nor that they'd struggled for years to attract decent teaching staff because who wanted to work in a sink school on a sink estate? Anyone who'd been at St Seb's for any length of time was worn out, ground down by the relentless conveyor belt of initiatives and strategies, of pressures and disappointments. *It's the hope that kills you*, or whatever the phrase was. She only got the job of acting head because there was nobody else to do it. Perhaps 'crap teacher' summed it up. All these years thinking she was doing a good job! Who was she kidding? ('Pride comes before a fall,' agreed her mother.) Nell felt her professional confidence leak away with every passing hour.

She was virtually in Park Town. Perhaps she'd go and knock on her friend Josh's door and ask him whether he'd ever managed to piss off the entire parent body of Liddells and what the consequences would be if he did. It was after 3.30 a.m., though, so of course she couldn't. She could just imagine Josh on the doorstep in his pyjamas. He was such a sweetheart he would almost certainly invite her in and make her a cup of tea. She suspected the parents he dealt with cared more about getting little Freddie into Eton or Winchester than anything else. They were probably far too focused on that even to notice that little Freddie's teachers might actually be human beings.

But Josh wouldn't have been as stupid as she'd been in the first place. He wasn't an idiot. She'd brought this on herself. ('You make your bed, you have to lie in it,' jeered her mother.) She sighed. Josh had no idea, no idea at all. He was a darned good teacher – they once had to observe each other on teaching practice and he was seriously impressive – but it was so bloody unfair. The advantages his kids had over hers through the simple accident of birth were massive. Incomprehensibly so. If you were to compare the home life of a St Seb's family and a Liddells family . . . Well, it was laughable. Except that it wasn't.

It was almost five in the morning when Nell came home. It would be getting light before long. She closed the front door behind her as quietly as she could, so as not to waken the neighbours, and tiptoed upstairs. Stepping inside, she caught sight of herself in the hall mirror and was surprised to see that her face was wet with tears. She hadn't realized she was crying. She almost didn't recognize her own reflection. Who was the wraith-like figure looking back at her?

I don't know who I am any more, she thought. *I'm so tired. And I'm so bloody ashamed*. She'd cocked up, earning every ounce of scorn that was being heaped on her. She was ashamed of her behaviour. Ashamed of having given the media another stick to beat St Seb's with. Ashamed that she *minded* what people were saying so much. ('Sticks and stones may break my bones, but words will never hurt me,' said her mother.) Ashamed of her weakness. Ashamed that she seemed to be falling apart.

When Ray Graham rang the following morning to request a second meeting, Nell was already resigned to her fate. She knew she was going to get the sack. She just couldn't bear the thought of that happening on school premises.

'Come to my office, then,' said Ray. 'Lunchtime. But look, Nell, it's good news. It's sorted.'

Nell, still foggy with sleep, failed to take in the phrase 'good news' and simply said she'd see him later. She took a long hot shower and then set about cleaning the flat from top to bottom. She wiped out the fridge and defrosted the freezer. She cleared her food cupboard of anything approaching its sell-by date. She went through her wardrobe and ruthlessly removed anything she hadn't worn in the last year. She boxed up some of the untouched Christmas presents she'd received from the children. However grateful she was for the thought, she would never drink the bottle of Baileys or use the geranium bubble bath or wear the charm bracelet she was given last year.

The World's Best Teacher mug – which she'd allowed into her kitchen, even though it didn't match, because she was so fond of Tara O'Neill, an eleven-year-old with cystic fibrosis – she could no longer bear to keep. She sorted her books and put a dozen or so into a carrier bag for the charity shop. She wondered if she'd need to sell the flat, move away. *At least I've put my affairs in order*, she thought, as she pulled into the Grahams' yard.

She emerged from Ray's office half an hour later shaking her head in disbelief. It was over. Finished and done with, as long as she was prepared to write a letter of apology to Kelly Meacher. She also had to take an assembly next week about saying sorry when you've made a mistake or hurt other people's feelings. The investigation had found that she had been careless, but in the light of her excellent track record, the governors had concluded there was no further case to answer. The *Daily Mail* ran a short piece about trends in children's names, citing Kar-ian as an extreme example, but with no mention of either St Seb's or her by name. It hadn't been in *The Sun*. Unbelievably, the St Seb's Facebook community page had come down, and Ray assured her that the Twitter campaign had fizzled out.

'How on earth . . .?' asked Nell.

'That's for me to know and for you to find out. Or not,' he said, tapping the side of his nose with his forefinger. He looked distinctly pleased with himself.

'But they were out of order, too, you know, Shaneece and her posse. Six of one, half a dozen of the other, if you look at our social media policy. Copy me into that letter, get it over to Kelly Meacher by the end of the day and you can be back in school tomorrow morning.'

Nell opened her mouth to speak, but couldn't think what to say. Had Ray sent round the heavies? Called in a few favours? She knew he had tentacles everywhere. 'Thanks,' was all she could muster. 'I'll get right on to it.'

'Oh, and Nell?' She paused at the door. 'Lay off Ryan Power, will you? I know he's a little tyke but cut him a bit of slack for a couple of weeks. It'll make life much easier.'

She left his office simultaneously relieved and fuming. Relieved that she was off the hook, obviously, but fuming at Ray's parting remark. She was the teacher, not him. It was surely not up to him to question her professional judgement on matters of discipline. It was going to be hard enough re-establishing her authority as it was. Well, perhaps as Chair of Governors it was *partly* up to him; he was the critical friend and it was right that she was accountable. But Ryan was a red herring in all this, surely? She'd had no option but to exclude him – from lunchtime on Thursday until Monday morning, for heaven's sake – over the knife incident. On that, at least, she didn't believe she had anything to reproach herself for. But when she was back, she'd talk it over with Fiona, who was Ryan's class teacher. See whether they needed to adjust their behaviour management strategy in Ryan's case. He certainly knew how to press all the buttons.

She also felt slightly . . . what? *Cheated*, she thought, as she did up her seat belt and switched on the engine. Was that it? After almost a fortnight of hell, her professional reputation in tatters, she had to write a grovelling letter and it would all be *over*, just like that? ('Least said, soonest mended,' said her mother through pursed lips.)

9
Edward, May 1932

Edward's first sight of Edith is almost too sublime to be true. To his delight, he has been allocated a curacy in Oxford. He fell in love with the city of dreaming spires when he came up to university, and has prolonged the association by training for ordination at Cuddesdon College, only a few miles away.

To know that he is to stay in the city for yet another three years is the icing on the cake. He suspects his uncle, a personal friend of the Bishop of Oxford, may have had some influence over the appointment. He is determined not to disappoint either Uncle Hubert or Dr Strong, an academic theologian who served as both dean of Christ Church and vice chancellor of the university before his consecration as bishop. But on a good day – and today is a good day – Edward feels this ambition is within reach. His sense of calling is powerful. He can think of no better way of living his life.

Edward may be no scholar, but he has not done too badly, all things considered. He somehow scraped through his School Certificate, which allowed him to abandon the dreaded mathematics and concentrate on more enjoyable subjects for his last two years of school. Unexpectedly, he won a place at Oxford and, even more unexpectedly, sailed through both university and theological college, uncovering an aptitude for his studies that surprised him and delighted his tutors.

He worked hard, devoting many happy hours to his studies in the Bodleian Library. Biblical studies, church history, philosophy ... even Hebrew and Greek came remarkably easily. He remembers with great fondness evenings spent debating the finer points of theology with his fellow students, something he attempted to replicate in the vacations, with mixed success, with Uncle Hubert, who tended to wander off into anecdotes and stories. ('The theory's all very well, dear boy, but you may find the practice a little different.') And for the first time in his life, it seemed, he had friends, two in particular. There was Gareth Evans, a bluff Welshman whose thickset figure housed a heart of gold, who was even now renouncing a promising career on the rugger pitch to return to the valleys of south Wales where he would serve as his own father's curate. The other was Ross Fergusson, fiercely academic, who spent his evenings learning Mandarin because he believed God was calling him to serve as a missionary in China.

Edward is the only one of the three hanging on to Oxford. His nagging conscience that this is too privileged an existence is salvaged by the fact that he will be working in an area of the city that is poor, if not quite a slum. The vicar under whom he is to serve has written asking Edward to call on him for tea a month or so before his ordination in the cathedral. Edward accepted the invitation with alacrity. It will be his first meeting with Archie Taylor, whose reputation for inspired preaching and energetic service to the poor is well known.

The day is sunny. Edward arrives a little early, over-warm in his formal clothes. He is wearing a white linen suit, once upon a time Uncle Hubert's, and passed on to him by Aunt Florence. ('A victim of your uncle's expanding waistline,' she said, conspir-atorially. 'But don't breathe a *word*.') The trousers have been let down, because at six foot two, Edward is some inches taller than his uncle. He could tell from his tailor's expression that the suit is of fine quality, although he nurses a faint suspicion that the cut is unfashionable. ('Dear Edward at his most Edwardian!' Edith will tease before too long.) For now, though, he allows himself a moment of vanity. He looks smart, dapper even. In honour of the occasion, he has splashed out on a bus fare, in the hope that his appearance will suffer less in the heat than a long walk might allow. Today, after all, is a portentous day.

He easily identifies the vicarage: a substantial nineteenth-century house, a little set back from the road, and to Edward's eyes inappropriately luxurious alongside the mean terraces that line the rest of the street. But he must not disapprove, he reminds himself. He is here to serve. And to learn. The church, of the same vintage, is right next door. The clock shows it is ten to four; he will fill in the time by looking around.

The interior is dark and cool after the brightness of the afternoon, and Edward's eyes take a moment or two to adjust to the dimness. There is a great deal of stained glass, late Victorian at a guess and tending towards the sentimental. His own tastes are more austere. He walks up the tiled aisle towards the altar, pausing to examine the priest's stall where before very long he will take his place. The pulpit seems curiously out of proportion with the rest of the furniture: it is imposing, octagonal in shape and up a set of unnecessarily grandiose wooden steps. The relic of a grander church elsewhere?

All of a sudden he is overwhelmed by what lies ahead. His earlier confidence vanishes in a puff of smoke. Can he possibly be up to the task before him? Can he conduct divine worship, preach and teach in a way that will have any meaning for his new parishioners? What does he have to say to the men and women of east Oxford? All at once his inadequacies are laid bare before him. Who is he fooling; what on earth has he to offer? There are times when the presence of God is very real, but there are so many more when he knows himself to be a fraud and a hypocrite.

He is overcome by an urgent need to pray. He dares not sit in the priest's stall, and sinks to his knees in a pew in the front row. *Oh Lord*, he prays. *I am your unworthy servant. Can it really be that you are calling me to this task?*

He lays himself bare before God, wordlessly imploring his Maker for reassurance. And then he remembers a verse from Isaiah. 'I heard the voice of the Lord, saying, Whom shall I send, and who will go for us? Then said I, Here am I; send me.'

Here I am, he thinks. *Send me. But what can the Lord want with such a miserable sinner? And do I want to be sent?* Suddenly he remembers the time. Oh Lord! He must not be late for Canon Taylor. He stands up so swiftly that his head swims, and he hurtles out of the church into the sunshine in the direction of the vicarage. The doorbell is answered by a maid, who leads him through the house into the garden, which is ablaze with May colour. A girl is setting out a flowered china tea set under the natural arbour of an apple tree in full blossom. A ray of sunlight falls on her head, almost halo-like. She is tall and slender, boy-like almost, and wearing a blue-and-white dress, vertically striped and made of some sort of filmy fabric that clings to her body as she moves. Her hair is fashionably bobbed and so blonde it is almost white.

'How do you do?' she says, holding out a slim hand. She is terribly young, barely more than a schoolgirl, and unquestionably striking. 'My father won't be long, I'm sure. He had an urgent summons to a dying man's bedside. I'm sure you get the picture. If not, you soon will!' She laughs, an unaffected, musical laugh. 'Edith Taylor, daughter of the house,' she continues. 'Oh, good! Here comes Molly with the teapot.'

Even before he speaks a word, Edward finds he is framing the image in his mind for safekeeping. He wishes that he had his camera. Edith – the sunlight – the tea things – the perfectly mown lawn – the apple blossom – she is picture perfect.

'I suppose you play croquet, too?' he gabbles.

'Croquet, Mr Meadows?' She raises her eyebrows the merest fraction, but appears otherwise unfazed by his non sequitur. 'Naturally. Do you? Shall we?'

He almost laughs out loud with delight. 'Miss Taylor, you must forgive me. It was simply that the sight of you in this glorious setting quite took my breath away. I would be delighted to play croquet, if it would bring you pleasure. But perhaps we should not let the tea go cold.'

'Better not,' she says, matter-of-factly. 'I'm parched in this heat. I'll be mother, shall I, and you can tell me all about yourself. They usually do.'

'They?'

66

'My father's curates.'

'Ah,' says Edward, immediately determined to be the exception. 'I'm rather more interested in hearing about you. If that isn't an impertinence, that is.'

By the time the Vicar arrives, out of breath and apologetic – the man he went to see had been horribly injured in an accident at the motor car factory and died in considerable pain – Edward has established that Edith is seventeen ('nearly eighteen') and has been running her father's household for the last two years since her mother died. Her older sister Mabel lives in Dorset with her farmer husband and two boys. Edith plays the piano and is fond of growing roses, but has less time for these lady-like hobbies than might be expected because she is much occupied in helping her father set up a soup kitchen for the unemployed. She and her old school friend Dorothy are teaching a group of young mothers to read in the Parish Rooms. 'You'd be surprised by the demand,' she says. 'Everyone seems to think that Oxford has escaped the worst of the Depression, thanks to the motor car. But there are poor people everywhere, even here.'

Edward, all too conscious of staring at this delightfully unexpected girl, is almost relieved when she excuses herself and leaves him to talk to her father. Otherwise, he fears he might be unable to pay attention. Canon Taylor – or Father Archie, as he must now think of him ('no need for formality') – sets out Edward's duties and his own expectations.

'You come highly recommended, but I'd advise you not to rely too much on your varsity education,' he says. 'You'll find ministry here requires certain other qualities. A toughness of character. Resilience.'

Edward's face must betray something, because Father Archie pauses. 'Having doubts?'

'Of course not, Father! But I confess . . . I feel inadequate. Unworthy.'

Father Archie laughs. 'We all do, from time to time. But it's not a matter of being good enough. Remember, "He is faithful who called you," as St Paul put it. Hang on to that, if I were

67

you.' He drains his teacup. 'No need to worry unduly. I've met softer specimens than you. I'm sure we can knock the corners off. We'll make a parson of you yet.'

Father Archie tells him about the other curate, Leonard Smith, who came to ordination later in life, and the Church Army worker, Philip Hodgkins, both of whom arrived in the parish a year ago to help meet the needs of the community springing up around the burgeoning motor industry.

'You'll meet them at our first staff meeting. Monday mornings, eight o'clock sharp, please.' Father Archie stands up, signalling that the meeting is at an end. 'Probably worth mentioning that they both rather moon after Edith,' he adds casually. 'She's pretty fond of them, in a sisterly way, though poor old Len has an ugly war wound. Left his right arm at the Front. Not that he makes a meal of it. Manages jolly well, all things considered. But it might be wise not to get your hopes up.'

Edward feels himself blush scarlet. Is he really so obvious? Has he made a total ass of himself already? He stumbles over his words of thanks and farewell as he makes a hasty departure.

He hurries up the road towards the bus stop, then abruptly changes his mind and decides to return to his lodgings on foot. The walk may clear his head, which is spinning. His confidence has been up and down like a yo-yo all afternoon. Until now, he's been so sure of his vocation. For almost as long as he can remember – a decade, at least – he's been certain that becoming a priest would make him the man he was born to be, in Papa's words. It is his calling. And he thought he wanted nothing more. What if he is making a terrible mistake? If the whole thing is a fiasco? The sooner his ordination is in the bag the better, he thinks angrily. Otherwise he might change his mind. And the trouble is, there's really no back-up plan.

Seven months later, Edward is exhausted and ill. It is late December, a dreary dark day, the dregs of the year. He has a hacking cough he can't seem to shift and fears he may be heading for a dose of the bronchitis that confined him to bed throughout the snowy Christmas holidays of 1927. He sits in his pyjamas, wrapped in the eiderdown he has pulled from his bed. His swollen throat is concealed under two scarves, one his college colours, and the other a welcome new muffler knitted by Mrs Appleton as a Christmas present and posted by his aunt. He is wearing three pairs of socks to stave off the creeping cold. He huddles slightly closer to the fire than is probably safe. He knows he ought to refill the coal scuttle but the effort of going out to the coal shed feels quite beyond him. He can't even face boiling the kettle on the gas ring.

Though wretched in body, his spirits are high. His curacy has been a roller coaster of learning and mistakes, of trials and triumphs. Yet for the first time in his life he feels like a round peg in a round hole. Conducting worship is a tremendous privilege. He has discovered that he loves preaching, relishes the challenge of taking a sacred text and making it live for the day. To his astonishment, he is becoming a confident public speaker. In private, he will admit he enjoys the performance of a sermon, the sense of holding the congregation in the palm of his hand, of taking them on a journey from beginning to end in his address. He must be doing something right because Father Archie invited him to preach at Midnight Mass.

He enjoys expounding the Bible too. After a slightly bumpy start when he assumed too much, his confirmation classes are now going well. A few weeks in, his pupils listen quite attentively, considering their lack of education, and with the right prompting, engage in discussion. Father Archie, sticking his head round the door and looking in on his class a fortnight ago, indicated his approval in a quiet nod and left him to it.

He is full of admiration for Father Archie on all counts, but perhaps particularly in the way he speaks out for the poor, and does constant battle with the authorities to improve their living conditions. Many of their parishioners live in appalling housing, at the mercy of brutal and greedy landlords. Father Archie is always prepared to fight their corner. He is currently part of a campaign calling on the government to give schoolchildren free milk. Edward is in awe of his tenacity and is trying to do his bit too by taking a regular turn in the soup kitchen.

What he finds harder is the everyday conversation with parishioners. The interest in the lives of others that characterizes Uncle Hubert's ministry seems to have passed him by. Where Len happily falls into banter over a pint with the workers as they clock off, Edward struggles to think of anything to say. He feels hampered by his Oxford degree, his educated voice, his natural reserve. Len is older, more experienced, and has been through the War, as have many of the factory hands. His disfigurement may even help. But Edward doesn't know where to start. He thinks again of Kipling's 'If –', the last stanza:

> If you can talk with crowds and keep your virtue
> Or walk with Kings – nor lose the common touch . . .

Edward isn't sure he ever had much of a common touch to lose. Len makes it look so easy. How does he do it?

He must not be jealous, he tells himself as he hears a knock at the door. Len is a good fellow, a generous and understanding colleague. This is almost certainly the man himself, having missed Edward at Evening Prayer and come to see what is wrong. He shuffles to the door like an old man, still swaddled in his layers.

'Ah! Miss Taylor!'

'Edith, please,' she replies, entering the hallway with a basket under her arm before he can object. 'Dear Mr Meadows, what a state you are in!'

Edward is mortified that she should find him in such chaos. It is the first time she has visited his lodgings, and he is painfully conscious of his shambolic appearance and the general muddle. The air is stale and he desperately needs a bath and a shave.

'Dear Miss Taylor . . . *Edith* . . . forgive me! I was not expecting visitors,' he says, and begins to cough again, an unpleasant phlegmy sound.

'You know perfectly well I've seen far worse,' she says serenely, setting her basket down on his table. She gathers his sermon notes, his commentaries and Bible into a neat pile, taking care not to lose the place in the open books, and unloads her wares. 'Soup, in case your throat's too sore to swallow, and a little stew for when you're feeling stronger,' she says. 'And if you really can't face either, there's some lemon barley water.

'Now, shall I tidy up a bit? Refill that coal scuttle? The fire's looking in need of a good stoke. I thought I might send Molly round later to change your sheets. Would that be a help?'

Edward collapses back into his chair, weak with relief. Gratitude replaces embarrassment. She is so impressively capable that all he can feel is thankfulness that she is here. She really is the most marvellous girl; indeed, she is right at the top of the list of reasons for his current happiness. *Oh dear Lord, thank you for Edith!*

The months since the apple-blossom tea have done nothing to diminish his first impressions. She is estimable in all ways: hard-working and practical, calm and kind. He knows her to be a woman of deep faith and regular prayer, and like her father, she never misses an opportunity to make life better for those around her. He is altogether charmed by her. No! he thinks in surprise. Surely he is in love with her! Even if she doesn't return his affections, he will adore her without hope, like a chivalrous knight bound by courtly love.

Yet, in truth, he dares to believe that perhaps she is rather fond of him. In spite of Father Archie's warning, he is cautiously confident that he has seen off his rivals. Disfigurement aside, surely Len is far too old for her; and on more than one occasion, he's noticed Edith's eyes glaze over when Hodgkins recounts yet another self-serving story about his work supporting an unemployment centre in his previous post in Liverpool.

Without exactly saying so, Edith has taken it on herself to show Edward the ropes. Whenever he finds himself at a loss, it seems that she is there to steer him, unobtrusively, in the right direction. She is his compass, his lodestar.

They have had long conversations about – well, anything and everything. Life, faith, hopes and dreams. She asked him all about

India, and he tried to paint the sights and sounds, the colours and scents of his early life. She was such a sympathetic listener that he found himself telling her about the snake, the appalling nightmares, and to his immense relief she didn't laugh. He shared precious memories of holidays with his aunt and uncle, his gratitude for the gift of a loving adoptive second family. In return, she entrusted him with her own confidences: her regret at leaving school early to nurse her mother through her long and difficult final illness, her sadness when her sister moved away, her delight in Mabel's weekly letters from Dorset. She's shown Edward snaps of her nephews, dear little chaps. Surely Edward can't be imagining the glances in his direction when she thinks no one is looking? The shared moments of amusement when their eyes meet across a crowded room? And is she not here now, an angel of mercy in his hour of need?

To his chagrin, Edward's eyes well up with unexpected tears. And then, because he is moved, and because she is so splendid, and probably, too, he thinks later, because he has a temperature and isn't thinking straight, he asks Edith if she could bear the thought of marrying him. And to his astonishment, Edith accepts without hesitation.

10
Nell, April 2016

This time a fortnight ago . . ., thought Nell. It seemed far longer. *If I could only turn back time.* ('No use crying over spilt milk,' said her mother.)

It was Friday afternoon again and time she went home. Nell had got through her first day back, but at some considerable cost. It had taken every ounce of her energy to go to work, as usual, to prepare for the day, as usual, to give every appearance of normality, when inside she was in pieces.

She'd been heartened by the response of her colleagues. 'Good to see you back,' was Fiona's cheerful greeting on arrival. 'Glad not to be the acting acting head any more. Know my place, and it's acting deputy, thank you.' No one else said anything much. She didn't know exactly what Ray had told them, but she hadn't picked up any sidelong looks. The conversation didn't suddenly stop when she entered the staffroom. Nonetheless, she tried to counter any gossip before it had a chance to start.

'I've had a bit of a fortnight and no doubt you have too,' she said. 'Sincere apologies for making extra work for you all, especially Fiona. But it's great to be back where I belong. Come and see me if you've got any questions. Otherwise it's onwards and upwards, and let's all keep doing what we know we need to do.'

The day ran pretty smoothly, all things considered. Nell even managed a cup of instant soup at lunchtime without throwing up. She avoided the playground at home time, telling herself she had far too much catching up to do to leave her desk. If anyone really wanted her, they could stop by her office. On Monday she would stand there, as usual, at the beginning and end of the day, ready to chat to parents and carers and children as they arrived and left. Just not today.

So she'd got through, if only by the skin of her teeth. She'd felt stretched taut all day, like an overtightened string on a violin. Drafting the advert for Rachel's maternity leave cover took far longer than it should have. And she dithered terribly over the budget, which needed to go back to the governors next week for signing off. She'd already spent hours on it – everything but everything needed realigning if they were going to pull themselves out of Special Measures – but she had a nagging feeling that she might have missed something. *This will all soon feel normal again*, she told herself. *It's bound to be a bit odd, coming back*. She was just thinking about packing up for the day when a head appeared round the door.

'Ah, Nell . . . I wasn't sure if you were still expecting me?' It was Father Hugh, the new parish priest from St Sebastian's next door. He was massive, tall and broad, with a beard and thick curly dark hair, and widely known as Father Hagrid. According to Diane, a churchgoer, he had a beautiful Nigerian wife called Precious. 'We can reschedule, if you like?'

Nell groaned. He'd come to talk about assembly themes for the term. The date had been in the diary since the end of last term, but she'd totally forgotten. 'I'm sorry. Come on in. Would you like a cup of tea?'

'Love one,' he said. 'But why don't I make it? You look done in.' Whether it was his kindness or his smile, Nell found herself in tears.

Father Hugh waved away her apology. 'Don't move,' he said. 'I'll be back in a minute.'

She had just about got herself under control when he returned with two mugs of tea and a couple of dark chocolate KitKats.

'My favourite! How did you know?'

'Had a hunch,' he said. 'I buy the multi-packs for emergencies. At least that way you get the proper wrappers. Call me old-fashioned, but KitKats taste much better out of foil and paper.'

'Oh come on!' said Nell. 'The plasticky ones have been around for ever.'

'The technical term is a flow-wrap-and-tear-strip,' said Father Hugh. 'And you're quite right. It was introduced in 2001 as a cost-saving measure. So none of the children here at St Seb's will have the pleasure if they buy them singly. A major hole in their education, I'm sure you'll agree. And you can't recycle the plastic chaps, either.'

Nell laughed for the first time in what seemed like months. 'What are you? Some kind of packaging nerd?'

'No. Just a pub quiz nerd.'

'Well, I'm very grateful. Just the sugar boost I needed,' she said. 'Shall we look at those assemblies? I've got a list somewhere.'

She printed it off, and they worked through the list together. Father Hugh had led an excellent assembly as part of his job interview in January. He'd stripped off his black shirt and clerical collar to reveal a T-shirt printed with 'Father Hagrid' – he'd had the kids eating out of his hand from that moment on – but he'd made a good point about finding out who we really are, under the surface. And you could hear a pin drop when he said a prayer at the end. But Nell was still keen to establish some ground rules. She was encouraged to discover that he understood the need to link in with school values and the targets they were working towards. Refreshingly, he didn't seem to have an agenda of his own.

'I don't know if you've had a chance to read the School Improvement Plan yet, but we've got a lot of work to do on promoting self-esteem,' she said. 'If we're going to raise achievement, we need to invest a heck of a lot in social and emotional learning. The messages we give out in our assemblies form a key strand in our approach.'

Father Hugh nodded. 'I'm right behind you on that one,' he said. 'If you can't crack self-esteem, you don't stand a chance.' He gathered up his papers into an old-fashioned brown leather

75

satchel. 'In fact, I'm right behind you on the whole shebang, if it helps at all. I hear you've had a bit of a time of it lately. Do you want to talk about it?'

'No,' she said, and promptly burst into tears. And, to her mortification, it all came pouring out. The Facebook nightmare, the vitriolic comments, the Twitter campaign, the calls for her to be sacked.

'I know it's pathetic, but I'm just not coping very well,' she said. 'It's as if all my years as a teacher . . . well, they count for nothing. How could I be so stupid? It's all my fault! I feel like a total waste of space. Useless. And now it's over, I should be happy as Larry, but I feel like shit. *Sorry*. I feel rubbish.'

'Don't mind me,' he said. 'Tell it as it is. It's not just shit, by the way. I'd say it was horseshit. Megashit. Whatever you like.'

She half laughed. 'When I came to work this morning, the one thing I wanted was that it wouldn't be an issue. That no one would mention it, that we'd all have moved on. And now I find I almost resent the fact that no one's said anything to me. No one seems to realize quite how . . . devastating this has been for me. Being suspended was bad enough. But the comments! They were so *personal* and so vicious! I've never known anything like it. Being vilified, and so publicly. You probably think I'm overreacting. Even I think I'm making a fuss about nothing!'

She blew her nose. 'That's a really stupid word, by the way. Megashit, I mean. It's so not a thing. And definitely not a word we should teach the children.'

He laughed. 'Then let's put it another way. My guess is you feel well and truly dumped on.'

She started crying again. 'God, I'm sorry about this. I never cry. Especially in front of people I barely know. And d'you know what? I don't even care.'

And now she couldn't speak any more. The tears poured from her eyes. The floodgates opened on a torrent of pent-up unhappiness and fear and anxiety. When she finally paused for breath, she saw that Father Hugh had pilfered the box of tissues that usually sat on Diane's desk. He came back into the room with a fresh cup of tea. *What a lovely man*, she thought.

'You know what I think?' he said, gently. 'I'm assuming you have a whole raft of other school policies alongside the social media one. Which I've read by the way. I ought to fess up that Ray gave me a run-down.'

She groaned again. She should have guessed. As the parish priest, Father Hugh was a foundation governor, even if he'd barely got his feet under the table.

'What's your point?'

'Your anti-bullying policy. It's not just about what goes on in the playground. Or at least it shouldn't be. From where I'm standing, I'd say what happened to you was bullying, Nell. Harassment, at the very least. The comments, all the Twitter rubbish . . . it's not just about one or two parents going against the social media policy. It was *bullying*. Clear as day. And the thing to remember about bullying is that it's *not* your fault. For what it's worth, the way you're reacting is par for the course.'

For all the awareness training she'd done over the years, it had never occurred to Nell that she might be the victim of bullying. 'Really? Do you think so?'

'I know so. It's cyberbullying and it's really nasty. Worse than that, it's dangerous. In my last job, a close colleague of mine – a friend really – she was targeted. It almost destroyed her.'

'So you don't think I'm making a fuss?'

'Absolutely not. And at the risk of being disloyal to the governors when I've only been here five minutes, I'm not sure this has been as well handled as it might have been. You should have had more support. You might want to contact your union. Do you want me to tackle Ray about it?'

Nell shuddered. 'I just want to put it all behind me. Get on with my job.'

'In that case, I think you need to go home and try and get some sleep. You look dog tired. Any plans for the weekend?'

Nell shook her head. There was always the Park Run but she hadn't bothered making any arrangements with friends.

'Well, I think you need to be kind to yourself. Regroup a little. Don't for goodness' sake spend the whole weekend working. And if you still feel this bad after a couple of good nights' sleep, you might think about going to the doctor. Maybe consider some counselling.'

'Counselling? So you really do think I'm losing the plot?'

'There's nothing wrong with counselling,' said Father Hugh. 'Well, there can be, I suppose, if it's not done well. But from my own experience, I can tell you that the right kind of therapy can be a great help. A lifesaver, even.' Nell found herself wondering what problems Father Hugh needed to take to therapy. He seemed so together.

He got up to leave, swinging his satchel across his body. 'It's not a weakness, you know, asking for help,' he said with a smile. 'You're only human. And if it helps at all, you're not a waste of space. Far from it. I can tell that, even after only forty-five minutes. Word on the street is that you're a great teacher. A dog with a bone, when it comes to St Seb's. Hang on to that if you possibly can.

'Piece of advice, though,' he added from the door. 'Stay off social media if you have a drink tonight.'

Nell laughed and made to throw a stapler at his retreating figure. He'd given her plenty to think about. A new perspective. Best of all, he'd offered a tiny flicker of hope.

Nell slept through the night for the first time in a week. As a result she woke up late and groggy on Saturday morning to find she'd missed the Park Run. After a shower she decided to take herself out for breakfast and make some plans for the rest of the day. She rang Susie for a quick chat, and arranged to go to the cinema with Fran. Work could wait. *See, Father Hagrid? I was listening. I'm being kind to myself.*

She set off for Luigi's, which was just far enough away from St Seb's in the opposite direction from the Binks that she was pretty confident she wouldn't bump into anyone she didn't want to see. *But I'm out of hibernation*, she told herself. *It's a start.* ('Fine words butter no parsnips,' mocked her mother.) Luigi's had long been a favourite haunt, although she would admit that the nightmare birthday dinner with Mark last year had taken the shine off it for a while. The place was done out like a 1950s Italian bistro, with metal chairs in bright colours and a vintage red Vespa in the window. They played Elvis and Johnny Cash on a top-notch sound system cleverly concealed behind a period jukebox. When the weather was nice, people spilled out on to a stretch of pavement just wide enough for a handful of tables and chairs.

'*Cara* Nell!' Luigi greeted her with a kiss on both cheeks. 'Where have you been, mia bella? I missed you. You are breaking my heart when you desert us!'

Luigi snapped his fingers and his daughter, Caterina, appeared with a menu. 'I 'ope that man has come to a horrible end,' he added in a stage whisper. '*Stronzo*! Son of a bitch. No good for you. Waste of time.'

Nell immediately felt better. She chatted for a few minutes to Caterina, asking about her studies, and then ordered poached egg, smoked salmon, avocado and spinach on sourdough toast, with a caffé latte. Some proper food would be good for her. She picked up a newspaper from the bar and took herself off to a corner. She'd been so absorbed in her own problems that she had no idea what was going on in the world. Her breakfast was brought by someone she didn't recognize: dark-haired, with a neatly trimmed beard, olive-skinned and around her own age. Presumably one of Luigi's extended family. Spending a few months brushing up their English in Oxford seemed to be a rite of passage, although they were usually school leavers or students when they came over. The food looked delicious, but there was no sign of the coffee.

'Um, do you mind checking on my latte, please?' she asked. The waiter nodded without speaking and she wondered if he had understood. He might only just have arrived in the country. But he returned a few moments later with the missing drink.

'*Grazie*,' she said, expecting the usual '*Prego*'.

'*Afwan*,' he replied with a slight smile. 'Welcome.' He pronounced the pleasantry as if it was two words – *well*

79

come – not one. *Afwan*? Possibly not Italian. 'Are you new?' she asked, speaking more slowly than usual. 'I don't think I've seen you here before.'

'Yes, I am new, and no, we have not met until this day,' he said, holding out his hand. 'My name is George, and it is my pleasure to meet you.'

Nell blushed as she shook his hand. His English was flawless – a little formal perhaps and just slightly accented. But perfect.

'And mine to meet you. I'm Nell. How long are you over here for?'

'That remains to be seen,' he said. 'Now, if you will please excuse me? I am needed at the bar.' He gave a little nod, and left Nell to her breakfast and her paper. She took a steadying breath. It was good to think there was life beyond her flat, beyond St Seb's. It was good to find you could speak to a stranger and not receive a mouthful of abuse in return. Not everyone was out to get her.

This is a treat and I will enjoy it, she thought as she started her breakfast. ('Hah!' said her mother. 'All right for some!') She caught Caterina's eye, and asked for a freshly squeezed orange juice on the side. *Perhaps I can get through this, after all.*

11
Hope, February 1959

Hope leaned backwards slightly, half turned her head to face the camera and smiled in what she hoped was a winning manner.

'Arms, darling, arms!' said Marco, the photographer's assistant.

'What am I supposed to do with them?'

Marco bustled over. He had already pushed her right leg out in front of the left, with the knee slightly bent. Now he put her left hand on her hip, which was slightly raised above the right because of the position of her feet. He took her right hand and curved it upwards.

'Touch your chin, darling!'

'Won't I look a frightful fool?'

Eric, the photographer, intervened. 'Touch the collar, Speedy G. Just with the fingertips, there's a good girl.'

Hope tried that, and although it felt awkward, Marco and Eric settled on her forefinger and middle finger just brushing the neckline of the jacket. It was rather a dear little knitted two-piece suit in navy blue. The jacket was collarless and had no lapels either: it had three-quarter-length sleeves and a border of white piping. The skirt was narrow, almost a pencil skirt, and clung to Hope's slender figure. A Chanel rip-off, but none the worse for that. She couldn't abide the sack dresses that were everywhere last year, though Faith used to say she could carry off the most outlandish of styles.

Now, her back ached, and she felt sure her smile was looking strained. It all felt terribly artificial. Did anyone actually stand like this in real life? Just when she thought she couldn't bear to hold the pose a moment longer, Eric pronounced himself satisfied and sent her off behind the screen to change into the next outfit. He patted her bottom as she went. Eric, with his slicked back hair and leather bomber jacket, must be at least forty, far too old to be of any interest, but she wiggled her behind anyway, because she fancied Marco, even if she knew in her heart of hearts he was as queer as a coot. And probably not even called Marco. It was terribly cold in the studio, and the corner behind the screen was thick with dust. Thank goodness there was room on the rail to hang up her work dress. She needed to look half decent when she got back to her desk, or someone in the office would be bound to smell a rat. This was moonlighting, technically, and could land her in trouble. Honestly, though! To think she'd nearly refused to give it a go, when Eric invited her along, just because it was knitwear. She'd had visions of her mother's ghastly knitting patterns and the frightful grey V-necks Mama used to make for the boys. Not elegant little suits like these. You lived and learned.

Mind you, it was a lot harder work, modelling, than you might think. All this standing about at funny angles and trying to make it look natural. And she was getting a teeny bit anxious about the time. Julia would give her an awful earful if she was late back at her desk, but luckily Julia was out at a lunch do, so fingers crossed. Being Julia's secretary was far and away the best job she'd ever had and she didn't want to lose it.

It had led to this, after all. Gracious, she was a model now! Who'd have thought it? Or almost. *Almost* a model. She mustn't get ahead of herself. These were trial shots, and Eric had made her no promises. But she thought it was going well and if the snaps got used . . . *if* they got used . . . maybe one thing would lead to another. If her picture appeared in print, who could tell what might happen next? For one thing, someone would be bound to see it and tell her parents. Then what would Father say? He was an archdeacon now, one step below a bishop. Which meant he was more insufferable than ever. Hah! He would be bound to disapprove because he'd disapproved of Hope all her life.

But she was an adult now, and she'd escaped, thank heavens. She stuck it out in Lancashire as long as she could bear – rather longer, actually – and even scraped her way through dreaded secretarial college, for heaven's sake. Partly to keep her parents happy, and partly because Betty convinced her a qualification was her best escape route. Her mood clouded a little at the thought of Betty. Hope really had imagined she would move back to Brum at the earliest opportunity, assumed that she and Betty would find a place together, but it hadn't turned out quite like that. Betty ended up having to get married in a hurry to Ron, who worked in the paint shop on the new Austin A55. Now Betty and Ron and baby Susan were all crammed into Betty's grandma's place. The old lady was totally doolally now, wrote Betty, but that was life, wasn't it?

So, Hope thought, in for a penny, in for a pound, and turned her gaze towards the capital, because there was certainly more chance of excitement in London than lousy Lancashire. As it happened, her parents couldn't really object to London, because both Prudence and Faith had gone to live there. Prue went first, to university, although she'd moved to Manchester by the time Hope arrived, for some unspeakably dull job in the civil service the parents were terribly impressed with. Faith was still here, though, working as a staff nurse at St Thomas's where she'd trained. At her mother's insistence, Hope agreed – a little reluctantly, it must be said – to lodge with Faith in the first instance. Faith had moved out of the nurses' home into a bedsit in Soho as soon as she qualified. Hope was surprised – and impressed – that Faith had lit on such a colourful part of London, but her sister claimed it was simply convenient for work and handy for the pictures. Either way, Hope was content to take the tiny attic room above Faith's, which had just become vacant because another girl was getting married.

To Hope's surprise, living on top of Faith hadn't been all that bad. Several times a week, they cooked for each other on the little gas ring in the passageway that masqueraded as a kitchen. If Faith wasn't working at weekends – and her shift pattern was erratic – they went to the pictures or, if they could get cheap seats, sometimes the theatre. Not that Hope ever really followed the plot, but she enjoyed the spectacle. And without Prue's influence overshadowing everything, Hope discovered a whole new side to Faith. She was far kinder than Hope remembered, took her under her wing and introduced Hope to her friends and colleagues. They weren't the most exciting crowd, perhaps, but it was a start in a city where she didn't know a soul.

'Just don't run off with Ted, because I've got high hopes of him,' said Faith the morning after a party at someone's digs a few weeks after Hope arrived.

'Ted? Which one's he?'

'Honestly, Hope! I know you're bad at faces, but *still*. You must remember Ted. Junior doctor. The one who spilt his beer. I helped him mop up in the kitchen. You saw me! Awfully clever and utterly dreamy.'

Hope racked her brains, but drew a blank. She dimly recalled the spilt beer, but no face to match. She would try and remember the name, though, because Faith was clearly in the grip of a pash, and Hope had to admit that men tended to pay her far more attention than they ever did Faith. It was all 'Good old Faith, what a *brick*,' whereas they bought Hope drinks, and asked her to dance. She adored dancing, always had. One or two made it plain it wasn't just a dance they were after, but Hope was keeping herself tidy. For now, at least. She didn't want to end up like Betty.

After a couple of dismal months working in a typing pool for an insurance firm in the City, Hope found the job at *Style* through someone she met at a party. *Style* was only round the corner, within walking distance in Wardour Street, and the features editor needed a secretary. Some of the work was the same – typing was typing, after all – but it was so much more glamorous being part of the fashion world. It was only *Style*, not *Vogue* or *Vanity Fair*, but Hope loved it with a passion. She understood what she was typing, for starters. Because Hope understood clothes. She was fascinated by design and colour, and instinctively knew what worked and what didn't. She'd even started voicing her opinions, cautiously at first, and then, encouraged by her boss, Miss Fenn, with greater confidence. Two years on, Miss Fenn – or Julia, she was supposed to call her, it was all first-name terms at *Style*, very informal – was starting to rely on her judgement, and always asked for her comments on new styles when they arrived in the office. Julia said Hope had a good eye. It was a novelty for Hope to be good at anything.

It was through work that she met Eric and the delectable Marco. She'd seen them several times from a distance, of course, but they'd never really spoken before, until one day Julia sent her round to the studio to pick up some photos because there was a panic on. A feature had fallen through and Julia was in for a dressing-down at the editorial meeting if she didn't come up with an alternative pretty fast.

'Why not do something on car coats?' Hope suggested.

'Car coats? Why on earth would we do that?'

'It's only an idea,' said Hope. 'But car ownership is going through the roof. The factories are battling to keep up with demand. And lots and lots of the new owners are women.'

'How on earth do you know that?'

'My friend Betty's husband works on the assembly line at Longbridge. Some of the newer models are specially designed for women. You know, a little runabout for the little woman. They're bringing in new paint colours specially. The other thing is . . . well, I don't think anyone else has done car coats recently. There's certainly been nothing in *Vogue*.'

Hope returned to her typing, confident that she'd hooked Julia's interest.

'I'll tell you what else,' she added as an afterthought. 'Say we do run with car coats. What about setting up the photoshoot differently? Don't have pictures of women driving cars on a country estate. Don't do it in town either. Why not take the car coats to the factory floor? Put our models alongside the production line? You could make a joke in the headline: *The*

85

latest model with the latest model. That'd be hip. Our readers would go mad for it.'

Julia had leapt at the idea. It had been a heck of a lot of work, sending out for samples and booking models and sorting things out with the factory. They'd worked flat out to turn the feature round in time, but they'd done it. They had to pay Eric over the odds, but Julia said it was worth it. They were right up to the wire when Hope took a phone call to say that the contact sheets were ready, and she hotfooted it over to the studio, a five-minute walk away. While she was waiting for the dozy receptionist to fish out the right package for her, Eric himself had appeared. There was the bomber jacket.

'Oh, it's you!' he said, looking her up and down. He had a distinctive gravelly voice, a sort of cockney drawl, and hairy hands. 'And what's a nice-looking girl like you doing in my studio?'

'The car coats pics, for *Style*,' she said, hearing an unfortunate primness in her own voice. 'Just collecting the contact sheets. We're up against it, timewise.'

'And you're Speedy Gonzales, huh?' He laughed. 'Know what? I'm always after new models. Dunno where you got those pins, but I reckon you might just fit the bill. What say you?'

Hope was taken aback. She knew she was tolerably good-looking – the pixie haircut she'd worn ever since the day she begged Rita to cut off her pigtails suited her features, and she'd long since grown into her height – but she'd never thought of herself as a mannequin. Or . . . gracious . . . had she got the wrong end of the stick altogether? Did he mean something else entirely? Something sleazy? Her face must have betrayed her thoughts, because he laughed.

'No funny business, honest!' he said. 'Got a knitwear feature coming up and my usual girl's gone off sick. Come at lunchtime tomorrow. We can give you a try-out. All above board. Bring your mum if you want. What d'you reckon?'

The thought of Edith here in Soho was risible – 'fish out of water' didn't come close – and Hope's head was too full of the car coats to linger now. She played for time.

86

'I'm in an awful rush. May I telephone? When I've had a chance to think about it.'

'Give you till 6 p.m. today.' He shrugged, losing interest. 'Plenty more fish in the sea, Speedy G.'

And now here she was, finally changing back into her navy day dress, and getting ready to go back to the office, her head in a total spin. Hope Meadows, a model! Not so Hopeless after all. She felt a pang that Faith wasn't there to share the moment. In fact, if Faith had still been around, she might have brought her along in place of her mother. Faith would have enjoyed it, shared a joke with her about Marco. Teased her about her poses. Celebrated her success, even. The few months they lived cheek by jowl in London had been precious. They'd even managed to exorcize some old ghosts.

'I was always so jealous of you!' Faith confessed over a cup of cocoa late one cold November night. Hope had run out of coins for her own meter, so they were curled up in the tired armchairs in front of the two-bar electric fire in Faith's room.

'Hah! Jealous of *me*?' Hope almost snorted. 'What in heaven's name did you have to be jealous about? You always made me feel so stupid! All of you!'

'But you were so *brave*. So defiant. The way you stood up to Father. I was in shock and awe!'

'But you and Prudence . . . You were always such a mouse!'

'Exactly! Imagine being sandwiched between Prue and you. I couldn't compete on either side. All I could do was cling on to Prue's coat-tails and hope for the best. And then of course there was Amazing Grace . . .'

The sisters exchanged a fond look. Grace was at teacher training college now, and by the end of the first term was engaged to a predictably nice man called John.

'Not to mention the boys,' said Hope, raising her eyebrows heavenwards. 'Father always wanted sons. Why else did he name the boys after kings, when we were all lumbered with mouldy old Christian virtues? Do you know what he once said to Uncle Lionel . . .?'

But Faith wasn't listening. 'Do you know what?' she said abruptly. 'I've realized I'm going to have to give up on Ted.'

'Why do you say that?'

'We've worked together for two years and he barely knows I'm there!' Faith shook her head. 'You wouldn't know what that's like,' she continued, not unkindly. 'You've simply no idea. You're annoyingly beautiful.'

Hope looked up, taken aback. 'I . . .'

'I know! You can't help it. It's just the cards we've been dealt. But actually, I've decided on something. I haven't told anyone else yet, but I'm going to become a missionary.'

Hope whooped. 'Faith! Just because one rather ordinary young man doesn't look your way . . . you can't be serious!'

'I'm perfectly serious,' said Faith, and Hope saw that she was. 'He's not ordinary, by the way. Not to me. I really thought he was the one. Ah well.' She shrugged. Then her eyes lit up as she told Hope about a visiting speaker who'd preached at St Anne's a couple of Sundays before. Hope hadn't been near a church since moving to London, but Faith was as regular as clockwork. 'He's home on furlough from the Far East and I must say, he was marvellous! So inspiring. I talked to his wife afterwards, and apparently mission societies snap up British nurses like nobody's business. Now I've just got to start applying. I'm convinced it's God's will for me.'

Hope was speechless. No sooner had she discovered her sister than she was losing her again.

'Besides, it might be an adventure,' added Faith with forced cheer. 'You wait, I'll be the one seeing the world and you'll be jealous of me for once when you read all my fascinating letters.'

Hope went over to hug Faith, who promptly burst into tears. And now she'd gone, off to India with a medical missionary society. She wrote once a week and, in truth, her letters were not terribly fascinating. But Hope missed her more than she imagined possible.

12
Edward, March 1940

Edward stands at the barriers on New Street station. His eyes scan the heaving platform, and he cranes his neck in the hope of catching sight of Uncle Hubert. The station, always busy, is swarming with life. Soldiers in khaki, airmen in blue, kitbags slung over their shoulders. Handsome young men in high spirits, shouting and cheering as they set off for the adventure of a lifetime. A gaggle of girls, dressed up to the nines to wave their menfolk goodbye, add to the festival atmosphere. A brass band is playing.

Edward feels a stab of envy so sharp it almost takes his breath away. These fine men will have the chance to put themselves to the test. To pit themselves against the forces of evil, to prove themselves on the battlefield. They are serving King and country. But do they have any idea what they are walking into? They seem so light hearted. And they are so young – barely out of school, it seems – too young to remember the Great War. Or is it all bravado?

Edward sighs. He is tired; the night was badly disrupted by a teething Grace. No wonder his thoughts are confused. He considers going in search of a cup of tea, but decides that the risk of missing Uncle Hubert is too great. Then right on cue, his uncle appears, an elderly lady on his arm, with whom he is in animated conversation.

'Edward, dear boy! You simply must meet Miss Jarvis. She has been telling me all about her work at the Oxford University Press. So very interesting. Retired, of course, now, but she worked on dear Dr Strong's marvellous *Lectures on the Method of*

Science. And today she's visiting her nephew in Edgbaston. Isn't that splendid?'

Edward politely shakes hands with Miss Jarvis, and helps steer her in the direction of the branch line to Edgbaston, doing his best to conceal his impatience. He assured Edith that he would be home in time to say goodnight prayers with the children, but he doesn't want to let slip the chance of speaking to Uncle Hubert. He wants his advice, badly. There is a tea shop around the corner and he is about to suggest it when his eye falls on the Station Tavern.

'Can I buy you a pint, Uncle?' he asks.

'I say! Now there's a thought,' says Uncle Hubert. 'A half perhaps. Might we do well to slip off our collars before we venture in?'

Inside, the Tavern is thick with the air of cigarette smoke and despair. The barstools are threadbare and the table is sticky. The beer, at least, is tolerable. Edward steers his uncle away from the knot of men playing darts – once in conversation he will be quite impossible to extract – and into a quiet corner.

'Well, I say!' Uncle Hubert's eyes light up like a child's at the sight of his beer. 'Isn't this marvellous? Your very good health, dear boy! Now, how are dear Edith and the quiverful?'

'Very well, thank you,' says Edward. 'Though the baby's new teeth are troubling her, and us too.'

Somehow, Edward and Edith have produced four daughters in the space of seven years. His quiver is indeed full, as the psalmist would say, and he needs to remember this. Prudence, Faith, Hope and Grace are a great blessing, even if at times he feels overwhelmed by the burden of fatherhood. Such a responsibility! And he longs, how he longs, for a son, the affirmation of his manhood. In an unguarded moment he said as much to Edith, and she was quite brisk with him. 'Shame on you, Edward! How can you be so Victorian? It's not as if there's a title or a fortune at stake. Our four darling girls are a gift from God and we should be thankful.'

He shares none of this with Uncle Hubert, who has never known the joy of family life. Years after Edward's first school holiday at the rectory, Mrs Appleton let slip that his original Christmas visit was postponed because Aunt Florence was suffering not from the influenza Edward imagined, but the last in a long line of miscarriages. Edward knows himself to be the undeserved recipient of Aunt Florence's spare maternal love, and all the better for it.

Having assured his uncle of his own domestic happiness and asked fondly after his aunt, Edward moves the conversation on.

'Uncle Hubert, I would value your advice. I need your wisdom.'

'About the parish? Run into difficulties, dear boy?'

'No! Not that. All that is . . . well, as well as can be expected, I suppose. We live in difficult times.' He took a long draught of his beer. 'It's more . . . I am struggling with my calling.'

'Having doubts? A tough parish can do that.'

'No. That is to say, I constantly doubt my abilities,' he says, recalling his crisis of confidence before ordination. Whenever the doubts return, he draws on his father-in-law's advice to remember the words of St Paul. Dear Father Archie, felled by a stroke last year at only sixty-one. Edward misses him acutely. But he has learned a great deal in the past eight years, and although he suspects a lifetime of learning is ahead of him, he would say he knows what he is doing.

'Ah. I can see I'm not explaining myself. I know without doubt I am called to serve God. It's more a question of *where* and *how*. I see all these fine young men going off to the War and I can't help wondering . . . Well, why not me? Why on earth am I not among them?'

'You know the answer to that,' says Uncle Hubert. 'And it's a perfectly respectable one. Ours is a reserved occupation, and you are a husband and father to boot. You have responsibilities aplenty. And never forget, war is an evil, filthy business. Our calling is to be peace-makers. Dear Lord, Edward, isn't that enough?'

Edward is taken aback by his uncle's passion. 'I thought . . . well, I thought, with your service record, you might understand.'

In fact, it strikes Edward now that he has taken for granted that Uncle Hubert will encourage him to put himself forward. And that he badly wants to take Uncle Hubert's certainty in the matter back to Edith. Too old himself for active service, Uncle Hubert is helping the war effort through his involvement with the Toc H organization. Hubert is an old friend of Tubby Clayton, who set up a club for soldiers in Belgium during the Great War. In the interwar years that soldiers' club – the first Toc H – became the model for a most admirable social movement. It is Toc H that brings Uncle Hubert to Birmingham today. He is exploring the possibility of setting up a series of Service Men's Clubs in the city.

'The Bishop said much the same in his letter,' sighs Edward. 'But I can't help thinking what Papa would expect of me. Ought I to stand aside when my country is at war and all my contemporaries are serving King and country? Surely it is my duty to volunteer myself?'

Uncle Hubert snorts. 'You're young, I know. Too young to know anything much about the pity of war. It's not all Woodbine Willie, you know! Of course you want to have a pop at Hitler. Quite right too. But believe me, dear boy, there are plenty of other ways of doing your bit in wartime. Sign up as an air-raid warden, for heaven's sake! Think of your parishioners, if not of Edith and the girls. What about all your factory workers? The mothers and sisters and sweethearts of our troops? It may not sound terribly glamorous, but in these dark days the Home Front needs good pastoral care more than ever. If you upped sticks, who would take on the cure of souls in Longbridge?'

Edward can't decide whether his uncle's words bring relief or disappointment. But if both Uncle Hubert and the Bishop – not to mention Edith, obviously – are convinced that humbly serving his parish is a worthwhile calling, he has little option but to listen.

He notices the time with a start. 'Uncle Hubert, you must go, and so must I,' he says, draining his glass and setting it down on the stained table more violently than he intended. Will Edith smell the beer on his breath? She disapproves of public houses and believes drinking sets a poor example to his parishioners. Edward steers his uncle out of the Tavern (filthy place really, Edith is quite right) and bids him an affectionate farewell before turning for home.

13
Nell, May 2016

Nell was out running, pounding the pavements in a rage. She was furious with school, furious with the doctor and, above all, furious with herself. Angry that she couldn't seem to get a handle on life. It seemed entirely beyond her.

She had tried to go back to school and carry on as normal, but she just couldn't do it. After her breakfast at Luigi's, she saw Shaneece Power in Tesco and it all went pear-shaped. She abandoned her half-filled basket in the aisle and left the store as fast as her legs could carry her. She hurtled into the car park, almost walking in front of a car in her haste. The driver rammed his horn and she leapt into the air as if electrocuted.

She spent the rest of the weekend barricaded in the flat and paralysed by a nameless apprehension. She cancelled Fran and stayed on the sofa, half watching TV. Even reading was too much effort, because the words seemed to float on the page. She mustered just enough energy to go online and cancel her gym membership – she would never darken its doors while there was a risk of running into Shaneece – but even that required a monumental effort of will. She left the flat only under the cover of darkness, when she drove to the twenty-four-hour supermarket on the other side of the city. What little sleep she had was interrupted by formless nightmares that she couldn't remember on waking.

After the weekend, she could barely cross the threshold at school. She could feel her heart begin to hammer in her chest as she walked up to the door. The thought of the day ahead felt insurmountable. Her hands were so sweaty that she dropped her keys twice while attempting to let herself in. *Get a grip*, she told herself fiercely, her eyes filling with tears. *For goodness' sake!* Luckily Fiona appeared, and held open the door for her. 'Thanks, Fiona! I'm all fingers and thumbs today,' she said in a shaky voice, and forced herself across the lobby into her office. *It will be fine, it will be fine, it will be fine.*

But it wasn't. She couldn't bring herself to switch on her computer, let alone check her emails. She kept imagining what she would find in her inbox if she did. 'Stupid cow. Crap teacher. What d'you expect of a fucking woman? Sack the stupid bitch. Go round her place and teach her a fucking lesson.' A tidal wave of nausea threatened to engulf her. She stood up, telling herself that there was no need to panic. The room was stuffy after the long weekend, and she'd feel better with the windows open. All she needed was a glass of water. But as she rose from her chair, her head began to swim so alarmingly she had to sit down again. She put her head in her hands and leaned forward on her elbows. *I can't do this. I just can't.* How could she possibly prepare for the day? Lead the weekly staff meeting? Let alone go out into the playground and greet the children, or take an assembly in front of the whole school. It was laughable. *She* was laughable.

When Fiona put her head round the door ten minutes later, Nell was still trembling uncontrollably.

'I'm calling a taxi and you're going straight home.' Fiona was brisk. 'You're clearly not well, Nell. You need an emergency appointment with your GP. As soon as possible. Make sure you ask them about post-traumatic stress disorder.' Fiona's husband, Andy, had been invalided out of the army with PTSD.

And the GP had been enormously sympathetic. She'd listened carefully and signed her off for a fortnight – in fact she wanted her to take four weeks, but Nell was insistent – and prescribed medication.

'Just to help with the anxiety, in the short term,' she said.

But what had really thrown Nell, enraged her, in fact, was Dr Walker's refusal to dismiss out of hand Fiona's suggestion that she might be suffering from PTSD.

'That's ridiculous!' she almost shouted. 'Surely that's what you get if you've been to war or had a terrible accident. Not had a bad week at work!'

'Well, there's lots of overlap between anxiety and PTSD,' said Dr Walker calmly. 'The insomnia, the difficulty concentrating. The sweating and the nausea. The hypervigilance, flashbacks and so on. Everything you've described. But look, let's not worry about that now. It's a bit of a red herring at this stage. You're clearly suffering the effects of severe stress. The most important thing is that you take some time off work and allow yourself to recover a bit. Try not to fight this, and you'll get better. You've taken the first step by coming here today. Come back and see me again next week and we'll talk about where we go next.'

Dr Walker suggested that Nell consider going away for a few days. 'A change of scene might be good for you,' she said. 'Put some distance between you and your workplace. Are there any family or friends who might offer a bit of TLC?'

Aunt Grace, thought Nell. *I'll ring Grace when I get home*. Remembering her conversation with Father Hugh, she asked about counselling, but Dr Walker pulled a face. 'I can certainly refer you. But I'm afraid there's always a waiting list. You might consider going private. Your employer might fund it. From what you've said, this is an occupational health issue.' Dr Walker also said that exercise might help, so Nell decided to run every day while she was off sick. Today she'd do six miles. She wore a cap pulled low over her forehead, and a pair of sunglasses. She'd taken the back route, avoiding the Binks Estate, down to the river because she thought she'd be safe there.

Twenty minutes in, she was feeling, if not exactly better, marginally less awful. She knew in her head there was no point being angry with Dr Walker. It was hardly her fault. Quite the opposite; she was trying to help. So what if she had got PTSD, unlikely as it sounded? What did it matter what you called it, this horrible tunnel of despair? She supposed there was some comfort in being told that the constant sense of dread might have a name. There probably wasn't much point being angry with school, either. She had been out of order and Ray was only doing his job.

And maybe, just maybe, there was no point being cross with herself, either. If Father Hagrid was right, perhaps this wasn't actually all her fault. ('Hah!' scoffed her mother. 'If the shoe fits, wear it.') OK, she did something silly, but not criminal. She'd been victimized. Attacked without due cause. Made a scapegoat for the decades of deprivation and underinvestment the residents of the Binks Estate had had to put up with. The armpit of Oxford, someone once called it. A neglected, forgotten corner of a famous city with a world-class reputation and extremes of poverty that were conveniently forgotten by most of its residents.

As she crossed the Donnington Bridge and descended to the towpath, she pondered what, if anything, to do next. The union rep she had spoken to that morning had taken her to task for not having got in touch when it all started. Somehow it had never occurred to her. He advised her that she might have grounds for a grievance against St Seb's. He was adamant that she shouldn't let the case drop. But Nell couldn't face it. For one thing, the Facebook page was down and the Twitter campaign had finished. Susie had promised to alert her if anything popped up again. For another, she still nursed the suspicion she was overreacting. And what could pursuing a grievance possibly achieve? It wouldn't do St Seb's any good, and she wasn't at all sure it would help her state of mind either. She would be stripped bare all over again, her idiocy publicly scrutinized. Whatever the outcome, her job at St Seb's would be untenable. All Nell wanted to do now was put as much distance as possible between herself and the whole incident. She'd concentrate on herself for once. Get properly well.

14
Edward, November 1942

Edward is setting up a makeshift altar in the desert. He spreads a cloth that was once white over the bonnet of his truck. Earlier, his batman Stevens presented him with a tin of army biscuits that would serve for the host and, miraculously, a flask of rough Italian wine. His portable Communion set, with its simple chalice and paten and some battered army prayer books, are all the equipment he has to celebrate the Eucharist. Somewhere in the last three weeks his cassock and surplice have gone missing and he is having to make do with a stole over his normal shirt and shorts. The altar cloth, tethered as it is only by a couple of stones and a small cross, threatens to take off at any moment. He doesn't have high hopes of the candles staying alight for more than a few minutes. Never has that mattered less. *Here I am, Lord; send me.* He has seldom felt so alive.

In the end, staying at home was simply not an option. The ruthless Birmingham Blitz hammered the final nail into the coffin of Edward's patience. At least he knew Edith and the family were safely out of harm's way in Dorset. It took months of coaxing before Edward could persuade her to leave. In fairness, the bombing was sporadic at first, and one could almost pretend it wasn't happening. Well, perhaps if one lacked imagination one could, and at his more honest moments, Edward feared that Edith fell into that category. She was one of the most literal-minded people he had ever encountered. The serenity that so impressed Edward in the early days he now ascribed to an almost wilful blindness. She would not, she said, be driven from her home. If bombs fell on the city centre, they would simply not go shopping. Her place was at Edward's side.

Edith's stubbornness held out through August, September and October 1940. His plea that Longbridge was bound to be a target for the bombers because of the Austin Works – the factory produced Hurricanes, Stirlings and Lancasters, not to mention 500 military vehicles a week – fell on deaf ears. Then in November two things happened. First, the Germans upped the ante and launched a full assault on the city. Five days after the devastating attack on Coventry, they launched a ferocious raid on Birmingham. In less than a fortnight, 800 people were killed, almost 2,500 injured, and around 20,000 civilians were made homeless. The demolition was so appalling it was almost unfathomable. And second, Edith discovered that she was expecting another baby. At last, she agreed to take the children to stay with her sister Mabel in the countryside. Not that Dorset was beyond the notice of the Luftwaffe, of course. But it was a matter of scale.

For Edward too, this was a line in the sand. He wrote to his bishop and begged his permission to offer himself for service as a military chaplain. 'I am unshaken in my belief that war is evil. But the greater evil is surely submitting to the tyranny that threatens to enslave the whole of Europe,' he wrote. 'This great battle we are called on to wage seems to me the very cruel and painful necessity St Augustine had in mind when he set out the conditions for what constitutes a just war.'

'Having witnessed first-hand the barbaric destruction of our great city, I cannot in all conscience remain at home and look my parishioners in the eye. I believe it is my duty to take my place alongside the men of my generation and attempt to bring the Church to them in the midst of all the horror and destruction of war. I respectfully ask you to release me from my parish that I may serve our Lord and His Majesty the King alongside our brave troops.'

Even after receiving his bishop's permission, Edward felt thwarted for several months. Naively, perhaps, he thought that the bishop's agreement would lead to an immediate commission. The tide of righteous anger that carried him off into war threatened to fizzle out in the face of the labyrinthine bureaucracy of the War Office. After months of waiting – spent tramping about the rubble of his parish by day and pacing his echoingly empty vicarage by night – he was finally summoned for interview, then a medical. Finally in April 1941 his papers came through saying that he had been accepted by the Royal Army Chaplains' Department.

He suspected his ideas about warfare, formed as they were by what he remembered of army life in India and his father's accounts of the Boer War, were outdated. Nonetheless, he was unprepared for the distance between his hopes and the reality of active service. There was, for starters, an awful lot of hanging about. His chaplaincy training should perhaps have lowered his expectations. He spent ten days in Chester at the teacher training college being instructed in his duties by a retired senior chaplain who persisted in wearing the uniform and long leather boots of the Great War, even going as far as to brandish a swagger stick. The first day was devoted to filling in a mind-numbing number of army forms. The next consisted of learning elementary drill under the supervision of a Sergeant Major McFadden, whose Scottish accent was so broad as to be almost unintelligible, until the moment Edward incurred his wrath. 'Your salute looks like a bloody papal benediction, Padre Meadows!' was the first utterance Edward fully understood.

Otherwise, the days were divided into blocks of map-reading (nothing he hadn't learned at Uncle Hubert's knee), anti-gas training, the simplest possible first aid, the basics of military law, the structures of the military units, and only the most cursory introduction to the duties of a chaplain. A lecture on moral welfare was delivered by a dry old stick who looked as if he should have been pensioned off long ago.

The course ended with a final interview. 'Piece of advice, Meadows,' said the Commandant of the Chaplains' School, as if imparting a remarkable insight. 'Speak to the men in their own language.' Edward supposed this might have been useful to the rest of his intake – at thirty-three he was certainly one of the oldest of the bunch – but there was uncommonly little in the training that left him feeling equipped for the job that eleven years in parish ministry among the factory workers of Oxford and Birmingham had not already taught him.

And then, just when he was champing at the bit to get started, he was deployed not as he'd anticipated to the Front but to the Royal Army Ordnance Corps depot in Shropshire, where stores of weaponry had been moved after the bombing of the Woolwich Arsenal. From Edward's point of view, the work was soul-destroying. The depot was constantly busy, testing and taking delivery of weaponry that was being churned out at a rate of knots to replace the stores destroyed in the Blitz and the arms abandoned in the hasty evacuation from Dunkirk. Yet it was hard to see where he fitted in. In reality, Edward spent a great deal of time wandering around, watching other people hard at work and feeling like a spare part.

There were Sunday services, obviously. Church parades were compulsory. There was also the Padre's Hour, the idea of which was to give the men the chance to get off their chests anything that was worrying them, in an environment supposedly free from army discipline. Beyond that, there were a few men who welcomed Bible study, and a tiny handful who signed up to join his confirmation class. The vast majority, officers and men alike, were simply busy preparing for war, and not interested. It was not so much that they resented the presence of a chaplain; it was rather that they couldn't really see the point of one cluttering up the place.

'Don't worry too much if none of the soldiers appears to need your services as a parson,' wrote Uncle Hubert in reply to a letter venting his frustration. 'Very few of them will not be prepared to regard you as a friend.' Things improved marginally a couple of months in when he found himself in charge of entertainment. He soon realized that the standard fare of whist drives and bingo wouldn't cut the mustard, and tried to think more imaginatively. He had a stroke of luck when, through a parishioner back in Birmingham, he managed to persuade a handful of variety stars to put on a show. Since the Prince of Wales Theatre had been flattened in the air raids, the actors were at a loose end and only too glad of a chance to entertain the troops. This modest achievement raised his standing a little among the men, no doubt helped by the fact that the performance was pretty bawdy.

The dreary long nine months in Shropshire were interrupted by a welcome few days of home leave after Christmas. At last Edward could meet his new son, named at his insistence Richard after the Lionheart King, on the grounds that courage was required of them all. He found the family happily ensconced in a labourer's cottage on his brother-in-law's farm near Wareham, just a stone's throw from the main farmhouse where Mabel and Lionel lived with Walter and Fred. Edith seemed well. Her figure was thickening, after five children. She was almost dumpy these days, no longer the androgynous girl of the apple-blossom tea. But calm as ever, and coping, as always, with what life threw at her.

Prudence and Faith were old enough to be of some help about the house, thank goodness; Prudence, just seven, seemed to have taken on herself the task of chief nursery-maid and took competent charge of the baby when needed. Even Hope, at four, had the responsibility of collecting the eggs every day from the hen house and delivering them to her aunt in the farmhouse. Grace pottered about cheerfully enough collecting fir cones for kindling. And dear little Richard, with his crown of golden curls! Edith claimed he was a fussy baby, but Edward found that hard to believe.

Living on the farm saved them from the worst privations of rationing, so supplies were not as tight as he had feared. Even in midwinter there seemed to be sufficient wood about the place – delivered to the door by one or other of Edith's nephews – to keep the fires well stoked and the little house tolerably warm. He spent happy evenings by the fire reading stories to the children and playing board games.

102

Looking back, his visit seemed charmed, a golden time. He returned to Shropshire thanking the Lord that his family were well provided for and safe. A couple of months later he received the news that his posting to the depot had come to an end, and he was sent to an army training camp in rural Wiltshire. Here he enjoyed the double bonus of friendship with the local vicar, an old-fashioned country parson in the style of Uncle Hubert, and proximity to the family, only 30 miles away. By this stage Edward had an army motorbike, supposedly to allow him to visit the sick. But whenever he could beg enough petrol, and permission from his commanding officer, he drove down to Wareham. Somehow he never quite recaptured the magic of his Christmas visit: it was harder to ignore the never-ceasing demands of the children, the tiredness around Edith's eyes, and the tight-lipped expression on Mabel's face. But that was the War; everyone had their own cross to bear.

Eventually, after far too long kicking his heels in England, the call to action came and now he finds himself in Egypt. At last he has a real job to do, and a difficult one at that. The first taste of battle has been a bitter experience. After a long journey living cheek by jowl – ten weeks on board ship, under constant threat of German submarines and bombers, six weeks travelling overland – the regiment is held together by glue. By now he has a pretty good understanding of what makes a soldier tick. And driving through the desert, the officers and men who make up B Company have bonded like brothers, as day after tedious day they feed on meal after meal of bully beef, biscuits and tea, and eke out their miserly water rations. Edward feels proud to be one of their number.

Today, B Company went into battle for the first time with high hopes. After so many months in preparation, the regiment was fired up with excitement and adventure. The sense of anticipation was tangible. At sunrise, the whole sky was bathed in scarlet and the desert was transformed into a place of magic and mystery. Edward felt the presence of God close at hand. And yet the day's events have left everyone, if not quite disgraced, severely shaken. The troops were forced to flee in humiliation with significant losses. Edward has conducted his first funerals of men killed in action. Men he knew and liked; friends and comrades. Judging by the wounds suffered, more funerals will follow. Tomorrow and the next day. What can he possibly say now, to those who remain?

But since it is Sunday, he has put the word about that he will celebrate the Eucharist here in the wadi. *If not now, when?* as the Jewish scholar, Hillel the Elder, said two thousand years ago. By the same token: *If not me, who?* Edward has spent the last hour pacing about, thinking of the Desert Fathers and praying for inspiration. Just at the point of turning back to camp, his foot struck something lying in the sand. Bending down, he picked up a belt, presumably once belonging to a soldier. He was about to throw it aside when he saw the inscription: GOTT MIT UNS. God with us. Not any old soldier, but a German soldier, who trusted in the same God as the men in Edward's care. A gift from the Almighty, his sermon came to him.

Edward gives the nod to Stevens, who lights the candles and hands out the prayer books. The candles blow out almost at once. Night is falling, rapidly as it does in the desert, but by now Edward is used to taking services in the dark. On the long journey over here, he took it on himself to learn the Communion service by heart, for just such an eventuality. Tonight they will begin with 'The King of Love My Shepherd Is' and end with 'Abide with Me', if only because the words are sufficiently familiar for the couple of dozen men gathered around the truck to make a reasonable fist of.

Inspired by the belt, he plans to preach on the love of God. The God who cares for all his children, and receives them into his loving hands, whichever side they fight on. He will remind the soldiers that the crucified Christ faced the cruelty of the world and built a bridge between man and God that remains firm in the midst of whatever horrors the War may pound them with. He will take as his text the words from St Paul's letter to the Romans: 'Neither death, nor life, nor angels, nor principalities, nor powers, nor things present, nor things to come, nor height, nor depth, nor any other creature, shall be able to separate us from the love of God, which is in Christ Jesus our Lord.'

15
Hope, October 1968

Hope wondered if she would ever stop vomiting. Surely there came a time when there was nothing left to throw up? At least the blood-flecked diarrhoea had stopped. Someone had given her some green pills that seemed to have acted like concrete. At that point she was feeling so ill that death seemed preferable to spending a single second longer writhing in agony under her mosquito net.

It was unbearably hot in Varanasi, far worse than anything she had endured so far on this ridiculous trip. The tiny room was a furnace. A ceiling fan slashed feebly through the fetid air, but the difference it made was negligible. The walls seemed to close in on her, threatening to crush her. Every mosquito in India appeared to have bitten her, and she itched from head to foot, a hundred times worse than from her childhood eczema. Some of the bites were crusted and weeping. She was plagued by violent nightmares. In one, which recurred, an army of devils was crawling out of a vivid doom-painting she remembered from the village church in Dorset. She could feel their spidery legs creeping through the hairs on her skin. She woke in panic just at the moment they reached her mouth. Her sheets were wet with sweat and the smell of her own body was repellent.

Twenty-four hours after the green pills, she felt fractionally better. As if she might actually live. She was still hot, but the worst of the fever seemed to have passed. And she'd made a decision. In a sudden rush of clarity, she realized that she'd had enough, more than enough. Enough of the road, enough of dodgy hostels and dodgier food. Enough of the filth and the flies and the foul heat. Enough of the stench of burning bodies on the banks of the Ganges. Enough of children with huge eyes and outstretched hands, and beggars with missing limbs. It was all utterly repulsive. The others could go on without her. She was bailing out. She'd go and find Faith and then after that, she'd see. Buoyed up by a long sleep and a few sips of the Coca-Cola that Maria had smuggled back from the market, it suddenly seemed the most obvious thing in the world. Why hadn't she thought of it sooner?

And so she waved them off, glad to see the back of them. Maria, Willem and Femke, who were all Dutch, Barry from Wigan with his dreary guitar, the two girls from Birmingham whose names she hadn't bothered to learn, and Pierre and Jean-Paul who were dark and French and interchangeable. And Larry from California, with his beard and ponytail, who she'd slept with between Tehran and Peshawar, until she got bored. It had taken until Rawalpindi to shrug him off completely, because he'd been thoroughly ill-tempered about the whole thing, haranguing her with appallingly tuneless love songs, until she'd caved in a couple of times simply to shut him up. At least now he seemed to have his sights set on Maria. Apparently it had escaped his notice that although Willem and Femke were technically a couple, Maria always shared their room. There was another pair of Americans they'd picked up in Delhi but she couldn't recall their names right now, let alone their faces.

Hah! Good luck to the lot of them. It was all very well pretending to be Jack Kerouac (Larry was obsessed with *On the Road*, another point against him) but the reality of the hippie trail wasn't anything like as glamorous as the theory. Let them all head for Goa in that bone-shaking excuse for a bus. The *Love Bus*, for heaven's sake! Couldn't they see it was held together by its blasted rainbow paint? She'd no idea how it had survived this long. Whatever you said about their driver – a former wrestler from Cardiff called Reg – and she could say a lot about Reg, quite frankly, and none of it particularly complimentary, he had an uncanny knack of keeping the Love Bus on the road when anyone else would have given up long since. When she first saw it – a rusty old school bus Reg bought on the cheap in Merthyr Tydfil because of its dodgy brakes – she thought they'd be lucky to make Dover.

Now, three days later, she wondered if she'd made the right decision. It was only after the Love Bus had disappeared over the horizon that she discovered someone (Larry, no doubt) had helped themselves to the contents of her money belt, presumably while she was too sick to notice. All her rupees and her last remaining roll of hash, the bastard. He didn't know about the emergency roll of pound notes in the lining of her rucksack, thank God, but that wasn't going to get her very far. It meant she couldn't afford to delay finding Faith a minute longer than necessary, so she set off a day earlier than she would have liked. She thought she'd be OK, because the diarrhoea was still holding off. Just as well, really, as all the public lavs were unspeakable.

She discovered she could take the train as far as Patna. But she was still very wobbly on her feet. Even buying a ticket felt like scaling a mountain. She went early in the morning to Varanasi station to find it heaving with people, even at the crack of dawn. Pilgrims flocking to bathe in the sewage-ridden Ganges, poor sods, or returning home in the belief that their sins were now washed way. Pathetic, really. Many of them appeared to have slept there overnight. She joined one queue, then another, passed from pillar to post until she grasped that she must write down the number of the train and her intended date of travel on a scrap of paper. She joined yet another queue, wondering how much longer her legs would hold up. When she reached the front, she had long since missed the train she intended to take. A young man in the queue behind her who spoke English took pity on her. He persuaded the ticket officer to allocate her the last seat on the next train to Patna, and showed her where she had to queue a fourth time to have her ticket validated.

By the time she folded herself into the corner of the scruffy carriage, she was almost wiped out with tiredness. But it was a minor triumph; they might be packed in like sardines, but other passengers were sitting on the roof or hanging out of the windows. And it wasn't too bad, all things considered. Hope closed her eyes and dozed until the train lurched into Patna. The very last leg of the journey meant a bus all the way to Raxaul. That was supposed to be six and a half hours, if she'd understood the man at Patna bus station, but she'd long since discovered that public transport in India rarely ran to time and that officials would tell you what they thought you wanted to hear.

And then she'd started to throw up again. Which wasn't making her flavour of the month with the other people on the bus, although she was doing her absolute best to contain it in a bucket she'd bought from a roadside stall, and rinsed out at every rest stop. The trouble was that India was a constant assault on the senses, so there was literally no escape. The slightest smell — sweat, shit, spices, scorched metal (and try avoiding any of those in this cesspool of a country) — seemed to set her off. She couldn't imagine ever wanting to eat a morsel.

It was only when they stopped at a one-horse town called Motihari — or should that be one-cow town, because in India cows were sacred and wandered the streets quite freely, bringing the traffic to a grinding halt — that she suddenly wondered what she would do if Faith wasn't at the Gordon Hospital when she arrived. She had her address, of course, but she hadn't been in touch with her for months. Longer, actually. Years. Ever since . . . well, Eric and everything. In the end it was easier for Hope to cut herself off. Sever ties with her disapproving family. Oh *God*! What if she'd moved? Or gone away? Hope dimly remembered Faith writing about sometimes taking a mobile healthcare clinic out to some of the outlying villages. The state of Bihar was just about the poorest state in India.

It's a Christian hospital, Hope told herself. *An Anglican foundation. They wouldn't turn away a woman in need.* She was . . . what was the expression? A distressed gentlewoman. A bishop's daughter, for heaven's sake! For all that she had turned her back on her Father and everything he represented, she knew how to play that card, at least. But Faith would be there. She had to be.

In the meantime, as the bus wove its way along the potholed roads past paddy fields where women worked in colourful cotton saris, she took little sips of Coca-Cola and concentrated what little energy she had on not being sick again. Larry had a violent objection to Coca-Cola on the grounds that it was the archetypal representation of all that was wrong with American materialism. He would be furious if he knew she was practically living on the stuff. Hah! He was as prejudiced as her father. It was a relief to drink it, free from his censorious eye. Everyone knew Coke was good for Delhi Belly.

When the bus finally heaved into Raxaul she had lost track of time but it was dark and the air was alive with insects. Hope was almost weeping with nausea and exhaustion. She was horribly hot again. Her limbs were sticking to the plastic seat and sweat was pouring from her forehead. Every now and again, her teeth started to chatter uncontrollably and she found herself shivering from head to foot. She ached all over.

She staggered off the bus and was immediately surrounded by a throng. She should be used to this by now: she was taller than most Indian women and her short blonde hair was a novelty. Besides which, Indians seemed to have no sense of personal space. Now they were swarming around her like mosquitoes. Men staring, unabashed and open-mouthed. Small children stretching out their filthy hands to touch her prickling skin. Her head spun. If only she could lie down.

'Gordon Hospital?' she said tentatively. And then in a firmer voice that sounded uncomfortably like her mother's, she asked: 'Please, can anyone take me to the Gordon Hospital?' The little crowd surged forward, a dozen people eager to help, all jabbering at her in a language she didn't understand. Did they really know where the hospital was? Perhaps they meant to do her harm. Sell her into slavery and steal her possessions, such as they were. Oh hell! She'd left her rucksack on the bus and

110

now it had driven off into the night. Did she even care? She felt herself sway, and then a hand took her elbow.

'Follow me,' said an authoritative voice. The man spoke a few words in Hindi, and the crowd scattered. 'Dr Kamal,' he said, holding out his hand. 'I work at the Gordon. I will escort you. This way.'

Dr Kamal shouted for a rickshaw. Hope was incoherent with gratitude.

'Thank you. I'm sorry . . . I can't . . .'

'Please!' he said. 'Do not trouble yourself. I can see you are ill.'

'Faith! I need to find Faith,' she said.

'You need a priest?'

I'm dying, she thought. *He's a doctor. He should know.* Then comprehension dawned. 'No! My sister. I need to find Faith. Faith Meadows.'

'Ah, Sister Faith! Our recently promoted Nursing Superintendent. I will take you to her. No need for speaking.'

The rest of the night was a blur. Dr Kamal shouting for the nightwatchman to open the gates. Hope stumbling out of the rickshaw, and promptly vomiting into a flower bed. Faith's face, uncertainty swiftly followed by the shock of recognition. An orderly bathing her with the utmost gentleness and giving her a clean gown.

She woke the next morning in a hospital ward with a drip in her arm. She must have slept for several hours, because even through the blinds she could tell the sun was high in the sky. Everything was bright and white and clean. The walls were plain, save for a simple cross over the doorway. There was a comforting smell of carbolic soap. Nurses in crisp uniforms were going about their business, checking charts and talking to patients in soft voices. After a few minutes, one spotted Hope stir, and fetched Faith, who bustled in and wordlessly reached under the mosquito net to check her pulse and take her temperature.

'Well, that's a slight improvement at least,' she said briskly. 'Your temperature's still up, but down on last night. You'll mend.'

111

'What's wrong with me, Nurse?' Hope attempted to inject a note of humour into the question, but even to her ears it sounded feeble. Her voice was wavery.

'Dysentery, by the look of things. Assuming you're not too stupid to take your anti-malarial tablets. You'll start feeling better once you're rehydrated.'

Hope reached for her hand. 'Faith . . . why are you so angry with me?'

'Do you really have to ask?'

Hope tried to nod, but her head hurt too much. 'I . . . I thought you'd be pleased to see me.'

'You thought you could turn up on my doorstep, completely out of the blue, looking like death and I'm going to say, "Come on in, Hope, how lovely to see you!" without batting an eyelid? And, oh yes, I work here, so it's "Hello, everyone, here's my sister. She's a fallen woman and a junkie but don't let that put you off. She used to be a nice person." Why on *earth* would I be angry with you?'

'Faith! I'm not . . . it's not like that . . .'

'Not like what, exactly?'

'I'm not . . . I'm still your sister,' said Hope weakly.

'That would be the sister I wrote to week after week after week, would it? Who hasn't deigned to let me know she's even *alive*.' Faith looked her in the eye for the first time. 'You know, I almost didn't recognize you. I thought you were supposed to be a model! Well, take it from me, girl. You look like *shit*.'

As the unfamiliar word burst out of her mouth, a hand flew up to Faith's lips, and she looked anxiously around to see if anyone else on the ward had heard. The tension snapped abruptly.

'Hah! I can't believe you just said that, Miss Missionary Meadows!'

'Well, you do!' said Faith, giggling. 'Have you looked in a mirror recently? You're skin and bone, and your eyes are all bloodshot. And look at your arms! You're more bite than flesh!' She sat cautiously on the edge of Hope's bed.

112

'Thank you! I do believe that's the first time I've ever heard you swear. I'm honoured to be the cause! And did you really call me a fallen woman? A bit Victorian, don't you think?'

'I believe I may have picked up the phrase from our esteemed father.'

'You're joking! He didn't really—'

'He might have.'

'Oh *God*!' Hope felt bone-tired. Hot tears leaked from her eyes on to the clean white pillow. At that moment, two doctors in white coats arrived on their ward rounds. One might have been Dr Kamal, but she wasn't sure.

Faith stood up. 'I must get back to work,' she whispered. 'You concentrate on getting well. We'll talk properly later.'

It was several weeks before Hope was fully better. She spent a week on the ward, and it was bliss, utter bliss, to be looked after. And to be clean. Out of the corner of her eye, she watched Faith at work. She found herself in awe of her sister's calm efficiency as she went about her business. Her unassuming authority. The esteem in which she was held by the doctors.

Gradually, Hope's temperature went down and the swollen bites receded. She began to eat, a little plain rice to start with, and in due course dhal, yoghurt, a mango. Her strength returned, although her legs still collapsed into jelly at the slightest provocation. She put on a little weight, though the spare clothes Faith found for her hung off her skinny frame.

When she was well enough to leave the ward, she was given a guest room. It was cell-like, but clean.

'You know I can't pay for it,' she told her sister.

'You're my guest,' said Faith, sounding hurt. 'Besides, this is a place of Christian hospitality.'

'Hah! Are you trying to make me feel bad on purpose?' asked Hope. 'Surely you're there for the deserving poor. I'm not sure I count.'

'Don't be silly,' said Faith. 'Although you could always help out.'

'You're not suggesting bedpans, are you?'

'Don't be daft! But you might try the garden.'

So Hope spent her days pottering about outside. She remembered little of her arrival, but now she saw that the approach to the hospital was lined with flowering plants in pots, beautifully cared for by the gardener, Ashok, who had lost several fingers to leprosy. There was an area of seating under a huge banyan tree, and smaller walnut and sal trees beyond. Tucked away behind the hospital there was a kitchen garden, where Ashok grew vegetables and salad. He showed her spinach, radishes, lettuce and tomatoes. There were other less familiar vegetables: brinjal, chillis, herbs such as coriander, *kadi patter*, *ajwain* and *chaangeri*. Under Ashok's instruction – all conveyed in sign language – Hope weeded, watered and planted out seedlings.

And at the end of the day, when Faith had finished her shift and attended Evening Prayer in the chapel, the sisters talked over cups of chai. Hope told her sister about the modelling. How it had started off quite innocently, and what a kick she'd got out of it. First it was catalogues and then it was advertisements, and before she knew it, glossy magazines and even the occasional fashion show. But magazines were what worked best, because there was something about the spark between her and Eric that meant he was somehow able to transform a perfectly ordinary shot into something magical. Added to which, Eric had all the right contacts, and by lucky chance she had just the right look for the moment. She gave up her day job, and he became her manager, and set her up in a little flat in Dean Street. One thing led to another, and he moved in, and all of a sudden they were in great demand, getting more bookings than they could keep up with. Crazily, the more jobs they turned down, the more desperately the editors seemed to want them.

'I can't tell you what a blast it was, at the beginning,' she said. 'Honestly, you've no idea what London's like these days. It's unrecognizable. It's been like coming alive after all the frightful drabness of the War. As if the world was suddenly full of possibilities. I felt like . . . I don't know, a butterfly maybe. Don't

114

laugh! I mean, finding my wings after years and years trapped in a furry brown chrysalis. Not just wings but multicoloured ones! For the first time in my life I was . . . *someone*.

'And it was all so classy! London was swinging and we were smack bang in the middle of it all. You know, dancing till dawn. People recognizing us when we went out, press men taking snaps. We were the couple everyone wanted at their party. Invitations flooded in, to film screenings and nightclubs and country house weekends. And enough money to do what we liked!'

'And you truly didn't know Eric was married?'

Hope looked at her hands. 'No. Not at the beginning. I know it sounds frightfully stupid but he never said.'

'And you didn't trouble to ask?'

How could Hope explain the Swinging Sixties to her innocent sister? The clothes and the cars and the music, and Purple Hearts to pep you up when you needed a boost. And the glorious, glorious freedom of pleasing herself after decades under her father's joyless roof. Faith lived in a different world.

She shook her head. 'I was having far too much fun to ask.' And it *had* been fun, until it wasn't any more. When Eric started wanting her to strip off, do glamour shots, in spite of her insistence that her good-girl image was central to her appeal. When they both started to play away from home, tit for tat. When the penny finally dropped that his increasingly erratic behaviour was down to a serious drug habit. When the allure of relentless hedonism began to lose its lustre. When the *Daily Sketch* ran a diary piece about Eric's wife, Sylvia, who'd once been to drama school and was now suing for divorce, under the clumsy headline 'As the actress said to the bishop's daughter' and Hope received a letter – a true stinker – from her father.

'It was all going wrong anyway when . . . when . . .' Hope stumbled to a halt. She could hardly bear to remember. The weekend she'd gone to Brighton with a man called Dennis, whom she didn't even like particularly, because she and Eric had had a row. The horrid phone call from Marco telling her

Eric had been found dead in a pool of his own vomit. The funeral, which Sylvia organized, deliberately giving Hope the wrong time so that she missed it and was then slammed by the press for staying away. The discovery that there was barely a penny left of her earnings, because he'd blown it all to feed his addiction.

'And I'm not a junkie, for the record,' she said, pulling herself together. She hadn't popped a pill for weeks, after all, and hash didn't really count.

'Really?' Faith raised her eyebrows.

'*Really*. I tried LSD once with Eric. But never again.' She shuddered at the memory. 'Trust me, I don't go near the hard stuff.'

'But isn't that the reason everyone comes to India these days? I thought it was all about the cheap drugs. You know, "turn on, tune in, drop out".'

Hope finds herself laughing out loud. 'Fancy you knowing about Timothy Leary!'

'Don't flatter yourself,' said Faith crisply. 'You're not the first beatnik to make it to Bihar, even if we are a bit off the beaten track. Sometimes they pass by this way on their way up to Kathmandu.'

Faith got up to refill their cups. 'So why did you come out to India? Not to see me, by the sound of things.'

Hope sighed. 'Father was so horrid. He implied I'd brought disgrace on the whole family. I thought it would be easier for everyone if I made myself scarce.'

'Not easier for me. I missed your letters. You suddenly dropped off the face of the earth.'

'I see that now.'

'It's just . . . Well, I love it here. I really do. I'm fulfilled in my work. I know it's my calling. But the evenings are long. I need to know you haven't all forgotten me.'

'Heavens, Faith. I'm sorry.'

'He's not all bad, you know. Father, I mean. The two of you bring out the worst in each other.'

116

'Hah! That's an understatement. I'll tell you when the rot started. D'you know . . . when I was little . . . when we were little . . .' She tailed off.

'What?' Faith sat down beside her. 'What happened?'

'You remember when Richard was born, and Father came home, just after Christmas? I must have been about four, so I suppose you were five or six.'

'Of course I do. He hadn't been home for months and we were all fearfully excited. Mama was in a terrible flap. He brought us a bag of marbles. We were thrilled to bits, but Mama was convinced one of the tinies was going to choke on them.'

'Well, you could see Father thought Richard was the best thing ever. He was so insufferably smug about having a son! I overheard him telling Uncle Lionel that he'd 'almost given up hope'. It took me years to work out that he meant hope of having a boy after us four girls. I assumed he meant Hope with a capital "H"! That he was about to give me up.' A note of hysteria crept into her voice. 'I mean, it sounds silly now, but at the time, I thought he'd been thinking about giving me up for adoption. Swapping me for a little boy. I really did! And I still think . . . well, he always preferred the boys, didn't he? We were always second class.'

'Lots of men aren't any good with women,' said Faith. 'Being in the army probably didn't help. And I sometimes wonder . . .'

'What?'

'What he went through in the War. The sights he must have witnessed. I'd have thought that was pretty brutalizing. But that's ancient history. You're here now. Even if I'm still none the wiser how you ended up in India.'

Hope thought for a minute. 'I'm not sure I know, either. It was all a bit sudden. I was cut to pieces about Eric. I was very fond of him. And it didn't take a genius to work out that without him, my career was down the pan. A couple of weeks after the funeral I happened to walk past a travel agent in London and I saw an advert for the Love Bus and I realized I could just about scrape together the cash for a ticket. And I thought, wouldn't it

117

be marvellous just to disappear? Leave this all behind. I suppose it seemed like a good idea at the time.'

She laughed, then went on. 'Don't you dare tell Father, but I think I was looking for something more spiritual after all that relentless pleasure-seeking. The chance to find myself. I'd discovered that all that glisters might not be gold, after all.'

'You and your adages!' said Faith affectionately.

'And now look what's happened!'

'What?'

'Despite my best efforts, I've ended up back in the bosom of the Church.'

16
Nell, May 2016

The drive to Grace's house in the Cotswolds took less than an hour, but she might as well have been in a different world. For as long as Nell could remember, Grace and her beloved John, who died the previous year, had lived in a honey-coloured former farmhouse, down the end of a narrow lane on the edge of a picture-postcard village. The Binks Estate seemed a very long way away.

Not that Lane End was remotely chichi. The interior was decidedly down-at-heel, and the kitchen hadn't been updated since the 1970s. And while the front of the house was awash with purple wisteria, and there were planters either side of the front door, at the back, where one might have expected a pretty cottage garden, lay what could best be described as a salvage yard. Uncle John had been obsessed with vintage vehicles of all sorts, especially tractors, and the stables were filled with farm machinery in various states of disrepair. On what had once been a small patch of lawn stood Bertha, a cream-and-white 1974 Bedford bus, alongside Uncle John's pride and joy, a 1948 grey TE-20 Ferguson tractor. Most of Nell's memories of John were of him in a boiler suit, tinkering under a bonnet, or dashing off to an auction in search of a new restoration project. Even on his deathbed, he was watching daily reruns of *Scrapheap Challenge* on TV.

'Nell, you're here!' Grace came out to meet her. She enfolded her in a hug and Nell promptly burst into tears.

'I'm sorry!' said Nell. 'I just don't seem to be able to stop crying. Honestly, it's pathetic! I don't know what's come over me. I need to pull myself together.'

'Whatever the trouble is, lovey, I think you need a bowl of my soup,' said Grace. 'Come on. You're here now. In you come.'

She led Nell into the house and sat her down at the familiar kitchen table, among the hideous mustard units and faded flowery wallpaper. And Nell was immediately, blissfully a child again, embraced in a warm blanket of love and acceptance. She knew she didn't need to say anything, unless or until she wanted to. It was enough that she was home, and she was safe.

True to expectation, Grace asked nothing of her. After giving her a bowl of home-made tomato and lentil soup, she sent Nell to bed with a hot-water bottle.

'You look as if you could do with a nap,' she said. 'Bet you haven't been sleeping again. Have a bit of shut-eye and then come and find me if you feel like it.'

'What are your plans?' asked Nell. It had only just occurred to her that her last-minute visit might be putting Grace out.

'I'm going to make some rhubarb jam,' she said. 'It's about the only thing in the veg patch that's survived your uncle's little hobby. And then I'm going to tackle the barn.'

'What needs doing in the barn?'

'Ah,' said Grace. 'I haven't told you, have I?'

'Told me what?'

'That I'm going to put the house on the market. I'm trying to get rid of as much junk as possible. Which as you can imagine is a bit of a challenge.'

'But why? Where are you going?'

'Cirencester. We should have moved years ago. Without the girls, we've been rattling around for decades,' said Grace. Nell's cousins, Emma and Kate, long since grown up, both lived in the town with their own families. 'But your uncle wouldn't hear of it, even when he was far too old and arthritic to be mucking about with all that farm machinery, the great lummox. And now it's all getting beyond me.'

'But what about Bertha? The grey Fergie? You can't just get rid of them.'

'Of course not. A friend of John's is sorting that out for me. They'll fetch a decent price, if I'm lucky. And someone else can have the pleasure.'

'So where . . .? When . . .?' Nell suddenly felt very bleak. She was thrown by the news. Grace and Lane End had been such a constant. 'Is there something you're not telling me?'

Grace reached out and took her hand. 'Nell, lovey. I'm just getting *old*. That's all. I'm going to be seventy-seven this year. I could stagger on a bit longer. But actually, why should I? Of course it's a wrench, leaving here. But it makes far more sense to move into town now I'm on my own. Emma's keeping her eyes out for a nice little bungalow. I've just got to get this place off my hands first. So when you've had your rest, I could do with your help.'

To her surprise, Nell slept for a couple of hours, sinking blissfully under the comfort of an old-fashioned feather eiderdown. But when she woke, her heart was thumping angrily in her chest. Her mouth was dry, she was on high alert, and she didn't know why. She took a few deep breaths and decided to get up and go in search of her aunt. The kitchen smelled enticingly of fruit and sugar, a tray of full jam jars on the table. Nell pulled on her boots and went out of the back door. Sunshine! She consciously paused for a moment on the doorstep, closing her eyes, and making an effort to breathe in the fresh air. Her heart was back in its normal rhythm. *No need to be scared*, she thought. *Try not to fight this, and you will get better.* Wasn't that what Dr Walker said?

She found Grace surrounded by apple crates and boxes and tools and bits of old furniture. There was a familiar log pile in the corner, beautifully stacked, presumably by John before his death. It was he who first taught her the word 'tessellation', when she was little and admired the way they fitted so neatly together. There was also a bicycle with flat tyres, an old pram, several rusting pots of paint, and what looked like a couple of rotting louvred doors. And goodness knows what else behind all that.

121

'Three piles,' said Grace. 'Keep, recycle and burn. I'm trying to make sure that the keep pile's the smallest. But it's not easy.'

'Well, you know me. I'm the queen of tidying. It's practically one of my hobbies,' said Nell.

'It always was,' said Grace with a smile. 'You were always after a bit of order. I remember you reorganizing my larder, lining up the tins alphabetically. Bit of a nuisance, if I'm honest. But I decided it was educational. And it kept you out of mischief.'

Nell had a flashback – she is seven, staying with Grace and John for the holidays for the very first time. She's in awe of Emma and Kate, who are sixteen and fourteen and so grown up it's not true. They read to her, and play endless games of Snakes and Ladders, and Ludo, and Kate has even taught her a card trick that she can't wait to try out on her brother when she goes home. She's missing him horribly. But they've been out in Bertha with the local Brownie pack to visit a village that has a river running through it, and lots of little bridges and sweet shops. When they're at home at Lane End, meals appear at regular times of day. There are proper puddings, dishes she's only read about in books – apple pie, rhubarb crumble, rice pudding – and at weekends, chocolate buttons after lunch. Aunt Grace hasn't exactly made her eat meat, but somehow because everyone else is and it smells so good she has done. 'Don't worry, Poppet, we won't tell Hope. Will we, girls?' says her aunt with a wink. And of course they chorus 'No' and it becomes their secret and Nell wriggles in her seat with pleasure.

'It was the first time I'd ever eaten chicken!' she said now. 'That first time I came to stay with you. And ham. And sausages! And proper puddings. It was bliss!'

'You needed feeding up. Little scrap of a thing,' said Grace. She sounded indignant, all these years later. 'Sent you home with a bit of colour in your cheeks, and the same every summer after that. Did you good. And I'll do the same again this time. Doesn't look to me as if you're eating properly.'

She tutted, and threw an old sack in the direction of the 'burn' pile. 'Well, are you?' she added.

'Not really. Can't face it,' said Nell.

'Still fretting over Mark?'

'God, no! Not really. I'm *cross* more than anything else,' said Nell, realizing as she spoke that this was true. 'Cross with myself, that I wasted my precious time on him. I can't even remember what I saw in him. What an idiot I am!'

Grace looked up. 'Don't be too hard on yourself, Nell. We all make mistakes. Mark was OK. Just not right for you. Or you for him. So what's laid you so low?'

Gradually, as the two of them worked away at sorting out the detritus of a lifetime, Nell spilled out tiny fragments of the sorry saga, as much as she could bear. If she said too much, she knew she'd start crying again. And she wasn't sure if she'd be able to stop. Where she could be more open, though, was on the subject of her job, and the challenges it presented, because that was safer ground. Grace had been a secondary school English teacher for thirty years and had a professional interest. She wanted to know all about the inspection and the changes Nell was trying to introduce, and what she thought about St Seb's becoming an academy.

'I try not to disapprove on principle,' said Grace, sitting down heavily on an apple crate. 'But I'm honestly very glad I'm out of teaching now. You wonder what they're going to come up with next. All this change feels like change for change's sake. Does it really help the children? Are their lives demonstrably better as a result?'

Nell couldn't help but agree. 'You have to wonder, don't you? And from a teacher's point of view, it's so exhausting because the goalposts keep moving. Talking of which, is it time for a break? Shall I go and put the kettle on?'

As Grace stood up, Nell spotted something behind her, under a tarpaulin. 'What's this?' she said. She pulled off the cover to reveal a small, square table, desk-height, made of dark brown wood. There was a little drawer in the front with a tiny keyhole and a dirty brass handle.

'Goodness! I'd forgotten all about that,' said Grace. 'It was my father's. Your grandfather's. Must have come my way in the dividing of the spoils after Mama died. Perhaps I thought I was going to do my marking at it, or something. Let's take it outside and have a look. Probably riddled with worm.'

They pulled the table out from under the tarpaulin, and Nell carried it into the sunshine. It was dusty, but seemed structurally sound, with none of the telltale holes that might suggest woodworm. She found a brush, and swept away the worst of the dirt. 'What do you want to do with it? It would be a shame to burn it.'

'I quite agree,' said Grace. 'I don't suppose you'd like it, would you?'

Slightly to her surprise, Nell heard herself accepting. Stylistically, it wouldn't remotely fit in with anything else in the flat, but there was something appealing about its squareness, its solidity. And she'd be doing Grace a favour.

'Is it something from your childhood, the table?' she asked as they sat down with a cup of tea.

'Mama used to write letters on it in the cottage, in the War,' said Grace. She smiled. 'Thinking about it, I suppose she was writing to our father. We were terribly squashed because there were so many of us, but it tucked into a corner. Then when Father came home . . . well, everything changed, of course.'

'What do you mean?'

'Well, for a start he was wounded, so that was hard for poor Mama. And for the rest of us, actually. I suppose he was in a lot of pain. He must have been. But he had these awful headaches and he used to lose his temper at the drop of a hat. Terrible rages. Quite frightening when you're little. Mama came up with this sort of code. She used to say, "Storm alert, everyone," when she could see an explosion building.'

She paused. 'He was in hospital at first. For quite a long time, I think, but I was quite little so I'm not sure, but I know Mama used to go off on the train to visit him. I remember she used to come back in tears.'

'That must have been tough for Grandma.'

'Undoubtedly. Luckily she was tough as old boots, so I suppose she found a way through.'

'What happened to him? I mean, how was he wounded?'

'I've no idea. He wouldn't talk about it. People didn't, by and large. There was a sense of the War being something their generation wanted to shake off, put behind them. And to be fair, he must have rallied. Recovered enough to make a success of his life. But whatever happened, it left him in a great deal of pain. He had a limp for the rest of his life. And thinking about the headaches, I suppose he may have had some sort of head injury. I do remember he had ugly great stitches on his face when he came home.'

'How old were you, then?'

'I must have been five or six, I suppose.'

'Did you remember him? From before he went away, I mean.'

'Just. Only just. He'd been home on leave not that long before he went off to France. And I suppose he may have come home at other times, too. But the poor boys! It wasn't so bad for Richard, but poor little William was petrified. He can only have been two or three.'

Nell found it hard to think of her Uncle William as either a little boy or petrified. To her, he was twinkly eyed and as solid as a rock. Always the same, whenever you met him.

'So where were you living then? Was this the Dorset idyll?'

Grace snorted. 'Hardly an idyll! Gracious! Is that what Hope told you? It was a tiny cottage. No heating and no running water. Six children and Mama in two bedrooms and a box room! We were squashed in like sardines. We were only there in the first place because they'd bombed Birmingham to smithereens and it wasn't safe to stay. I can't speak for Hope, but I can assure you I was quite happy when we moved.'

'Back to Birmingham?'

'Yes, for a while. I don't remember anyone telling us what was going on, but then perhaps it didn't occur to them. You didn't consult children in those days. But one day there were packing crates and trunks and we were on our way. I'm sure we missed running about on the farm, but the house was huge. A great barn of a place! And apart from the boys who shared, we girls had our own bedrooms. The bliss of being able to read in peace! Not having to share a bed. It was so exciting. Until that awful next winter when it snowed for months and everyone in the country was frozen stiff.'

Grace drained her cup. 'But that's all a very long time ago. You wanted to know about the table. Now I think about it, Father must have claimed it back from Mama when he came home from the War, because it was always in his study after that. Wherever we lived. I'm not sure what he used it for because he had a full-sized desk as well. And now it's your turn. I'm glad to think of you making use of it.'

She stood up. 'Now enough of all that. Let's think about supper.'

17
Edward, March 1944

Edward cannot decide if he is pleased or annoyed to be sent on a battle training course. After almost three years as a padre it seems too little, too late. He reckons that if he got by in Egypt and the short time he served in Italy on what little he learned at Chester, he has a pretty good idea of what is required of him. In truth, he almost can't remember what it was like being a parish priest: it is as if this long War is all he's ever known. What began as something temporary, a sort of limbo, has become his new normality. He is hard put to picture another way of life.

On the other hand, the word is that this is specialist training ahead of the long-awaited invasion of Europe. According to the rumour mill, dozens of chaplains have got themselves killed in battle by taking stupid risks. He has it on good authority that out of the eighteen men in his intake at Chester, seven are dead. Seven! Not every serving Army chaplain has been called up, either, so it is perhaps to his credit that he's received his orders to attend the training. He is a mite concerned about his fitness because he's been warned the course will be tough: anyone who fails to make the grade will be left behind. Edward cannot countenance this. To be kept at arm's length from the men he serves at this kairos moment would be cruel indeed. He'd been acutely disappointed to be turned down by the Parachute Division on the grounds of age (he is thirty-six) so he knows he needs to be on his mettle now.

After a tedious journey on a series of overcrowded trains, he finally arrives at Church Stowe, a small village nestling deep in the rolling Northamptonshire hills. They are to stay in the rectory, a squat, self-confident Victorian building reminiscent of Uncle Hubert's house in Devon. Edward experiences a pang for Aunt Florence, who died while he was in North Africa. He'd missed her funeral. How on earth will his uncle manage without her?

He is just helping himself to a cup of tea from a trolley in the dining room when he feels a slap on his shoulder.

'Meadows, boyo! Well, I'll be blowed!' It is Gareth Evans, his friend from Oxford.

'Evans, by heavens!' says Edward, using an old sobriquet. 'What a relief to see a friendly face! And it means I won't be the only old man here.'

Edward is immensely heartened to discover his old friend among the thirty-five men on the course. The next five days will be infinitely richer for his company. They talk companionably about where life has taken them in the years since Cuddesdon. Evans served his curacy with his father, as planned, but stayed on in the parish unexpectedly when his father died suddenly from a heart attack. He married his childhood sweetheart, Bronwyn, and they have a son and a daughter. Edward is half proud and half embarrassed to confess that he is now the father of six. His brother-in-law gave him quite a talking to, last time he was home on leave. Lionel pointed out that Edith is exhausted by child-bearing and that it is increasingly hard to feed such a large family in wartime. Edward was quite taken aback. He was simply doing his duty! How can he explain to Lionel what it is like to lose your entire family? His unequivocal need for safety in numbers?

'The interwar years have not been kind to south Wales,' says Evans. 'After the economic boom of the early part of the twentieth century, recession struck, and these days unemployment is the only thing booming in the valleys. You could say that the War has saved our bacon,' he says. 'At least our young men have something useful to do nowadays.'

Evans has spent the last eighteen months as Chaplain to the 53rd Welsh Infantry Division, mostly based in Kent as part of the anti-invasion force. Like Edward, he has served under Field

Marshal Montgomery and takes comfort from his championing of chaplains. For Monty, the son of a bishop, Christian values and patriotism go hand in hand, and he has declared that he relies on chaplains to bring about a higher standard of discipline and morale in his army.

'You heard what the great man said in Cairo, I assume?' says Evans. '"I would as soon think of going into battle without my artillery as without my chaplains."'

Edward raises his eyebrows. 'Ah . . .' he begins, and then checks himself. Personally, he thinks Monty is an out-and-out egotist, with a tendency towards a doctrine of papal infallibility. But Evans has clearly swallowed his rousing rhetoric, hook, line and sinker. 'You're quite right, of course. Nice to be appreciated. And nothing like having an advocate at the top of the tree.'

Evans is about to reply when they are called to order. The chaplains are briefed about the coming days. The course is designed to prepare them to cope with the conditions of intensive warfare. The emphasis is most definitely on military training: there are eleven army instructors to the two senior chaplains running the show. Topics will include mine-lifting, digging slit trenches, and identifying battle sounds so that they can safely distinguish between rounds passing close by and the general noise of battle. Live ammo will be used and they will be trained in evacuating wounded soldiers while under fire. There will be a night exercise and a vigorous assault course. Their days will be framed by Morning and Evening Prayer in the parish church.

Just how demanding the assault course is becomes apparent on the second day as they find themselves crawling under barbed wire while machine guns fire overhead, jumping into a stream and clambering along trenches. It is bitterly cold, pouring with rain and the going is highly unpleasant. Edward and Evans emerge drenched and covered in mud, but triumphant at having met the time target set by the instructors. Edward is relieved to see that he has more than kept up with his rugger-playing friend; he begins to suspect that he has the edge on Evans in having seen enemy action first-hand while Evans was marooned in Kent. Thank goodness he finally escaped the depot! He is just allowing himself a moment of exhilaration when there is an almighty explosion and an animal scream of pain. One of their number – a man whose name Edward has not even had time to learn – has had his hand blown off while using his helmet to smother a stick of explosive that fell in front of him.

Watching the poor fellow being carted off on a stretcher, his bloodied stump raised heavenwards, Edward offers a fervent prayer for his recovery, and a guilty postscript of thanksgiving for his own safety. He can't help noticing that Evans looks positively green about the gills. In truth, the whole intake is badly shaken and so too, he thinks, are the instructors. All he can think, as he turns in for the night, is that he must attend to the training with an eagle eye. This is not a game in any sense of the word. It is not a dress rehearsal. There is no room for complacency. Whatever lies ahead, he is determined to survive. He owes it to Edith, to the children. He will not leave them fatherless.

18
Nell, May 2016

When Nell went to see Dr Walker a week or so later, she was certainly feeling slightly calmer. Whether it was the medication, the daily running through the lanes or simply Grace's loving-kindness, the anxiety seemed to have receded, just a little. It had been a relief to be away from Oxford, and a relief to talk about things other than her own problems. She and Grace had made steady progress with the clear-out of the barn, and Nell had offered to go back and work on the stables in half-term.

'If it fits in for you,' said Grace. 'It's always lovely to see you. But only come if it would bring you pleasure. I'll chip away in the meantime. I think you need to concentrate on *you* for a bit. Let yourself off the hook. Maybe even live a little. Take a holiday.'

Nell gave her a hug, and left hurriedly, in case she started crying again. Just being with Grace made her feel safer. Now she needed to get back to Oxford and her appointment.

As luck would have it, she managed to park right outside the flat, which meant she had just enough time before her appointment to carry the writing table inside. There was one obvious place for it in the corner of her bedroom, to serve as a sort of dressing table. If anyone had one of those any more. She took a step back and studied it as objectively as she could. Yes, the dark wood looked a bit out of place in among her grey-and-white Swedish minimalism. But she liked it. Perhaps a jug would help. Terracotta, maybe? She smiled at the thought that this represented a radical departure in taste. Was this what Grace meant by living a little?

She lined up the table's edges so that they were exactly parallel to the corner walls. As she did so, she remembered the drawer, which she'd tried and failed to open at Lane End. Was it locked or simply warped with age and stuck fast? She was just wondering if she should fetch a knife when she spotted there was something taped to the underside of the drawer. She peeled back a strip of masking tape and a small brass key fell into her hand. She wiggled it in the lock, gave it a twist, and to her satisfaction, heard the mechanism give way. In the drawer lay a yellowing envelope. The stamp was French, and there was a PAR AVION sticker. The address – written in cursive handwriting – was to 'Le Révérend Père E. Meadows', care of a hospital in Southampton. The grandfather she never knew. Suddenly noticing the time, she took the envelope and shoved it into her handbag. Stopping only to pick up her keys and a French dictionary, she headed out of the door. She mustn't miss her appointment.

What she now recognized as panic attacks were becoming less frequent, she told Dr Walker. They were still paralysing when they arrived – the pounding heart, the surge of fear, the terrible sense of doom – but there'd been no repeat of the complete meltdown she'd experienced on that awful Monday morning. Nonetheless, she couldn't vouch for what would happen when she next had to go into school. Even the thought of going in set her heart racing. And the leaden sense of dread remained.

'I don't even know what I'm frightened of. But it's there the whole time. A sort of blank terror. I can't remember what it feels like to look forward to something. Everything feels . . . well, *heavy*, somehow. Literally – I mean physically as well as emotionally. It's ridiculous, but I seem to ache with the effort of breathing.'

Dr Walker assured her that there was nothing ridiculous about this. The symptoms, while unpleasant and distressing, were very common, normal even, in someone suffering from anxiety and depression. She talked about possible routes forward: antidepressants, cognitive behaviour therapy, self-management including regular and healthy eating. 'I think you need to be

132

prepared for the long haul,' she said. 'It's worth considering that this has been building up for years. That recent events have just been the trigger.'

'But I've got to go back to work! It's SATS next week. Just the thought of everything that's piling up, waiting for me . . . I can't bear to think about it. I feel awful. So guilty! I'm letting everyone down. They're short-staffed as it is, and if I don't go back next week . . .'

'If you don't go back next week, what exactly? What's the worst that can happen?'

'They'll think I can't cope!'

'If they've got any sense at all, they'll think you're *ill*. It's not about coping. It's about your health. And I can tell you I've seen enough patients over the years to be able to say, hand on heart, that you won't be doing yourself or your workplace any favours by going back too soon. I'm going to sign you off until half-term at the earliest. In my opinion, professional to professional, you're simply not fit for work yet.'

Dr Walker must have seen the panic in her eyes because she added, 'You will be, one day. If you give yourself the chance. Just not yet. I'm afraid you need to be patient.'

So what now? thought Nell as she left the surgery. She'd have to send in the sick note, take the new prescription to the chemist, and try to resign herself to the long haul. She just wanted to get back to normal. *If I do what normal people do, will I start to feel normal?* she wondered. Everything felt such an effort. She decided to have a late lunch at Luigi's. Dr Walker and Grace had both stressed the need to keep eating well. Furthermore she would walk. For the exercise, and because that was the *normal* thing to do. *No need to be scared,* she told herself. *Act normal, feel normal.* She had her running cap and sunglasses in her bag, and she could wear them until she was safely out of the Binks orbit. *No,* she thought. *The Binks is a long way away and I don't have to hide.* Nell hovered in indecision for a moment, and then compromised on the sunglasses. It was

133

sunny. If she wanted to wear sunglasses on a sunny day, she would. She wasn't hiding.

It was still sunny when she reached Luigi's but her bravery didn't extend to choosing a table on the pavement. She went inside and received the usual warm welcome from Luigi. 'Nell, *mia bella*! 'Ow are you? I send George to serve you. Giorgio!'

She ordered a superfood salad and a drink of sparkling water, and as she waited for her order to arrive, remembered the envelope. She took it out of the bag, along with the dictionary. Inside the envelope she found a letter, in French, and two faded black-and-white photographs.

In the larger one, a couple stood side by side, not quite touching, in front of a tree. The tree was in full leaf so it was probably summer. Behind them she could make out a low stone wall, and what looked to be a farmhouse. The man wore army uniform and a clerical collar. Her grandfather, surely? He was a clergyman, a bishop in the end. The woman appeared to be a nurse. She was slight, dark-haired and looked very young, but it was hard to tell because her face was half in shadow, as if she was avoiding the camera. The man, on the other hand, was looking straight at the person taking the picture, and clearly laughing. He was tall, with a prominent hooked nose, but handsome in an aquiline way. He reminded Nell of one of those statues of the Roman emperors in Broad Street. Even in an old picture like this, you got a sense of . . . what? Charisma? Force of character? Or was she imagining that, because of what Grace had told her?

The second photograph was smaller, and showed a woman holding a baby. The same woman? Yes; on this occasion she was facing the camera, and smiling. Not in her nurse's uniform this time, but wearing a dark floral dress. The baby was swaddled in white, with a little bonnet to match, and although Nell couldn't be sure, looked very young. Not a new-born, but less than three months old? The mother seemed to be supporting the baby's head in her elbow.

She turned to the letter. The paper was cracked along the folds, as if it had been folded and unfolded many times over. The handwriting – upright and looping – matched the address on the envelope. It was beautifully written, and hard to read only because the ink had faded almost to brown.

29 août 1944
Mon cher Edouard,
J'espère que vous allez bientôt récupérer. Mon cœur s'est brisé en mille morceaux lorsque nous nous sommes quittés. Naturellement, le devoir vous appelle auprès de votre famille en Angleterre. Bien sûr, ils ont besoin de vous.
Je ne vous oublierai jamais. Je vous serai éternellement reconnaissante. Tout va bien ici.
Hélène

'My dear Edward,' she could manage, though whoever wrote this didn't know the name was spelt differently in English. 'I hope that you are going to recuperate soon.' Recover? Something about 'my heart'?

At that moment George, the new waiter, arrived with her salad. 'Sorry!' she said. 'Let me clear some space on the table.'

'You are studying French?' he asked, spotting the dictionary.

'No. Not really,' she said, a little embarrassed. The dictionary was a children's edition, with brightly coloured cartoon figures on the cover. It was aimed at complete beginners and probably wouldn't be much help, but it was all she had. 'It's just that I've found an old letter, in French. I'm trying to puzzle it out but my French is horribly rusty.'

'Can I be of assistance, perhaps?' asked George diffidently.

'Only if you speak French!' said Nell without thinking. 'Oh my goodness, don't tell me you *are* French?'

'I am not French, but I will do my best,' he said with the shy smile she noticed last time she was here. He glanced up at the bar as he did so. He had the most beautiful green eyes. Pale green, outlined with a dark circle around the iris. Unusual.

'I'm sure Luigi won't mind. It's quiet in here today. Please – take a seat.'

George pulled up a chair from another table and sat beside her. He read the letter in silence. 'It is, how do you say? A love letter, I think. Let me read it to you.

'"My dear Edouard, I hope that you will soon recover. My heart broke into a thousand pieces when we parted." That is romantic, I think. "Naturally, duty calls you to your family in England. For sure, they need you. I will never forget you. I will be", how do you say, "eternally grateful to you. All is going well here. Hélène."'

Nell found herself moved, whether by the words or his wistful delivery, she was unsure. 'Thank you,' she said.

'If you do not mind me asking,' asked George. 'Who are Edouard and Hélène?'

'Well, I know who Edward is. He's my grandfather. Or was. He died a long time ago. I never knew him. But Hélène . . . well, I can only assume that this is Hélène.'

Nell passed the photographs across the table to George. He picked them up and studied them carefully. 'Your grandmother, perhaps?'

'Definitely not,' said Nell. 'I knew her when I was little, and she looked nothing like that. And her name was Grandma Edie. Edith, I think.'

'What about the baby?' he asked.

'Not a clue.'

He turned both pictures over. The mother-and-baby one had writing on the back. Louis Edouard, 1 juillet 1945. The other was blank.

'That's odd,' said Nell. She picked up the envelope, and checked the postmark. 'The letter and the envelope are both dated 1944. The baby picture must have been sent later. But this one – I suppose it could have come with the letter?'

'Who knows? It is a mystery, I think.' George got up from the table. 'I must return to my work now. And you must enjoy your salad. It is very excellent.'

'Thank you,' said Nell. 'You've been a great help. Your French is very good. How many languages do you speak?'

'Ah,' said George, almost apologetically. 'Just the four. Arabic, Hebrew, English and a little French.'

'But not Italian?'

'*Solo un po*'. Just a little. Caterina is trying to teach me.

I bet she is, thought Nell. He really was very charming. 'I'm sorry. I just assumed you were one of the family.'

George gave a little bow. 'Luigi is very kind. He makes me part of the family while I am here. Please excuse me now.'

Nell was almost home, deep in thought, when she ran into Father Hagrid.

'Nell! It's good to see you,' he said. 'How are you? I've just put a card through your door.'

'Is everything all right?' said Nell, her pulse racing. 'Did you need me for something? Is it bad news?'

'Bad news?'

Nell felt silly. 'Sorry! I thought the whole ... *thing* ... might have started again. That you were coming to tell me something awful.'

'Well, I suppose that's an occupational hazard of wearing black. And knocking on unsuspecting people's doors. Like a policeman breaking bad news.'

The memory hit her in the solar plexus. '*Don't!*' she said, far too forcibly. She was shaking. *Breathe. Breathe. Breathe.*

He reached out and touched her arm. 'Are you all right?'

She shook him off. 'Sorry. *Sorry* about that.' She squeezed out the words, then took a few more steadying breaths. 'My apologies. A bad memory. Not your fault. Can I ... offer you a cup of tea?'

'Only if you're sure,' he said, looking concerned. 'I honestly only came by to see how you were. Nothing more, nothing less. But I have brought KitKats. If it makes a difference.'

Nell forced herself to smile and led him up to her flat. *When did I last have a visitor?* she thought as she showed him in. He seemed to fill the place. *And is it weird inviting in a man I barely know?* At least she knew it would be spotless. *No, it's what normal people do. Act normal.* They chatted as she boiled the kettle, found mugs and just enough milk left over from before she went away. She sniffed it for freshness, explaining that she'd been to stay with her aunt and that she felt better for it.

She didn't mention St Seb's till they were sitting in her living room with their tea. 'Everything all right at school?' she asked, tentatively. She wasn't sure she wanted to know the answer. If things were going badly, she'd feel responsible. If everything was fine and dandy without her, that would be almost as bad.

Father Hagrid seemed to understand this without being told. 'Fine, as far as I can see,' he said. 'In fact, in some ways, you going off sick may even have been the wake-up call everyone needed. There's no sign of Rob coming back, I'm afraid, so now there's talk about bringing in a full-time super-head till we're on our feet again.'

Nell pondered how she felt about this.

'Look, from what I can see, anyone else would have thrown in the towel months ago,' he went on. 'You need to let yourself off the hook a bit. Anyway, I'm not here to talk about school. I'm here to ask how you are. See if there's anything I can do to help.'

'Look . . . that's very kind. But I probably ought to tell you that . . . I'm not, well . . . religious or anything.'

'Thank goodness for that!' said Father Hagrid, draining his cup. 'Can't stand religious people, by and large. Just thought you might appreciate a chat. But you can tell me to mind my own business. For all I know, you may have all the support you need.'

Nell let out a long breath. Was her loneliness so obvious? Did he think she was a tragic spinster, living alone without even a cat for company? She wondered if she should be offended, but found she couldn't summon the energy. Besides, he was kind. His concern was genuine. So she told him about the visit to the doctor, the new sick note. How she was now running ten miles a day, and putting herself on a healthy eating programme.

'I know I'm better than I was, but I'm a long way from feeling myself,' she said. 'My GP warned me it will take a while for the medication to kick in. But it's so frustrating! I've almost never had a day off sick in my life – and now look at me. I feel such a failure!'

'Failure? That's a pretty emotive word. Would you say you were a "failure" if you'd broken your leg?'

'Of course not! But that's not the same at all.'

'Not quite, I know. But I'm not sure that failure's a very helpful way of thinking about your health. It kind of suggests that you'd get better, if only you tried harder. My . . . my first wife died from cancer. And one of the things she hated – well, we both did – was the idea that she was fighting a battle with cancer. Take that argument to its logical end and you're in a place where it's your fault if you don't recover, because you didn't fight hard enough. Really unhelpful. There are some things you just can't control. Including illness.'

Nell considered this. 'Perhaps that's why I hate feeling like this so much. I like to be in control.'

'Possibly. But objectively, I'd say you've also had a really horrible time. And talking of trying harder . . . ten miles a day? Are you *mad*?'

She laughed in spite of herself. 'Exercise is good for you! Everyone knows that.'

'That's as may be. But ten miles a day . . . Are you sure you're not driving yourself too hard? Forgive me if I'm speaking out of turn, but it sounds as if you're, well, punishing yourself.'

'It's *fine*,' said Nell crossly. 'It's about doing something. Taking charge.'

Father Hagrid changed tack. 'Did you have any joy with the union, by the way?'

Nell relayed the conversation. 'I suppose it was helpful in some ways. I mean, it reinforced the idea that . . . what happened wasn't all my fault. But all I want to do now is put this behind me.'

'Did you think about the idea of counselling?'

'Dr Walker says there's a waiting list.' An idea struck her. 'I . . . I don't suppose you know of anyone I could see privately, do you?'

Father Hagrid shook his head. 'I can ask around, but I'm a bit too new in the area, I'm afraid. But I've got another thought. Have you heard of mindfulness?'

'Who hasn't?' said Nell. 'I don't know much about it, but it's everywhere. The silver bullet.'

'Very *now*, you mean. Enough to put anyone off, isn't it? I felt much the same, until I tried it. Now I find it invaluable. And there's some good evidence that it's as effective as antidepressants in many cases. You can even get it on the NHS in some parts of the country. It's been used in prisons to good effect. Anyway, I've just started a course in the church hall, if you'd be interested in giving it a go.'

'Really?' Nell was surprised. 'I thought it was a Buddhist thing. You know, lots of sitting around cross-legged and chanting. Meditation. Balancing your chakras. And you should know right now that I'm completely and utterly allergic to hippies.'

'Oh?'

'Yes. My childhood . . . well, you don't want to know. Let's just say I don't do floaty.'

Father Hagrid smiled. 'I'd never have guessed,' he said, glancing around the immaculate room. 'Well, there's overlap with Buddhism, certainly. But Christians would argue it's only what we've been doing for years. Centuries, even. There's a whole strand of spirituality that's all about contemplative prayer, and mindfulness fits right into that. But it doesn't have to be practised as a spiritual discipline at all. No religion necessary. It's really about awareness. Paying attention, with compassion and kindness. Drop in, if you feel like it. No commitment.'

'Thank you for coming,' she said politely as he heaved himself up off the sofa. He gave her a look. 'No, I mean it. I know you're busy and you've been very kind.'

'You know where I am, Nell. Here's my card, if you need me. Look after yourself.'

19
Hope, May 1975

The last person, the very last person, Hope expected to see at visiting time was her father. She was sitting by the incubator in which her tiny baby lay, wired up to the nines, when the sister-in-charge told her she had a visitor. There was something in her tone that made Hope sit up. And then she saw that it was her father, not quite dressed in full episcopal regalia, thank God, but wearing a purple clerical shirt and sporting his large pectoral cross. Otherwise, she almost didn't recognize him. That was to say, she might have passed him in the street if he'd been in mufti. Edward was a shadow of himself. It had only been three years since she'd seen him, at a summer lunch at Grace and John's house when Willow was a baby. And three years was no time at all, given the lengths she generally went to to avoid her family. But the man walking towards her was no longer the towering figure of her childhood. He looked old and stooped, and as if his clothes were too big for him.

'Father!' she said. 'This is a surprise. I wasn't expecting you.'

'Ah, Hope,' he said, and kissed her awkwardly on the cheek. 'Ah' was one of his words. So much could be conveyed in a single syllable, depending on inflection. 'This the little scrap, then?'

'I'd have thought that much was obvious.'

'Ah yes. Well. Silly thing to say, I suppose.' He peered into the crib and tickled her cheek with his little finger. 'Hello, grand-daughter. Very small, isn't she?'

'Of course she's small,' said Hope tartly. 'She's premature. That's why we're still stuck in here, for God's sake.' She swallowed the tears she could feel pricking her eyes. Bloody, bloody hormones.

'How's Mama?' she tried, when he didn't reply. 'Not with you?'

'She's well, thank you, my dear. Well and busy. As always. She's holding the fort for Grace today. Looking after Emma and Kate.'

Hope's nieces were nine and seven. Edith had gone to stay while Grace was in hospital having her wisdom teeth extracted. Fort-holding was her mother's speciality, unless of course you happened to live in sin with a Danish wastrel called Per. ('Pear, dear? Like the fruit?' said Edith, when Hope phoned her parents on her return from India.) Hope couldn't picture Edith holding the fort at the Crabapple Collective. Aside from having to tear herself away from her countless good works, she'd never put up with the muddy track or the mould in the bathroom, or the perpetual fug of weed. On the other hand, decades of enduring draughty rectories would have prepared her for the chill wind that sliced through the hole in the roof. The hole that Per had been on the point of mending for about six months. In Edith's absence, Hope was counting on Daff to step into the breach. That was the plus of living in a commune, because it turned out that Per found it remarkably easy to forget he had a three-year-old son, let alone a premature baby daughter facing surgery. She supposed she should be grateful that at least the hospital was warm and dry.

Hope noticed her father was unusually quiet. He hovered awkwardly at her side. 'Are you all right, Father? Why don't you sit down?'

Edward pulled up a plastic chair next to Hope's. 'What do the doctors say about the little one, then?'

Hope explained that she had a hole in her heart that needed an operation.

'Well, you'll be relieved when it's over, I'm sure,' said her father. 'And . . . the little chap? How's he?'

'*Willow*. He has a *name*, Father. Willow is fine, thank you. Or was, last time I saw him.' The tears welled up again, and her voice trembled.

'My dear! Is everything all right?'

'Of course it's not bloody all right! For heaven's sake! My baby's life is in danger and they won't let children in here, so I haven't seen Willow for a week. And as for Per. *Bloody* Per!'

Her father opened his mouth to reply, but she cut him off before he could speak. 'Don't you dare say a word against him. Don't you *dare*! If you've come to criticize and carp you can get lost. Just go home!'

'Ah . . .' her father said, and made to take her hand. 'I really wasn't . . .'

They sat in silence for a few moments as hot tears spilled down Hope's cheeks. 'I'm just so frightened,' she whispered eventually. 'Look at her! She's so *tiny*. So fragile. I can't bear the thought of some horrid man with a knife slicing her open. What if she dies? I wish Faith was here.'

'That would be a comfort, wouldn't it? Have you thought about ringing Ruth, for a medical perspective? Might that help?'

She shook her head. In truth, it hadn't occurred to Hope to ring her sister-in-law, who was a doctor, though currently at home bringing up babies. Hope barely knew her, and while on balance she would probably trust William's good sense in his choice of wife, Ruth had always struck her as fearsomely competent.

'I just want Faith. I don't know what I would have done without her when I was ill in India.'

'An answer to all our prayers,' said her father. Hope glanced up. 'Sorry, old thing. But it's true. I was so worried when you took off like that.'

'Were you?'

'Naturally! Believe it or not, I've never stopped loving you. Even if I can't always approve of your choices.'

Hope snorted. *Hah! Funny way of showing it*, she thought.

'Ah . . . Hope . . .' His voice was uncharacteristically tentative. 'It occurs to me . . . well, if this little scrap really is in danger . . . Would it be any comfort to you if I baptize her while I'm here? Just quietly, with the two of us?'

'Are you allowed to do that?' Hope couldn't believe she was even entertaining the idea. But all of a sudden it seemed as if her baby girl needed all the help she could get. Even mumbo-jumbo.

'I am. But only if that's what you want.'

Hope was suddenly suspicious. 'Is that why you're here?'

Her father barked, a sort of laugh. 'No! There's something I need to tell you. But that can wait. Why don't I go and get us a cup of tea, and you can take a moment to think about it? Don't say yes to please me. It's entirely your choice.'

'When have I ever done anything to please you?'

The hint of a smile crossed his face. 'Fair point,' he said, and stood up. He hesitated for a moment. 'You know, I only wanted to . . . Ah, never mind.' He shook his head, turned and went in search of the drinks machine.

When Edward returned, carrying two cups of pretty disgusting tea and a briefcase that he must have fetched from his car, Hope surprised herself by accepting his offer. He took out a white stole, a tiny flask of oil and a little bowl which he asked a nurse to fill with water. For the first time since she fled for London all those years ago, Hope was reminded that he was a priest, as well as her tyrannical father. Against all her instincts, she glimpsed a tender side to him that had eluded her all her childhood. Perhaps this was what the adoring hordes of parishioners saw. A gentle shepherd, if she could believe it, not an irascible monster.

There was a dicey moment when it almost fell apart before he'd even started. As Edward put the stole around his neck, he asked Hope the baby's name.

'Buttercup.'

'Anything else?' he asked.

'Why? What the hell's wrong with Buttercup?'

'I only wondered if she had a second name. If that might be . . . a kindness.'

'Hah! How about Chastity?' Hope said waspishly. 'And I've heard Modesty and Patience are going spare, too. A *kindness*, for heaven's sake!'

Edward didn't rise to the bait. 'I meant something ordinary,' he said humbly. 'Just in case she finds Buttercup . . . ah . . . Meadows is a bit, well, flowery. How about Helen?'

'Helen?' she said irritably. 'Oh, why not. Just get on and do it.' She wanted it over. She was beginning to wonder why she'd agreed to this nonsense in the first place.

But then he reached into the incubator and she saw him wrestling with his emotions as he cradled her beautiful baby Buttercup and performed the ceremony with the utmost tenderness. By the end they were both in tears.

'Thank you,' she said, and they sat for a few minutes without speaking.

She remembered something. 'What was it? The thing you wanted to tell me?'

Almost apologetically, Edward told her then that he was dying. That he'd been diagnosed with cancer and the doctors had warned him it was incurable. He didn't know how long he'd got, but he imagined it was a matter of months. He planned to go on working as long as possible. He knew Hope was very busy with her own life (a euphemism, surely, for *never visits her parents*) so he wanted to say goodbye while he had the chance.

'You mean, while you had me cornered?' Hope's voice trembled.

Edward smiled, though now she knew he was ill, she saw the tiredness behind his eyes. 'Indeed! I arranged it all specially,' he said with forced jollity. 'Anyway, I couldn't toddle off without seeing my new granddaughter. Without meeting dear little Buttercup.'

'Is there any hope?'

'There's always hope, I suppose. But I'm not optimistic.'

Always Hope, she thought. Hah! She didn't know what to say next. She should probably tell him she was sorry to hear the news, and ask if he was in pain. For all the intimacy of the last hour, a lifetime's combat had carved a chasm between them that was too deep to cross. She was embarrassed by this new, vulnerable version of her father. He was diminished.

'How is Mama taking the news?' she said eventually.

145

'Ah,' said Edward.

'You haven't told her, have you? And she doesn't know you're here, either! You coward! How could you?'

Edward blinked. He looked very frail all of a sudden, as if she'd kicked him. 'I don't know how to begin.'

Conversation petered out after that. He stayed only another few minutes. As he stood up to take his leave, something else occurred to her. 'Why Helen?'

'Ah.'

'Ah *what*?'

'I knew a dear girl called Helen in the War. Well, *Hélène*, really. French. Sweet little thing. Had a brother. Jacques. Fine young man. Lost touch, when it was all over. Dear people. I often wonder what became of them.' His tone was wistful. 'Anyway. All a long time ago. Mustn't keep you. I'll be off now. Goodbye, my dear.'

20
Nell, May 2016

'Does the name Hélène mean anything to you?' Nell asked Grace on the phone some days later.

'Elaine? Why?'

'No. *Hélène.* The French name, with accents. You remember the writing table you gave me? There was a letter to Grandpa in the little drawer. From someone called Hélène.'

'A parishioner, perhaps?'

'I don't think so. It's in French. Dated 1944.'

'Goodness!' said Grace. 'I've really no idea. How mysterious. What does it say?'

Nell decided to be vague. 'My French is a bit rusty. But something about wishing him a speedy recovery. I wondered if she was someone who knew him during the War, when he was wounded. Perhaps a nurse who treated him? Does that ring any bells?'

'None at all,' said Grace cheerfully. 'As I said when you were here, no one talked about the War once it was over. I know that sounds odd to modern ears, but it just wasn't done.'

What a shame, thought Nell. *I really want to know.*

'Why the interest?' asked Grace.

Nell didn't want to mention the photographs at this stage, although they were in her hand right now. She stared at the faded images, as she had for the last two days, in the hope of spotting a clue, something she'd missed. She'd noticed a tarpaulin over the top left corner of the farmhouse, perhaps covering some missing tiles or a hole in the roof.

But she wasn't sure how Grace might react to the sudden appearance of a young woman who once wrote a passionate

147

letter to her father. The photographs – the baby – the evidence is all pointing in one direction. An affair. A love child. A buried secret?

'Oh, I don't know. Just curious, I suppose. I've got his desk, but I don't know anything about him. He was my only grandfather, after all. I can only just remember Grandma Edie.'

'Well, if you're really interested, you'd better get on with it,' said Grace. 'We're none of us getting any younger.'

Prudence, Grace's oldest sister, died of heart failure many years ago. And Faith, the next in line, had Alzheimer's, according to the nuns who cared for her in India, where she had lived as a missionary nurse all her adult life. That left Grace, Richard and William.

'And then there were three,' said Nell.

'Four, Nell. There are *four* of us.'

'I *can't*,' said Nell. 'I don't . . . It's not . . .'

'I'm sure—'

'The uncles,' interrupted Nell. 'Might the uncles know anything, do you think? Do you have their numbers?'

She heard Grace rustling in her address book and pictured her looking out into the yard. Was Bertha still there, she wondered? The grey Fergie? Or had they both been sold, leaving a yellow shadow where the grass might now at long last grow?

'The thing is,' said Grace, 'they may well know even less than me, because they're younger. Unless they thought to ask, later on. But give them a ring, by all means. Let me know if you turn up anything interesting.'

Uncle Richard was little use. He could add nothing to the bare facts that Edward served in the Battle for Normandy but was invalided out as a result of his wounds. He thought his father might have served in the Western Desert campaign before that. He certainly didn't remember the name Hélène, or any mention of Edward keeping in touch with a friend from France. There was no answer from William's landline, so she left a voicemail and another on his mobile.

She wondered – all over again – if she was right to keep the photographs to herself, and decided – yet again – that until she knew more, this was indeed the right decision. She quite liked the idea that she was the accidental guardian of a long-buried secret, but at the same time, she needed someone to pick over the mystery with. Then she remembered there was one other person who knew about the pictures. And, conveniently, had no vested interest. She decided to go in search of George.

Luigi's was quiet. There was no sign of George, and she found herself disproportionately disappointed. She ordered an Americano, and when Luigi brought it over to her himself, she asked – as casually as she could – where he was.

'Ah, *mia bella*! I see you are liking Giorgio! 'E is a good man, no?'

'He's helping me with my French,' said Nell primly. Luigi's eyebrows rose in surprise. She ploughed on, conscious that she was blushing. 'So where is he today? Is it his day off?'

'*All'università*. He must study today. He will be back on Saturday. I will tell him you are looking for him, no?'

Why not? 'Thanks, Luigi. I need his help.'

'So do I,' said Luigi conspiratorially. ''E is very good waiter. And 'e is working very hard at his studies as well. '*E disciplinato*.'

Nell felt obscurely cheated. She had been relying on George being here and available to chat. Which she knew was unreasonable. They barely knew each other. Instead, she decided she would try to drink her coffee mindfully. See if it worked. She had gone to Father Hagrid's class at the church hall last night. She really hadn't meant to, but decided to go on a whim. Partly because she wanted to show him she was open-minded. And partly because she was beginning to think she was prepared to try anything that might help her feel better. *Act normal.*

And it really had been OK. Nothing too weird and not a hippie in sight, though the church hall had seen better days. The paint on the windows was peeling, and inside there was a pervasive smell of jumble sales and damp. She hadn't known quite what to wear, and had settled on leggings and a loose sweatshirt. She arrived to find a dozen or so people there, all quite ordinary looking. A couple had clearly come straight from work, some were in jeans, and others dressed as she was. Better still, among the group she recognized Annie, a former colleague who was currently taking a career break after the birth of her third child.

'Nell, how lovely to see you!' she said, and gave her a hug. 'It's been too long. How are you? I'd heard you weren't well.'

'I'm off sick, but I'm making progress, thanks,' said Nell firmly. 'What about you? Is this your first time, too?'

'I came last week,' said Annie. 'It was brilliant. A real treat to take some time out. I hadn't realized how stressed I am. The kids run me ragged, bless them! Mind you, I've got a long way to go. I've been trying to practise all week and I'm definitely in the *"could do better"* category. And promise me you'll nudge me if I fall asleep. Or at least if I start snoring.'

Feeling immediately less anxious, Nell sat down next to Annie. Father Hagrid welcomed them and explained that it was all too easy to rush through life on autopilot, and that this often led to stress-related problems. 'Mindfulness helps us to pay attention to and see clearly what's happening in our lives,' he said. 'It's not the answer to everything and it can't get rid of the pressures in life, but it can be a good way to help us deal with those pressures in a calmer way. And that's good for our overall well-being.'

He went on to introduce a series of exercises, the three-minute breathing space and the body scan, all designed to foster awareness. The hour disappeared far faster than Nell had dared believe. She was sure she was calmer at the end of it. Now, she put her hands around the mug and focused on the physical experience of the warmth radiating through the china. She tried to breathe deeply. She set herself the challenge of sipping slowly, savouring each taste of her coffee. Enjoying the moment. Not thinking about the past, or the future, but simply dwelling in the here and now.

150

Nell's hand hesitated over her phone. She wanted to call but she knew Father Hagrid was a busy man. Email would, perhaps, be less intrusive, but she still couldn't face email. It was too threatening. Apart from setting up an out-of-office message she hadn't been online since Dr Walker signed her off sick. She took courage; Father Hagrid wouldn't have given her his mobile number if he hadn't meant her to ring.

'Father Hugh, I'm sorry to bother you. It's Nell Meadows,' she said.

'Nell! Good to hear your voice. How are you? Everything OK?'

'Not bad, thanks,' she said. 'I wanted to ask you a favour.'

'That's a relief. You're not going to tell me off for being too hippie-dippie, then?'

She laughed. 'No! Actually, I kind of enjoyed it. Thank you. If that's the right word.'

'Use whatever word you want. Now, what's the favour?'

'I'm on the detective trail,' she said. 'There's something . . . Well, could I call round some time? Meet you at St Sebastian's when you've got half an hour to spare?'

'Well, that was quick!'

'What do you mean?'

'You come to one mindfulness class and now you want to take religious instruction? Good grief, I'll get a reputation for myself if I don't look out!'

Nell laughed again. 'Not quite,' she said. 'Sorry to disappoint. I'll explain when I see you.'

When they met the next morning – Saturday, so Nell was confident that the coast would be clear when she walked past school – she explained that she was in search of information about her grandfather.

'He died the year I was born,' she said. 'But I spoke to my uncle on Thursday, and he told me something really spooky.'

'Oh?'

'I knew he was a bishop when he died. I guess that means he

151

had to be a vicar first. But Uncle William says he was here at St Sebastian's! I assumed you'd have records or something.'

'And you really had no idea?'

'Not a clue,' she said. 'I'm amazed no one thought to mention it when I moved here. But then, why would they? I suppose I just said I'd got a job in Oxford.'

'OK,' said Father Hagrid. 'Follow me. There's a board with a list of clergy at the back. What was his name? And this would have been when? Roughly.'

'Edward Meadows. I'm afraid I don't know the dates. But he died in 1975, so we could work backwards.'

On the wall at the back of the church there was a wooden board with the names of the clergy painted on it, their dates alongside. She'd been in the church any number of times with the school, obviously, but it had never occurred to her to read it. In fact, she couldn't help but look round the church with new eyes. Her grandfather – the tall, aquiline Roman emperor of a grandfather – once took services here. He must have stood at the altar, preached from the pulpit. She scanned the board, which began in 1843 with the Revd John Henry Browne. The twentieth century listed Edgar Milner, Arthur Jones, Archibald Taylor, Reginald Smythe, Harry Weston, Anthony Baker, James Roberts, David Blackmore and Phillip Owen.

'No Meadows,' said Nell. 'That's weird. Uncle William was so certain.'

'Hmm,' said Father Hagrid. 'Look, if he was a bishop, he's not going to be difficult to track down. Follow me.'

He unlocked the door into the vestry and fired up his laptop. 'We can check *Crockford's* for a start,' he said. 'It's a directory. Lists all C of E clergy, dead and alive. I assume you've tried Google?'

Nell shook her head, embarrassed. 'I'm . . . well, I'm kind of offline right now.'

'Very sensible,' he said. 'Digital detox. Do you know which year that phrase first appeared in the Oxford English Dictionary, by the way?'

'No, but I sense you're about to tell me.'

'It was 2013. Other words added that year include FOMO and emoji. And *phablet*, which is one of my personal favourites. It sounds like a speech impediment.' He blew a raspberry. 'Phablet, phablet, phablet.'

Nell chuckled in spite of herself. 'Well, that's good to know,' she said. 'Any sign?'

'OK. *P-s-a-l-m-3-2-7* . . .'

'Sorry?'

'My password. Psalm 32.7. It's a verse from the Bible: "You are my hiding place." I use it for most things on the assumption that your average cybercriminal probably doesn't know his Bible very well. Bingo! I'm in. Right . . . Edward Randolph Meadows, Bishop of Walsall 1962 to 1975, died in office. Would that be our man?'

'Yes! What does it say?'

'Ah . . . that explains it. Look, here on the screen. Ordination training down the road at Cuddesdon. Ordained here in Oxford in 1932, and then he served his title at St Seb's until 1936, when he moved to Birmingham. That explains why he's not on the board.'

'I don't follow.'

'Well, when you're first ordained you serve as an assistant to the vicar. You're a curate. It's a sort of apprenticeship. You're not the boss so you don't get on to the board. But I might be able to dig out some old parish registers if you want any more information.'

'What would they tell me?'

'Not all that much, really, beyond a list of services he'd taken. That long ago they might be in the county archives, anyway, rather than here. So let's scrap that idea. What else? I suppose there could be some parish magazines somewhere, but I can't promise.'

'Actually, what I really want to know about is what he did in the War. Is there anything about that?'

'Let's have a look,' said Father Hagrid. 'Here we are. Army Chaplain CF (EC), 1942 to 1944. What the heck does that

153

mean?' He clicked a couple more times. 'It looks as if CF stands for "Chaplain to the Forces" and EC for "Emergency Commission". Well, that makes sense, I suppose. Would you like a printout?'

'Thank you,' said Nell. She pondered for a moment. 'Is there any more detail? Like where he was posted?'

'No. It's more of a listing really. The bare minimum. But give me a minute. I'll see if there's anything else online.' Father Hagrid tapped away for a few minutes. He found a short obituary in the *Daily Telegraph* and a longer one in the *Church Times*, printed both out and gave them to her. 'The other thing you might consider is contacting the MOD,' he said. 'I'd have thought they might have records, especially now everything's digitized. Isn't the internet miraculous?'

'Yes,' said Nell flatly. 'Quite miraculous.'

'I'm sorry. That was tactless! How are you doing?'

Nell thought about it. 'I think . . . well, a bit better. It's not that it's gone away. I still have this great . . . sort of *weight* on my shoulders. The feeling that my chest is full of lead. But I'm not quite as panicky as I was. I have good days and bad days. I don't know if that's the medication or the passage of time or the running . . . but I'm trying to hang on to that, as some kind of progress. Even if it's a bit up and down.'

'Well done. I think you're doing really well. And where does this quest to find out about your grandfather fit in?'

Nell considered. 'Well, it's given me something else to think about. And that's a relief, I can tell you. I'm bored to tears by looking inwards. Only thinking about myself and my own little world.'

'It sounds like a good project. Let me know if I can do anything else to help.'

Lunch, thought Nell. *Lunch at Luigi's*. It would give her a chance to order another healthy salad and read the obituaries. And if George happened to be there . . . well, it would be nice to see him. That was all. Always good to have a chat.

In the end, the café was busy, and she was served by Caterina. It was only by spinning out her spinach salad far longer than was reasonable and ignoring the glares of other customers waiting for tables that she managed to speak to George at all. By then she'd read the two obituaries. The one in the *Church Times* included a black-and-white photograph: a smiling Edward, in a cassock and wearing a large pectoral cross. In his sixties? Certainly towards the end of his life. Some facts she knew: that he died leaving a wife and six children. Both obituaries described him as a 'devoted family man'. The fact that he met Grandma Edie during his curacy in Oxford, and that she was the vicar's daughter, was new to her. That meant her great-grandfather, at least, was a predecessor of Father Hugh's. She must have another look at that board. Also new to her was the fact that her grandfather spent the first few years of his life in India before being sent to school in England. It appeared that he saw action – if that was the right phrase for a chaplain – in Egypt and Italy before the Battle for Normandy. And he'd actually been part of the expeditionary forces that landed on the beaches at D-Day.

'He based himself at a Regimental Aid Post to help with the wounded and to do anything required of him, bar fight,' read the *Church Times* piece. 'He performed his clerical duties with great diligence, counselling men suffering from shock, dispensing tea and holding open-air services, although the size of the gatherings was necessarily limited by the constant threat of air attack. In many ways, the war was the making of Edward Meadows, although it was not without its challenges. Many years afterwards, he confessed to a colleague that he found himself weeping while conducting the burial service for a friend who had fallen in battle. However, by far the greatest strain came from scraping charred bodies out of burned tanks.'

Nell felt herself shiver. Horrible! The obituary went on to say that the regiment Edward had landed with was disbanded in late July 1944 because of heavy losses. Along with a number of his colleagues in the field dressing station, he was transferred to support another unit which was involved in the final push into the Falaise Gap. 'During the Battle of the Falaise Pocket the enemy's command of the road made it very difficult and dangerous to evacuate casualties, but Padre Meadows insisted that every possible effort must be made. Against the advice of his superiors he insisted on going to collect the dead and wounded, and it was on one such occasion that the ambulance in which he was travelling was hit by a shell. Meadows alone survived the explosion, and was afterwards awarded the MC for his bravery. In his citation, his Commanding Officer wrote that gallantry and quick leadership displayed by Padre Meadows enabled many casualties to be evacuated far more quickly than would otherwise have been possible. "His indifference to danger has earned him high merit, and I can personally vouch for the inspiration which he gave during this battle."'

A war hero, then! The obituary added that Edward was sent home to England and spent several months in hospital recuperating. 'Fears that he would lose his leg through infection fortunately proved unfounded, but he was to be troubled for the rest of his life by pain in his knee and severe headaches.' That tied in with what Grace had told her. There was little more of immediate interest to Nell. At some point after the War, Edward returned to his parish in Birmingham, before moving to another post in Leyland in Lancashire in 1957. In both parishes he was respected for his drive and determination, especially for his work in working men's clubs. In 1957 he became an archdeacon – a promotion, presumably, though she wasn't really sure what an archdeacon did – and five years later he was made a bishop, where apparently he devoted a great deal of energy to the cause of ecumenism.

The only bit of colour came in a reference to his driving. 'Bishop Meadows once joked that although he had spent most of his working life serving parishes associated with the motor industry he had never learned to drive. He set about rectifying this oversight on his consecration. It should be said that this new venture was not an unalloyed success. More than one car perished at his hands. It was not unknown for him to knock on the door of the parsonage nearest his latest mishap to commandeer the vicar's car. His wiser clergy offered instead to chauffeur him to his destination.'

The *Daily Telegraph* added that Edward was known for his trenchant views on the moral decline of Britain since the end of the War, and was an outspoken critic of the Divorce Reform Act of 1969, whatever that meant. 'The phrase "He didn't suffer fools gladly" could have been invented for Edward Meadows,' said the writer of the obituary. 'He demanded high standards of his staff, but never higher than those he himself aspired to.'

Hmm, thought Nell. *I think I prefer the dashing war hero.* George appeared at her table to clear away her empty plate. 'Good afternoon,' he said with his sweet smile. 'May I bring you something else to eat or drink? Some coffee perhaps?'

'Yes, please,' she said, smiling back. 'But . . . can you . . . will you join me now it's quietened down a bit in here? I have news to share.'

Luigi waved his permission with a wink in Nell's direction, which fortunately George couldn't see, and George returned with two cups of coffee, a latte for her and an espresso for himself. 'It is more like the coffee in my country,' he said by way of explanation.

'And where is your country?' asked Nell, realizing she'd been too self-absorbed to ask until now.

'Palestine.'

'What brings you here?'

'Now that is a long story.' George took a sip of coffee. 'I could start with the Second Intifada. Or perhaps I should go back to 1967 and the Six-Day War, or to 1948 and the Arab–Israeli conflict. But for you to have a true understanding, I cannot really ignore the British Mandate in the 1920s. Or the scandalous behaviour of the Ottoman Empire in the nineteenth century.'

'Um . . . I don't know quite what to say,' said Nell. 'Would "sorry" help at all?'

George smiled again. 'I am only teasing you. A more suitable answer to your question might be that things are very difficult in my country. It is not easy for my people, not easy at all. We are

157

sometimes feeling the forgotten people. What is the expression? Out of the sight, out of the mind. But I am here because it seems, after all, that we are *not* forgotten.' He explained that a scholarship had been established to bring a student from Gaza over to study in Oxford every year. George was studying for an MA in Education.

'You're a teacher,' said Nell, delighted. 'Like me!'

'A teacher, yes. But possibly not quite like you. I think perhaps the circumstances are a little different.' He explained the realities of life in the Gaza Strip, where the population were virtual prisoners, under semi-permanent siege. Hemmed in on all sides: by Egypt, by the State of Israel, by the Mediterranean Sea. 'Last year my cousin Maryam was not permitted to travel through Israel to Jordan even to attend her own wedding,' he said. 'Believe it or not, the authorities found that she did not meet the criteria for travel. It is possible only in exceptional humanitarian cases.'

'You must miss your family,' said Nell, carefully. There would be a wife, olive-skinned children, anxiously awaiting his return. 'And they you.'

'Sadly, apart from Maryam there is now almost no one left.' George fiddled with his coffee spoon. 'My mother bled to death giving birth to my sister because the Israeli soldiers would not let her through the checkpoint and she could not reach medical help in time. And my father was killed almost ten years ago.'

'By the Israelis?'

'Ironically not. Our family business was a bookstore. Our shop was firebombed by Muslim extremists because he used to sell Christian books. Bibles and prayer books.'

'You're a Christian? I didn't realize . . .'

'You think all Palestinians are Muslims, and all Arabs are terrorists, perhaps? No, we are Christian family. Though truth to tell, there are almost no Christian families left in Gaza. It is too hard. When we lost my father, it was the end for my brother. Isah is now in United States.'

'And . . . the baby? Your sister?'

'Layla. She died too, in my mother's arms. The bombing . . . it seems the shelling sent my mother into labour too early. Layla was too small to live. She could not breathe properly.'

There was a short silence. George wiped a single tear from his face with a paper napkin. 'I'm so very sorry,' said Nell. 'That's a terrible story. I . . . I know . . . well, I lost my brother . . . but nothing, nothing. *Nothing* like this.'

'Meanwhile everyone in Gaza is becoming poorer by the day,' George continued as if he hadn't heard. 'The economy is shot to pieces. That is hardly a great surprise. But far more serious for my people's future is that our children are traumatized by what they have seen and heard. They have seen the most terrible things. More terrible than you can imagine. They have grown up with the sound of shelling, not birdsong. They are looking at bloodshed, not flowers. Is it surprising that our young men grow up with a hunger for justice? Or a thirst for violence? It is tragedy for my people.'

Nell shook her head in disbelief. 'I . . . I don't know what to say. Nothing I say can possibly make any difference. Except that I can't imagine how you cope with something like this.'

There was another pause. 'May I ask about your studies?' Nell ventured. 'What's your particular interest?'

'I am focusing on the effects of trauma on learning. Then I will have something good to take back to my country.' He brightened. 'I am also, how do you say? Enjoying a change of scenery. I mean that I find I am very tired of the daily difficulties. It is good to be in a place where it rains a lot. And where peace is taken for granted.'

'You don't mind? That we're all going about our business, oblivious to what's going on in Gaza? Isn't that shameful?'

'On the contrary, I find that most refreshing. It is how the world ought to be. Now, let us speak of other things. You said you had news. And you have some papers. Have you found out more about the missing grandfather?'

Nell showed George the obituaries, pointing out the new photograph, the older Edward. She explained that she knew a little more about her grandfather, and that he had a connection with Oxford. 'But still nothing about Hélène,' she said. 'Assuming that the young woman in the picture *is* Hélène.'

'You have asked your mother and your father?'

'No father,' said Nell shortly. 'And my mother . . . well. We don't . . . It's complicated. I spoke to my aunt, my uncles. No one seems to recognize her name.'

'Perhaps it was not a . . . friendship he wanted to bring home from the War. If he was already married, with a family.'

'I know. Presumably it would have been a terrible scandal. The obituaries both refer to his devotion to his family. Listen to this: "It was in Oxford that he met Edith Taylor, the formidable young woman who was to become his beloved wife. Their long and happy marriage was a great blessing to all who knew them."' She handed him the picture of Edward and the woman. 'Look at this one again. It could be perfectly innocent, couldn't it? They could be colleagues or friends. If it wasn't for the letter. And the picture with the baby. She called her baby *Edouard*, for heaven's sake. Surely that can only mean one thing?'

'*Louis* Edouard,' he said. 'Is it possible perhaps that she just liked the name? Are you, how do you say, jumping into conclusions?'

'Oh, I don't know. What's it got to do with you, anyway?' Nell was surprised how cross she felt all of a sudden. She stood up hurriedly and snatched back the photo. 'I must get going. I'm sure you've got more important things to do than listen to me banging on.'

George's face fell. 'I do not think there are many more important things than making friendships in a new country. But I am sorry if I am misunderstanding you.'

Nell was mortified. 'I'm so sorry. That was really rude of me.' And because he looked so crestfallen, and because he'd shared with her so openly his life story, she found herself sitting back down and telling him, haltingly at first, that she had been ill. Was still ill, in fact, a bit of a mess, and subject to mood swings.

160

'I'm being treated for anxiety and depression,' she said apologetically. It felt good to name her condition, say those two taboo words aloud. 'I've had some . . . work problems. Nothing like what you've been through. But I'm not myself. I go up and down, like a yo-yo on some days. Please be assured . . . there is no misunderstanding. You have been kind and generous with your time. You were a great help with the translation. And I very much enjoy talking to you. I'm sorry I snapped.'

'That is very excellent news,' said George. 'I am wondering. Is it possible that you would like to go on a date with me?'

21
Edward, May 1944

Everyone is keenly anticipating the invasion. Edward is sent home on embarkation leave, acutely aware that up and down the land, soldiers are trying to pretend that this is just ordinary, run-of-the-mill leave, to be enjoyed, naturally, but of no particular moment. Mothers and wives and sweethearts are presumably pretending, too, not wanting to mar these precious days with histrionics.

He himself is on tenterhooks, half dreading, half longing for the moment. He can't settle; the cottage seems too small, the children too noisy, Edith too exacting. He is jittery, eager to know what lies ahead. One day he takes the bus to Studland, and finds both heath and beach littered with the detritus of recent pre-invasion exercises. Otherwise it is eerily quiet, the air heavy with anticipation. He takes himself off for long walks, knowing as he does so that he is being neglectful. He tells himself he needs to know that he is spiritually prepared, up to the undertaking he is being called to. The details are still clouded in mystery, and Edward is increasingly annoyed that he is of insufficient rank to be in the know.

At long last, when his patience is stretched to snapping point, he is ordered to report for duty. His regiment awaits him in Bournemouth. Bournemouth! It sounds so genteel, so respectable, so stuffy! And yet the moment has come. He says his farewells with almost indecent haste, and takes a bus, then the train, eastwards along the coast. He finds the grand old lady of a town in a state of siege. The attractions are all closed and the beach is smothered in barbed wire. Everywhere, there are signs directing traffic to military camps.

Edward is instructed that he will be part of 15 Field Dressing Station. Casualties will be brought in, and while the walking wounded will be sent to the rear for treatment at the Regional Aid Post, the seriously injured will receive treatment in field hospitals or be evacuated back to England by air or ship. He shudders to think of the extensive preparations under way; that there will be casualties is in no doubt. He shudders again when he takes delivery of a large box of crosses and a bale of body bags. It is his job not only to comfort the sick but also to bury the dead, as he had in the desert.

Up and down the south coast, units are hard at work, training for landing. Tanks, three-ton lorries, trucks and jeeps crawl through unsuspecting villages. Soldiers are sent by bus through tiny country lanes − without a thought for the farmers intent on ploughing, drilling and threshing − and ordered to find their way back to base, through dummy shellfire. Others endure daily swimming drills in unheated outdoor baths, fully dressed and equipped. Units pile on to landing craft which are sent out into the sea, and then, mid-Channel, brought back to shore so that the men can practise disembarking. When they are not rehearsing their landings, the troops are kept busy putting their tents up and down. They have to do this at high speed, again and again and again.

Edward's unit is made up of a ragbag of young men barely out of the schoolroom and old crocks like himself. A couple of dozen medics and orderlies, a single padre. The senior medic and officer in charge is Dr Johnson, a London GP with a dour look about him. 'Hope you're not going to get under foot, Padre,' he says on meeting Edward. 'Can't afford to be tripping over God-botherers when Jerry's got all guns blazing. We'll have enough going on as it is.'

Edward resists the temptation to tell Dr Johnson that he has seen action in Egypt, that he's served − informally of course, and out of sheer necessity − as a medical orderly. He simply makes a mental note to make himself useful when the time comes. He greets the others: the quartermaster, the stretcher-bearer officer, the general purpose officer, none of whom appears to be a doctor, although they all wear the uniform of the Royal Army Medical Corps.

Three of the officers in 15 FDS come from the same small fishing village on the west coast of Scotland. McMasters used to be the village GP. Drummond, the son of the Minister, started life as a ship's officer, but because of the slump in shipping during the Depression retrained as a doctor. Fairbairn, the third, is a pharmacist with a shop in Glasgow. Somehow they have contrived to serve in the same unit. There is even a dentist, along with his chair. Edward remembers hearing that Monty suffered such terrible toothache in the desert that the War was stopped until he could have his tooth extracted. He now insists that the army has dentists on hand.

Meanwhile, the countryside revels in early summer blossom: lilac, laburnum, fruit trees. England seems heartbreakingly beautiful, the massive build-up of military equipment totally incongruous. As May comes to an end, a sense of unreality begins to build. It seems as if they are suspended in time, with nothing for the troops to do but put up and down the tents and go out to sea and back again. They are all quietly going stir-crazy, trapped in an over-rehearsed play, longing for the relief of curtain-up.

One day they are ordered to move a few miles east, into a camp just outside Southampton. Security is high: the camp is encased in barbed wire and heavily guarded. All outside communication ceases. Word goes out that any letters written now will not be posted until after the invasion.

And then, just as they are poised for action, everything jerks to an abrupt halt. No information; nothing to do but to check and recheck their equipment. The weather turns; suddenly it is hot and sweaty. Tempers flare. The men are bored and crotchety. They sit around rickety tables playing increasingly impassioned games of cards. Edward is just thinking he ought to reprimand the men for gambling when a white-faced runner appears for him with the dreadful news that a private has shot himself in the heart while cleaning his rifle. He arrives at the scene only moments after Dr Johnson. Blood is spurting from the wound so dramatically that if it wasn't so shocking, it might almost be comical.

'Not a hope,' said Johnson. 'Poor bastard! An accident, one assumes. Suggest you sit on this one, Padre.'

Edward nods. There is nothing to be gained by notifying the next of kin now. He makes a note of the details; the man's family will be told that Private Smith was killed in action. The truth would be unnecessarily cruel. Meanwhile he will give the man a decent funeral, with minimal fuss so as not to spook the lad's friends. Edward squashes the unworthy thought that at least it gives him something to occupy himself with during this infernal waiting.

Eventually, when the suspense has become insupportable, they are called together and issued with battle orders. It turns out that they will be landing on the beaches of Normandy, on the grounds that Hitler is expecting something else entirely. Since the spring the Allies have been going to great lengths to convince listening German ears that any invasion will arrive at Pas de Calais, across the Strait of Dover. Dummy landing craft and gliders litter the Kent coast to reinforce the impression. And the secret plans are breathtakingly ambitious. An immense aerial and naval bombardment will be followed by wave after wave of troops landing on a 50-mile stretch of wide sandy beaches north of Caen. They should be under no illusions; the coast is heavily fortified. But the US First Army will take the western beaches, the British Second Army and its Canadian allies the east. It is to be the largest amphibious military assault in history.

With the battle orders, the mood shifts markedly. The news provides an almost electric charge that crackles through the camp and breaks the tension. Relief sweeps away the sullen sense of powerlessness that has dominated the camp during the long days they've been holed up. Now they know what is expected of them, there is a new clarity. A fresh sense of purpose. They are part of what General Eisenhower is calling a great crusade.

At last, everyone has a job to do. The officers are briefed and become absorbed in memorizing maps, studying models, consulting photographic intelligence reports. Edward's unit is shown charts indicating the site allocated for the field dressing station, the point for the water wagon, the burial area, the prisoner of war camp. They are issued with French francs.

Edward feels propelled forwards on a surge of adrenalin. His head is clear, his focus on the task ahead. While others go over and over the fine details of their last orders, he begins to plan the Eucharist he will conduct before they set out. The words of General Eisenhower's battle orders are ringing in his ears. The Supreme Commander has assured the armies that they go into battle with the hopes and prayers of liberty-loving people everywhere. 'The tide has turned!' the General's message concludes. 'The free men of the world are marching together to Victory. I have full confidence in your courage, devotion to duty and skill in battle. We will accept nothing less than full victory. Good luck! And let us all beseech the blessing of Almighty God upon this great and noble undertaking.'

If Monty is to be believed, it is Edward's job now to capitalize on this sentiment, to fire up the resolve of men facing serious danger and possible – no: all too likely – death. It is his duty to prepare the men, to offer comfort where he can. He must do everything in his power to preach a powerful, humane and inspiring message. He anticipates a pretty full house, a mini religious revival even, however busy everyone is. There are no atheists in foxholes, as the old saying goes.

He sets off purposefully in search of Stevens, his batman, pondering as he walks on the best text to choose. He considers – and rejects – a passage from St Matthew's Gospel. 'Take no thought for your life . . .' is too stark a message on the eve of battle. He settles instead on a fiery passage from the Old

166

Testament, the book of Joshua. 'Have not I commanded thee? Be strong and of a good courage; be not afraid, neither be thou dismayed: for the LORD thy God is with thee whithersoever thou goest.'

22
Hope, July 1982

Hope had a hunch she shouldn't be rejoicing quite so much in the absence of her children. Of course at one level she was sad to see them disappear off for the summer, Willow in one direction to stay with William and Ruth – his cousins were much the same age – and Buttercup in the other, to Grace and John. Emma and Kate were older, but they adored Buttercup and were terribly patient with her. Even when she was at her most annoying.

Which she could be. Honestly, when Hope thought back to the restrictions of her own childhood and the absolute freedom afforded to her own children, you would think they might be grateful. The minimum of rules, and ten acres of woodland and meadowland to run about in. What could be more idyllic? *Sharper than a serpent's tooth it is to have a thankless child*, she thought. (Was that the Bible? Was there no escape? It sounded like Proverbs, but she wasn't one hundred per cent certain. Prue would know.) She sometimes wondered if she'd spoiled Buttercup when she was little. She was still so tiny when they were finally allowed home. Maybe that was why she was so clingy now. Willow, thank heavens, was more robust. Sunday's child, bonny and blithe, to Buttercup's woeful Wednesday. He roamed the grounds without a care in the world, a piglet in clover. Cowboys and Indians, hide-and-seek, kick the can: Willow was king of the castle, the leader of the little gang of Crabapplets. On good days – good for *him*, obviously – she didn't see him from dawn till dusk.

They would have a good time with their cousins, she told herself. Old-fashioned Enid Blyton holidays with picnics on tartan rugs and sea-bathing. Her siblings were so conventional. Well, it wouldn't do the children any harm for a week or two. She wouldn't allow herself to feel guilty. Surely she deserved a break. It wasn't easy being a single parent, even in a commune. Ever since Per buggered off back to Denmark it had been a constant trial to keep it all together. Thank heavens for Daff, who'd been an absolute brick and did most of the cooking – organic and vegan, obviously – and thank heavens for Valerie, who used to be a teacher and had pretty much taken on the home-schooling of the kids. All seven of them. That left Hope pretty much free to concentrate on the garden.

The market garden was technically under the supervision of Valerie's partner, Ziggy. Somehow he was in charge, even though Valerie and Ziggy (real name Derek, she happened to know) arrived a good two years after she and Per did. That was men for you. He went on and on about his degree in horticulture, as if hands-on learning counted for nothing. Altogether, Ziggy radiated a sense of male entitlement that drove her up the wall. Especially when he scorned her efforts to introduce some of the more exotic herbs Ashok used to cultivate at the Gordon Hospital. It hadn't been easy, because she didn't always know the correct English name and it had been a bit trial and error, getting the conditions right. True enough, some of them hadn't really taken off, even in the glasshouse, but the coriander was going great guns now. Even Ziggy couldn't argue with that. And that was a bit of a feather in her cap, because actually it had helped him negotiate a contract supplying the new Indian restaurant in Pershore, which meant that things were on a more sustainable footing. Well, slightly.

They were working towards self-sufficiency, and it was always touch and go, even in the Vale of Evesham, which was famous for its fertility and well known as the fruit-and-vegetable basket of England. To be fair (though why she should be fair to Ziggy, she didn't know) Valerie could be bossy, too. It was all rotas and schedules and house meetings these days. It was so much freer in the early days. She wasn't sure that Valerie and Ziggy entirely grasped the Collective principle of egalitarianism. Not to mention the fact that they were the ones responsible for bringing in a string of gawping volunteers. As if Crabapple was some kind of freak show! WWOOFers, you were supposed to call them. World–Wide–Something–Organic. And look where that led.

They all had part-time jobs outside Crabapple, too. Ziggy taught at the local FE college and Daff was a cleaner, and some of the others did odd jobs like coppicing and bricklaying. Hope had her yoga classes in the village hall, thank heavens. She didn't know where she'd be without it. Discovering yoga in India had been her salvation. It had transformed her life, as well as giving her a means of earning a living. Well, almost. Contributing to the common purse, at least, which is what the Collective required. From each according to her ability, to each according to her needs, and all that.

She began to practise yoga while she was still in Raxaul, following the exercises out of a book left behind by one of Faith's beatnik visitors. Although Faith pursed her lips, she could see it was making Hope calmer and stronger. Through a stroke of luck – the Gordon Hospital's administrator left at short notice to nurse her dying mother – she got a secretarial job in the office for a few months, and thanks to that managed to scrape together enough money to travel to Pune and study with B. K. S. Iyengar. What a privilege! Not only was he one of the greatest yoga teachers of all time but he'd had a whole strand of yoga named after him. Based on the ancient yoga sutras of Patanjali, naturally, but made marvellously his own. So now she was teaching the more enlightened residents of the Evesham Vale a series of asanas as prescribed by the great man. It was all about precision and postural alignment. And pranayama, of course. Breath control. If the breath was balanced, then the mind, emotions and senses all became balanced too.

She always arrived an hour early for her class, because you couldn't teach if you weren't in the zone, as it were. You had to leave any distractions behind you. Luckily Daff seemed to appreciate this, and gave the children their breakfast. It was hard work, but such bliss to escape the chaos of Crabapple for a few hours each week. 'Crapapple', Per used to call it, but that might have been his accent. She was better off without Per, she knew that now. Bloody man. She could see now she had been hoodwinked by him, just because he'd shown up at her yoga class in Pune. A freeloader, a waste of space! What did he ever contribute to the Collective? Finding him in bed with a WWOOFer half his age (Hazel, Daff told her kindly, afterwards) was the final straw. But there was no point crying over spilt milk, was there? What didn't kill you made you stronger and all that. (Somewhere along the way, she seemed to have ingested a string of aphorisms, and every now and again caught herself muttering one under her breath. Or out loud. A secular substitute for all those frightful Bible verses she had to learn as a child, no doubt. And probably about as much use. Hah! Not Proverbs, but Shakespeare, she remembered. The serpent's tooth, that was. *Macbeth*? Hmm. She wasn't sure.)

Now her classes had stopped for the summer and three weeks' uninterrupted child-free time stretched invitingly ahead of her. She'd had a letter from her friend Nancy inviting her to visit. (Nancy was a founder member of the Crabapple Collective, but left six months after Hope and Per arrived, saying that as a radical lesbian, she wanted to live in a man-free environment. Hah! Per could have that effect on people.) Nancy and her girlfriend Marsha were living in a peace camp in Berkshire, newly set up to protest against the cruise missiles, which the British government in its wisdom was stockpiling at an RAF base. In May there was a big demonstration and a whole lot of people were arrested. Outrageous! It was all perfectly peaceful, but the military were jumpy, and now the jobsworths from the local authority were threatening to evict the women. Nancy and Marsha and their friends were planning to chain themselves to the fence if necessary. They might even invade the base.

Hope felt a duty to see for herself. It was female only (hence Nancy and Marsha) and that was partly because the women were protesting in the name of the safety of their own children and generations to come. Hope wanted to find out more. A change was as good as a rest, as the saying went. Crabapple was beginning to pall and at the very back of her mind a plan was starting to form.

23
Nell, June 2016

Nell strolled on the deck of the ferry, enjoying the sensation of a gentle breeze on her cheeks. She could smell the sea. Hear seagulls *mewing*. France was in sight – no, far better, *Normandy* was in sight – and she was beginning to feel excited.

Excited! She realized with a jolt that she was actually looking forward to something. For the first time since . . . well, probably since she saw Mark and Ellie at the Ashmolean. Two months ago, almost three? What an oddly literal figure of speech 'looking forward' was. When she was at her lowest, it was as if she actually, physically, couldn't look forward, couldn't see anything ahead of her. No glimmer of light at the end of the tunnel. If there was a tunnel at all – and there was, when she thought about it, a long, dark, narrow one – it was blocked at both ends and she was trapped inside, turned in on herself. Unable to see her way out. What a relief! She must savour the moment. Tune into it. Be mindful, as she was learning at Father Hagrid's weekly sessions in his dreary church hall.

She closed her eyes and concentrated on her breathing for a moment or two. Then she poked about a bit in her mind, but without judgement, as Father Hagrid would say. With compassion. She probed her emotions, wary that this sense of anticipation might be too good to be true. But no; it *was* true. Admittedly, she was a bit anxious. On the shaky side. Sort of job-interview-alert. But no more than that; not heart-in-mouth, not holding her breath, not hypervigilant. Good. In her mind, this trip was a kind of toe-in-the-water test, to see what she could cope with before she faced the bigger hurdle of returning

173

to work for the last few weeks of term. She was pushing herself, but gently. ('Hah!' said her mother. 'Hard work never did anyone any harm.')

Anxiety aside – and, remarkably, she could put it aside, sort of – she was definitely looking forward to being in France. The sun was shining and the sea was sparkling and it felt like a holiday rather than a field trip. Better still: an extra, if overdue, holiday taken in term time when everyone else she knew was hard at work. It felt pleasurably illicit, although it honestly wasn't. She had accepted Dr Walker's advice, and was resigned to taking at least another fortnight's sick leave. Right now, St Seb's and possible academization wasn't her problem. Nor were Kelly Meacher or how the SATS had gone or anything else to do with school. Apparently, the new super-head was going great guns, and a thoroughly reliable supply teacher was covering her class. Which meant that she had no to-do list, no paperwork, no timetable to think about, no lesson planning.

And no guilt, she reminded herself. This was something her counsellor was very strong on. Paula – like Father Hagrid before her – had helped her to see the absurdity of feeling guilty about being off sick. Paula had been . . . helpful, Nell supposed. Although the sessions were no picnic. Paula had an uncanny ability to put her finger on spots in Nell's psyche that were extremely tender. For starters, she seemed to think that Nell needed to discuss her childhood, in all its dysfunctional splendour, in spite of Nell's insistence that this was ancient history. Paula's theory was that the cyberbullying had been so devastating because it pressed buttons from her past, and although this was patently absurd, Nell had found herself talking about . . . well, her upbringing. Which she never, ever did, for obvious reasons.

Each time the hour seemed to fly past. The first session passed in a haze of tears, and she could remember nothing of what was said, only that the dread lifted, just a little, that the weight in her chest was a fraction lighter afterwards. Even now, she emerged from their sessions exhausted, drained even, but somehow rinsed through and cleansed. It was as if she was slowly dismantling a dam, allowing a tide of pent-up emotion to break through the barricades. Though it hurt, she knew she'd go back again, for as long as it took. She knew she had unfinished business.

She'd had four sessions with Paula now, in her high-ceilinged consulting room on the first floor of a tall house on the Iffley Road. Nell almost walked out, the first time, because there was a scented candle burning in the corner, lavender and jasmine by the smell of it, and Nell didn't hold with aroma-therapy, thank you very much. But Paula noticed her frown, and calmly said she would blow it out if it was troubling her. An offer Nell accepted and later almost regretted as the soothing scent began to fade. In the most recent session, she summoned up courage and asked Paula to light it, which she did without comment.

'Tell me a bit more about Will,' said Paula in her honeyed tones. And Nell found she was powerless to resist. She told Paula about the days playing hide-and-seek in the woods together. The adventures, the games. His quicksilver mind. His ability to conjure joy out of the most alarming situation. Her certainty that whatever happened, he would fight her corner, be on her side, keep her safe in a deeply uncertain world. His extraordinary, magical *Will*-ness. Until it all went sour and everything spiralled horribly, irreversibly out of control. How appallingly guilty she still felt. And how *angry* his death had left her. Incensed by the negligence, the sheer irresponsibility of their upbringing. How she couldn't . . . *wouldn't* . . . forgive or forget.

The next week, she told Paula about her fourteenth birthday, when she'd made the decision to leave home. If you could call it home. Home was supposed to be where people actually *cared* what you were doing and noticed if you'd gone to school or not. Where mums were called 'Mum' and set bedtimes. Turned up to parents' evening. Maybe, just maybe, a place where the grown-ups *did* something, if someone in the house was being seriously weird. Like Will.

When her mother first told her they were moving in with Maurice, she'd been so relieved she almost cried. Surely anything

175

was better than living in that horrible tent in the horrible camp. She hadn't known until then it was possible to be so cold and still alive. And it was terrifying, being on guard the whole time. Like that time, the first winter, when all those women from other parts of the country descended for a big demo. The police came with horses and truncheons and riot shields, and there was shouting and screaming and people being rounded up in vans, and Hope was beside herself, furious that she hadn't been arrested. Of course Nell was happy to leave all that behind. Will wasn't so keen, even though he'd always said he hated the camp, too.

'I don't want to live in a fucking cul-de-sac,' he said.

'Willow, my raggle taggle gypsy, oh!' Hope laughed and ruffled his hair. She never minded them swearing, and that really wasn't normal, was it?

At not quite eight, Nell didn't know what a cul-de-sac was, and she wasn't going to ask. It was probably something Will had overheard a grown-up saying. The women were cross with Hope because she had a boyfriend, and apparently you weren't supposed to do that. Hope met Maurice because he was a reporter on the local paper. They said she was betraying the sisterhood. Nancy and Marsha weren't even speaking to her, which was a shame because Marsha was teaching Nell to knit and they were making a scarf.

Mind you, in Maurice's house she probably wouldn't need the scarf because there was less chance of freezing to death. For the first time in her life, she had her own bedroom. Maurice called it the box room, which was a way of saying it was tiny, but Nell was thrilled to bits. At Crabapple she'd always shared, first with her mother and then, when she got too big ('Out of the nest, little chick,' declared Hope out of the blue one day), with Rainbow and Saffron, who were shouty like their mum, who was called Valerie and was her teacher. So a room with proper walls, instead of smelly damp canvas, where she was warm and dry and could shut the door and be on her own, was brilliant. Even better, they finally went to a real school. Orchard Primary

School in Newbury. ('Orchard!' scoffed Hope. 'They wish!') And that had been wonderful, because Mrs Gilbert was so much nicer than Valerie, and they actually had proper workbooks and pencils. There was a uniform with a green sweatshirt with a little tree symbol that she really liked because it was smart and cosy at the same time, and the badge showed she belonged. Willow hadn't liked Orchard Primary and he got into a lot of trouble at first with Mr Gee because of his bad language and his inability to sit still.

So to begin with, it had been fine. Maurice was OK and because he worked for a newspaper he sometimes got free tickets to things. He took her to a sort of puppet show for her eighth birthday, which was a bit babyish, but still a treat, because Hope never bothered with birthdays, and Maurice promised they'd go back again at Christmas to the pantomime. Which meant that she actually had something to look forward to, and that was a first because Hope didn't like making plans. She preferred to be a free spirit. Nell tried not to set her heart on the pantomime in case it didn't happen, but amazingly, they were still in Maurice's house in Newbury at Christmas, which meant she was in the nativity play at Orchard Primary. ('Stuff and nonsense!' snorted Hope, but still.)

Hope was still going to the peace camp at Greenham Common (Nancy and Marsha had forgiven her, apparently) but she was also teaching yoga and she had a part-time job in the Nut Shop, which was a health food store in the town centre. Maurice teased her and called it the Nut Case, and Hope let him, mostly, which was unusual because it was just the sort of thing she could get quite cross about. She got a discount at the Nut Shop so there was always lots of slightly gritty muesli in the house, which had its advantages as Hope was the worst cook in the world and often didn't bother with meals. She said she refused to be a slave to the stove. ('Have you looked in the fridge? Can't you *forage*?' she said irritably, if asked.) It was better in term time, because she and Willow had school dinners, and it was all right for Maurice, because there was a staff canteen where he worked, but Nell had decided she was going to ask Aunt Grace to teach her to cook.

By the time she was in Year 5, she'd stopped looking over her shoulder the whole time, waiting for Hope to spring something new on them. ('Nothing ventured, nothing gained' was one of her favourite expressions. Especially when she wanted you to do something horrible.) She cried when she left Oak Class (she loved Mrs Gilbert, had had her for two precious years) but actually Cedar Class with Mr Gee was fine, too. She didn't really understand why Will hated him so much. But they'd lived with Maurice in the cul-de-sac for long enough now that she allowed herself to relax. She made friends and did normal things like swimming lessons, even if that meant wheedling Maurice to get up early on a Saturday morning to take her, because Hope would just sigh, and say, 'Must you be so *boring*, Buttercup?'

It was when she left Orchard Primary that it started to go pear-shaped. She was dreading secondary school, because Will (he'd long discarded the 'oh') hated it so much. About the time she moved up to Dr Bacon's, he'd started to go spotty and sullen, and alternated between locking himself away in his bedroom with his Walkman on and taking himself out of the house for hours on end. He wouldn't tell her what he was doing, but she knew by the smell he was smoking and thought he was probably shoplifting, too, judging by his music collection. ('Boys will be boys!' said Hope.) Nell would wake up in the night, terrified that he would be arrested and locked up in prison, leaving her to fend for herself.

Dr Bacon's High was a nightmare. The teaching was poor and discipline was worse; the teachers seemed ineffectual against the hordes of hormone-charged teenagers. And so the name-calling began. While 'Buttercup' had seemed quite sweet at Orchard Primary (maybe that's why she ended up being best friends with Daisy), now she was Butthead. B-Cup. Buttocks. Buttercunt. To say nothing of the casual violence, the shoving in the corridor, the leg stuck out to make her trip and fall. The homework that mysteriously went missing before it could be marked. The can of Coke emptied into her brand-new school bag.

Hope was oblivious. ('Ignore them, for heaven's sake! Sticks and stones, sticks and stones . . .') Maurice, who usually had a bit more time for her, was caught up at work because they were making redundancies and it looked as if his job might be on the line. He kept volunteering for extra shifts in the hope of impressing the bosses with his commitment. In the end, it was easier to stop going to school altogether. To hang around in the park if it wasn't raining. To hide in the public library, where at least she could read.

It broke her heart, but she'd come to the realization that Will was lost to her. He left school at sixteen, having flunked all his exams. He was on the dole now, and spent his days lying on his bed, smoking weed or sleeping. Occasionally he disappeared for a few days, and was always vague afterwards about where he'd been. Apart from the occasional barbed comment ('The apple never falls far from the tree') Hope took no notice. So Nell made up her mind. She needed GCSEs and A levels and she wasn't going to get them at Dr Bacon's. And she needed a proper family, where people looked out for each other and ate proper meals at proper times of the day.

So she made a plan. She would go and live with Aunt Grace and Uncle John; not that she'd asked them, but she'd been there every summer since she was seven and she'd got it all worked out. She'd go to Aunt Grace's school, which was definitely not like Dr Bacon's because Emma and Kate went there and they were perfectly normal. She'd been to the station to find out about trains, and worked out she could get almost all the way to Lane End if she changed at Reading. She'd take money for a phone box and ring when she arrived at Kemble station and either her aunt or her uncle or maybe Kate, if she was home from university, would pick her up. She could even walk, if she absolutely had to.

When she got there she would tell them that she wasn't Buttercup any more. She was going to use her middle name. She

179

wasn't all that keen on Helen – there was a Helen at Greenham with a moustache and garlicky breath – so she would shorten it. From now on, she was going to be Nell.

What else was she looking forward to in France? Following her grandfather's footsteps. Learning something about D-Day, seeing the beaches where it all happened. It was a gap in her knowledge, an embarrassing one, really: St Seb's wasn't the kind of school that could muster a residential trip to Normandy and she'd never been. She'd borrowed a couple of books on D-Day from the library and had begun reading.

Thanks to a bit of digging, she now knew a little more about Edward's movements, too. A few days after her visit to the church, Father Hagrid had phoned Nell to give her the details of the Museum of Army Chaplaincy, with the suggestion that it might be a good source of information. The curator, David, had been terribly helpful, took her details and promised to dig out any information he could. Chaplains, he explained, were deployed according to need, and frequently moved regiments. Two days later, he sent her photocopies of the index cards detailing Edward's service in Egypt, Italy and Normandy. It appeared he had landed at Sword Beach on D-Day, and was stationed in the area for a while afterwards, before moving south into Calvados as part of Operation Tractable. The record – handwritten, faded and full of mystifying abbreviations – ended with the words, 'Returned UK (Battle Casualty) Disemb. 22.8.44'.

Now she was looking forward to bringing to three-dimensional life the places she'd so far only located on the map. They had booked a room in the Hotel de Normandie in the little seaside resort of Luc-sur-Mer, very near Sword Beach. She envisaged herself going for early-morning runs along the shoreline. She was also looking forward to tracking down Hélène, if that was remotely possible. There was so little to go on – not even a surname – and it seemed highly unlikely, but it was worth a shot. Surely. If by any chance she was still alive, she would be very old indeed. Say she was twenty in the picture, she'd be in her nineties now. Nell's hopes were pinned on Louis Edouard, who'd be not much more than seventy. And might or might not be her uncle. George had warned her, repeatedly, not to get her hopes up. 'People go missing in wartime,' he said. 'I am sorry, Nell, but that is the truth.'

And that, it went without saying, was the other thing she was looking forward to. Spending the next few days with George. It had been his idea to come over here. True, his initial suggestion was that she go alone, but somehow she managed to persuade him to accompany her.

'Please, George. *Please* come with me,' she begged. 'I'm not sure I'm up to going on my own. I need your help.' They had taken a picnic to the Botanic Garden on her birthday. Their fourth date. She was determined to show him that there was more to Oxford than ancient buildings and streets crowded with traffic and bicycles. She thought he would like the luscious green space, especially the Lower Garden with its herbaceous borders. So very English. And he did, but curiously, it was the seven glasshouses that really captured his imagination. He spent at least an hour exclaiming over the unfamiliar and exotic plants on display, and following a trail more properly designed for families that led from tropical jungles to oozing swamp.

'We should have picked you up one of those Big Botanic Backpacks!' said Nell. She went back to the information desk and returned with a leaflet. 'Look, there's an "At Home in the Garden" for Key Stage One, and an "Egyptian Explorer" theme for older children. I can't think why we haven't brought the St Seb's kids here.'

'You are laughing at me!' said George. 'I would like to bring my students too. We do not have this in my country. You have no idea.'

'Not really laughing,' said Nell. 'Teasing, perhaps, as you like to tease me. I love seeing you enjoying yourself.' And it was true: she was touched to her core by his enthusiasm, his passion for learning, the childlike delight he took in the world before him. His ability to live in the present, to take joy where joy is on offer. Where he could be angry and jealous and bitter that the children she taught had endless possibilities, when his own students had so little, he was happy simply to bask in the knowledge that such opportunities existed.

'How about it, though? Will you come?' Sensing his hesitation, she took his hand, and added: 'I can pay for the tickets if that's a problem. It's no more to take two passengers than one. It's the car that costs.'

'It is less that than . . . well, I must not neglect my studies. Or my job.'

'Surely it would be OK, just for a few days? I bet Luigi would give you the time off if you ask.'

'I'm sure he would, too, if he knows I am travelling with you. He has, how do you say, a soft spot for you.' George kissed her hand and smiled. A heart-melting smile. 'But in actual fact, the biggest stumbling block may be the visa situation,' he said more seriously. 'It is not always easy for a Palestinian person to travel freely. Even if they let me into France, I must know I can come back again to UK. Or else I'll have a big problem on my hands.'

Nell silently castigated herself for not thinking of this. There was so much she took for granted. 'How do we find out?' she said.

'I will perhaps ask the Oxford Brookes immigration office. But first you must tell me exactly why my presence is so necessary on this visit.'

'Oh,' said Nell, returning his smile. 'Well, it's the French, really. You speak it so well.'

'No good,' said George, shaking his head. 'You know that one of your main attractions for me is so that I can, how do you say, brush up my English. Improve my use of idioms. Why do you think I picked a teacher for my girlfriend?'

'In that case, you should know that coming to France with me will be strictly educational! It gives me the chance to put the record straight about our history. Show you that the British aren't all bad. We have our moments of glory, too. And I might need someone to carry my bag. I can't think of any other good reason, can you?'

The international students office had been helpful, and once George understood what was required it took another three weeks to get the correct visa. He was uncharacteristically jumpy when he had to hand over his passport to be checked at Portsmouth, and she suspected he would be jumpy again on arrival at Caen, although he had checked and double-checked with the university that all his paperwork was in order. Was this what it was going to be like for UK citizens travelling to Europe, post-Brexit? Nell was still shaken by the Referendum result, considering no one she knew would admit to having voted to leave.

But here they were, almost in France. Together. George – gorgeous George, with his tentative smile and beautiful eyes – was walking towards her, carrying two cups of coffee. How was it possible to feel so deeply for someone after just a few weeks?

'Here you are, *habibti*,' he said now, handing her a paper cup. 'Not the real thing, perhaps, and not how we drink coffee in my country, but better than nothing I think.'

She took a sip and made a face. 'Not as good as Luigi's, certainly. Look, though. We can see the harbour! We're nearly there! Do we have a plan?'

'Do we always need a plan?'

Nell laughed. 'But of course! I have to have a plan. How else do I know what to do next? You know I like to be in control.'

'I am thinking perhaps we should be prepared to, how do you say, go with the flow?'

'That sounds very risky,' she said. She was only half joking.

'Life is risky, Nell.' He put his arm around her shoulders. 'I think maybe you will be a little happier if you are prepared to expect the unexpected.'

She tested out the idea for a moment in silence. 'I can try,' she said in a small voice.

'That is good. I know it can be alarming. But let us both try. I am here to give you courage.'

24
Edward, June 1944

Four days after D-Day, the terrible reality is beginning to sink in. Edward goes down to the beach early in the morning, in the hope of finding a clue to Stevens's whereabouts. His batman hasn't been seen or heard from since the invasion. It is Edward's responsibility to search for any members of the battalion still missing. As things stand, the battalion has been decimated. Worse than decimated; reduced by a third. For the first time today, he is doing his rounds on a borrowed motorbike.

Yesterday, when he was on foot, a sudden burst of enemy machine-gun fire saw him diving into a slit trench. He landed on top of a young soldier, who swore violently, apparently as shaken by Edward's sudden arrival as by the firing. Edward recognized him as Private Ronald Wright, a friend of Smith, the man who had accidentally shot himself before embarkation. Wright was trembling from head to toe; it was clearly his first show and he was all alone.

'Rest easy, Private,' he said. 'It's way up in the air. We're safe down here.'

Wright swore violently, and to prove his own assessment of affairs, picked up a ration-box lid, which he held above the ground. A burst of machine-gun fire cut it clean in two. Wright began to sob. 'Our Father, who art in heaven,' prayed Edward. 'Yea, though I walk in the valley of the shadow of death, I will fear no evil. For thou art with me; thy rod and thy staff they comfort me.' When eventually the firing stopped, he had to prise his hand away from Wright's as he climbed out of the trench.

All is quiet this morning. But the sight that greets him on the beach is truly shocking. The wreckage on the beaches is apocalyptic, a hideous vision from the book of Revelation. Broken vehicles, burnt-out tanks, shattered jeeps lie stranded in ugly tangles of twisted metal. Odd items of office equipment – typewriters, telephones and files – are snarled up with abandoned lifebelts and ration boxes. And for all his experience in North Africa and Italy, Edward has never witnessed slaughter on such a scale. The numbers of dead and wounded appear to be far worse than even the most pessimistic predictions. The carnage is unspeakable.

Edward has been working round the clock and his head is buzzing with exhaustion. When he finally found his way to the rendezvous – and as it turned out, he had strayed badly off course, fetching up on Juno Beach with the Canadians when he was supposed to be on Sword – the tents were already up and the FDS in action. Someone told him later that the British Field Dressing Stations were in operation only 90 minutes after the first assault troops splashed ashore. Certainly by day two, the system was a well-oiled machine. Casualties – and they come in their untold hundreds – are passed through a Regional Aid Post to the casualty-clearing post and then back to units further to the rear. By now, only the sick and lightly wounded are treated at the FDS, while serious cases are being handled in field hospitals. Nonetheless, demand far outstrips what they can provide. The field hospitals are full to overflowing. Two days of rough seas made evacuation next to impossible; the weather has only now improved enough to ship men home for treatment. It is finally possible to imagine that the log jam is beginning to ease.

Edward works like a Trojan, determined to prove his worth to Johnson. He is furious with himself for getting separated from the unit for the first few hours and wants to make up for lost time. He serves as a stretcher-bearer, working in partnership with Hillman, a Quaker conscientious objector whose courage under fire is inspirational. He administers dressings. He assists as a medical orderly in minor surgery. Johnson is too busy to notice or to care, as long as he doesn't get in the way. On day four, he and Hillman ferry in a man whose armpit has been pierced by a shell fragment.

'What have we got?' barks Johnson.

'Underarm wound,' says Edward. 'Lung was exposed. I tried a field dressing but it didn't come close. So I . . . ah . . .' He hesitates.

Johnson raises an impatient eyebrow. 'And?'

Hillman replies before Edward can get a word in. 'Cow pat, doc!' he says. 'He only went and plastered a cow pat on the wound!'

'Only way I could think of restoring the vacuum,' says Edward, not letting on that he'd seen a doctor attempt this with camel dung in Egypt. Johnson looks impressed, against his better judgement.

'Morphine please, nurse!' he says, dismissing Edward and Hillman with a curt nod. They have been joined, oddly, by a young Frenchwoman, a student nurse. It turns out that she left her swimming costume on the beach the day before the invasion, and returned on her bicycle that very morning to reclaim it, only to find the seaside transformed into a battlefield. Her name is Hélène Duval. According to Fairbairn, she showed extraordinary bravery, ignoring the wolf whistles of the amazed squaddies and calmly setting about the business of bandaging wounds. Once the FDS was operational, she simply carried on and is now assisting Drummond and Johnson. While Edward is vastly relieved to see Fairbairn alive and well and hard at work, there is still no news of Stevens, which pains him deeply. His return to the beach yielded little. The casualties of the landing have been removed, although it is apparent that bodies of men who drowned or died at sea will be washing up for days, if not weeks, to come.

His most pressing job now is to begin burials. The trouble is that the proposed site at Hermanville, a mile or so from the FDS, is quite out of the question. A quick recce by motorbike brought him face to face with a huge sign: ACHTUNG MINEN. There's no hope of burying the dead until it has been

186

cleared of mines. He is just wondering what to do when he sees Hélène standing outside the tent, smoking. When she spots him approaching, she abruptly snuffs out her cigarette.

'*Ne vous inquiétez pas, mademoiselle*,' he says in his best schoolboy French. '*Nous avons tous besoin d'une cigarette maintenant et encore, non?*' He lights up as if to prove the point: we all need a cigarette every now and again.

'*Merci, mon Père*,' Hélène replies. She smiles, a beam of sunlight illuminating a face that has until now betrayed only seriousness, so far as he has noticed. '*Vous êtes très tolérant.* I'm not certain that Monsieur le Curé would agree.'

Edward laughs, delighted by the idea that he might be tolerant. He's not sure that anyone else has ever thought so. The fact that a pretty French girl does gladdens his heart. She has dark hair, neat features and almost violet eyes. He notices that she looks very young and very tired.

'*Vous êtes fatiguée, je crois?*'

'Please, mon Père. Let us speak in English. It is good for me to practise, no?'

'Of course, mademoiselle.' Edward suspects this is intended as a kindness. She has guessed that his knowledge of French has almost run its course. 'But perhaps you can help me. Are you local to this area?'

'*Mais bien sûr!* Of course. I have lived all my life here. How can I help?'

Edward explains the problem of the burial ground, the urgent need to find an alternative site as quickly as possible. The weather has taken a turn for the better and the temperature is rising. 'We cannot afford any delay.'

'Ah, oui!' she says. She explains that her father is a farmer, and she is sure he will understand the necessity. At that moment Drummond calls her name, and Hélène excuses herself, promising to speak to her father as a matter of some urgency as soon as Docteur Drummond can spare her.

Later, she takes him to the farmhouse. They walk together in silence for half a mile. It is utter bliss to be away from the

FDS, out of the tent in the fresh air, away from the stench of death. Edward is struck by the loveliness of the countryside. Hedges, orchards and meadows dressed in the rich green of early summer fire off vivid memories of school holidays in Devon, of his last walk over the Purbecks on his embarkation leave. Only the distant rumble of guns and the occasional explosion of mortars are out of place. Yet so used to the sound is he now that it is surprisingly possible to ignore it altogether.

Monsieur Duval, a stooped figure with a face weathered by the elements and dressed in blue overalls, is as wizened as his daughter is fresh-faced. For a moment he simply stares, and then he seizes Edward's hand in his own and clasps it. Silent tears stream down his face. He pours out a torrent of words of which Edward can catch only one in four.

'You must excuse Papa. He does not speak English,' says Hélène, clearly a little embarrassed as her father leaves the room. 'But he is very glad to see you. We all are.'

'Please. There's nothing to apologize for,' says Edward, moved by the man's display of emotion. 'Is it just the two of you, you and your father?'

'Non. J'ai un frère. A brother. Jacques. He is . . . away from home right now.'

The old man ushers them into the kitchen, reaches into a cupboard and retrieves three glasses and a bottle. He pours generous measures of an amber-coloured spirit and raises his glass to meet Edward's. 'A la libération!' he says. 'Dieu, merci pour la libération!'

The rest of the day is spent laying the dead to rest. It is a painstaking and demanding task, and Edward is scrupulous in the execution. Surely the only thing worse than hearing that your beloved son or husband or brother is dead is not knowing where his body lies. It is almost certain that the bodies will be exhumed and reburied when the mines in Hermanville have been cleared, and Edward therefore needs to make sure he knows the precise resting place of each fallen soldier. It may take him all day and half the night, too, but he owes it to the men of the regiment and their families to do right by them. They deserve dignity in death. Once he has said the services, marked the graves and plotted the burials on his map, he has one further impossible duty: to write to the families in such terms as make the unbearable just slightly more bearable.

25
Nell, June 2016

Three days after arriving in France, Nell and George had more or less drawn a blank. Having checked into the Hotel de Normandie, their first port of call was the Office de Tourisme, where an achingly elegant young woman behind the desk looked at the photographs, shrugged her shoulders and shook her head.

'*Désolée*,' she said. 'I'm sorry, but I don't think I can help you. These photographs are very old.' She gave them a tranche of booklets about the D-Day landings, drawing their attention to the list of individuals offering guided tours of the battlefields. 'These are most popular with our visitors. Would you like me to arrange for you a tour?'

Nell and George exchanged a look. 'Were any of the guides here during the War?' asked Nell.

'*Je crois que non.* I believe not,' she replied. 'They would be too old. But they are very well informed. In France, our guides must meet the highest possible standards in order to hold the licence *professionnelle de guide conférencier*.'

George thanked her, and they exchanged a few more swift sentences in French. Nell recognized that George was exercising the full force of his charm on the young woman. He appeared to be explaining that there was a family secret – possibly even a tragedy – behind their enquiries. At his urging, the young woman took the photographs and ran them through her scanner.

'*Ce serait très gentil, mademoiselle*,' said George, and scribbled something on the back of the photocopies. '*A bientôt*.' With another smile and a slight bow, he steered Nell out of the office.

'Camille's going to make some calls,' he said. 'She'll try to get hold of her old history teacher, who she says was an expert on the Normandy landings. And she's going to speak to her great-uncle. He's lived here all his life and may possibly know something. She'll call us if she comes up with anything. The other thing she suggests is that we ask around in the hotels. Show the pictures, and see if anyone recognizes anything.'

'Does she know we're only here for a few days?'

'Of course. And I've given her my number. If we hear nothing, we can drop in again.'

In the meantime they had visited some of the sites recommended by Camille. It turned out that there were scores of museums and memorials along the coast and just inland. There were 27 war cemeteries alone, containing the remains of 110,000 dead from both sides of the conflict. Nell was taken aback by the sheer scale of the Battle for Normandy. She was unaware that it had lasted a full three months after D-Day.

From her reading, she had discovered that around 156,000 troops landed on D-Day itself, and by 11 June, this number totalled more than 326,000, along with 54,000 vehicles and 104,000 tons of supplies. Not to mention the huge number of naval forces – almost 7,000 vessels – and more than 3,000 aircraft. The casualties were staggering: more than 425,000 Allied and German troops were killed, wounded or went missing between June and August 1944. And somewhere between 15,000 and 20,000 French civilians were killed, mainly as a result of Allied bombing.

They started at Bayeux, the site of the largest Second World War Commonwealth military cemetery in France. Next door to the cemetery there was a museum that offered a basic intro-duction to the key stages of the conflict. Alongside information boards and display cases, there were military vehicles, including a tank, and various pieces of equipment on show. After watching a short film of archived footage, they wandered across the road to the cemetery. It was stark but beautifully kept: four thousand soldiers of different nationalities were buried here, marked by row on row of white gravestones.

'They're all so *young*,' Nell said to George. 'Barely men. Look at this: "Private L. Jordan, 18. Flying Officer T. Ross, 21. Trooper E. Harris, 20." and so on, and so on.' She read the inscriptions, which varied from the patriotic ('For king and country') to the bland ('Cherished memories of a beloved son'), from the poetic ('Years will not darken nor shadows dim the beautiful memories I have of him') to the plainly bewildered ('Some day we will understand').

'Have you seen these, Nell?'

Scattered among the names were a number of gravestones dedicated simply to 'A soldier of the 1939–1945 war known unto God'. Once she noticed them, the unknown soldiers were everywhere.

'There are more than 300 in this cemetery alone,' said George. 'But there is another inscription you must see.' He steered her over to the pediment of the main memorial and pointed out the carved words 'Nos a Gulielmo Victi victoris patriam liberavimus'. 'It means more or less "Once conquered by William, today we liberate the Conqueror's native land",' he says, and laughs. 'I think your English want to, how do you say, score points off their neighbours. Even on a war memorial!'

'You might think we'd scored quite enough points by bombing the locals to bits in the campaign to liberate them,' said Nell, indignant. 'Some of those pictures in the museum were terrible. Towns and villages reduced to rubble. And by the Allies! We were supposed to be setting them free, not killing them. I had no idea.'

'War is a messy business, I am sorry to say.'

'Oh God, I'm sorry. I've done it again, haven't I?'

'You have done what, *habibti*?'

'Been thoughtless and naive. I'm sorry. Was it . . . did your home . . . is it like that in Gaza?'

'Yes. At times. And I fear that improvements in the technology since the Second World War have not made the experience any

192

more enjoyable for the civilian population,' he said. 'But come, we are here today, safe and well. Better still, you are holding my hand and the sun is shining. That is very excellent. Let us see if we can find somewhere nice to eat lunch.'

It was their last full day. Nell was beginning to think she'd had enough of war, while feeling ashamed of herself for voicing such a thought, even in her head. Particularly given everything that George had told her about his life in Gaza. For him, conflict was a recent memory and an ever-present threat, not distant history. Meanwhile, they'd visited the Mont-Ormel Memorial, high above the Dives valley, which commemorated the encirclement of 100,000 Germans in the Falaise-Chambois Pocket. It had become apparent that the final fight to end the Battle for Normandy was gory in the extreme. Indeed, Eisenhower called it 'one of the greatest killing fields in the War'. The outcome was decisive but bloody. Edward was lucky to escape with his life.

They'd been to the highly informative Visitor Center at the Normandy American Cemetery on Omaha Beach. They'd walked on three of the other beaches, too: Sword and Gold, where the British landed, and, sandwiched between them, Juno, targeted by the Canadians. For all the memorials, for all the cemeteries, for all her knowledge that an estimated 10,000 Allied troops died on D-Day alone, today the beaches were just beaches. Innocent swathes of golden sand, overlooked by pretty villas and elegant hotels and blue-and-white beach huts. For miles along the coast the shoreline stretched invitingly, beckoning families with buckets and spades to enjoy the spotless sand and gentle waves.

Meanwhile, they'd turned up precisely nothing in their search for Hélène. No one in the hotels or shops recognized the photographs. Their own landlady even seemed irritated by the enquiry. The War, she told them, was a very long time ago, and the people of Luc-sur-Mer would most definitely like to put it behind them.

'Considering her income depends on battlefield visitors, you'd think she'd be more helpful,' said Nell, indicating the bunting behind the reception desk, which was made up of alternating British, American and Canadian flags.

There was a brief flurry of excitement when, true to her word, Camille from the Office de Tourisme phoned to tell them that her Oncle Henri would be happy to meet them. But when they met Henri he explained he was only five during 1944, and while he remembered the tanks and the soldiers only too well, he shook his head when shown the pictures. '*Non. Je ne les connais pas*,' he said. He didn't recognize them. Camille added that she had emailed the pictures to her history *prof* and that his response had been the same. She agreed to put her copies of the photographs on her noticeboard, in the hope that someone might come in who recognized the faces, but Nell could tell that she was making the offer as a kindness, rather than because she actually believed it would bear fruit.

Over a lazy breakfast, they debated how to spend the day. They had got up late – Nell hadn't bothered with her run – and were sitting close to each other at the round table in the corner with the sea view that they had commandeered as their own. It was almost too small to accommodate two, but the position was unrivalled. Besides, Nell had no complaints about being snug with George.

'We're not going to find her, are we?' said Nell.

'It looks that way.' George refilled her coffee cup, and took her hand. 'I'm sorry, *habibti*. It was always a risk.'

'I know. You warned me. It's like looking for a needle in a haystack.'

'And why exactly would you look for a needle in a haystack? Is that a usual place for storing needles in your country?'

Nell laughed. 'I've no idea. But you're quite right. It's a daft expression. Like "pigs might fly". I mean, it's an impossible search.'

'In my country, we are not so keen on pig-related idioms. Instead we might say, we'll find her "when salt glows".'

'I like that one!'

'Me too. So . . . what next? We have only today.'

Nell pondered. The sun was shining, as it had every day since they'd arrived. They had woken up to another perfect June day: blue sky, a few clouds scudding gently in the sea breeze. She felt unbelievably, unrecognizably better. She had missed her run and, remarkably, the sky hadn't fallen on her head. 'I think we should give ourselves a holiday,' she said. 'I think we probably both need a break. Why don't we just amble along the beach? For all the history, there's something so . . . healing about being by the sea. We could swim? Maybe find some lunch in the next village along?'

'That sounds perfect to me,' said George. His face was radiant.

'*What*? What have I said?'

George laughed with pleasure. 'Maybe it is more what you have *not* said. It is almost not-a-plan. And you seem so much happier. If I may say so. I'm sorry we have not solved your mystery. But I'm glad you do not seem heartbroken.'

'In my heart of hearts, I'd still like to find her,' said Nell. 'But I'm reconciled to that not happening. At least not on this trip. And I feel closer to Edward, somehow. I've certainly got more of an idea of his world. Maybe your world, too.'

'Not a wasted journey, then?' He met her eye with such a look of intensity that every nerve ending on Nell's skin quivered. She felt herself colour.

'Oh no,' she said, and leaned in to kiss his cheek. 'Quite the opposite.'

26
Edward, July 1944

Edward is lying in a ditch behind a hedge. He and Hillman were forced to the ground by Major Robinson, who took charge of the battalion when the CO died in a mortar attack. Robinson cannot be more than twenty-five: a decent and kind young man who was training for the law when he was called up. He is surely more suited to the life of a country solicitor than a soldier in this hellhole. Robinson has seen friend after friend fall beside him since the beginning of the Battle for Normandy. Now his best friend from school, Captain Stuart Franklin, is lying injured, possibly dead, on the other side of the bocage.

Edward has made it his unfailing mission to trace the dead and rescue the wounded. He and Hillman have become quite a double act here. Since Stevens's disappearance – Edward fears his is one of the unrecognizably grotesque and unidentifiable bodies that wash up daily on the shore – Hillman has become his batman. And a good thing, too. A fine man. Not that Stevens is really replaceable. But he and Hillman have become each other's talisman.

Although unfailingly polite, Robinson is clearly infuriated by their persistence. It can't be easy for him to remonstrate with them when he is a decade younger. In general Edward finds it easier not to ask anyone's permission beforehand. Now Robinson is in a double bind because the wounded man they are trying to rescue is Franklin. Robinson has left them to it with strict instructions not to do anything stupid.

The burnt-out tank sits in a field between the two hedge-rows. Edward is reasonably confident there are no Germans behind the other hedgerow. He can just see a man lying in the grass. If it really is Franklin – and that is surely his blond hair – he can't bear to leave him there in the open, alive or dead. After half an hour without a squeak from the enemy, he decides it is safe to crawl his way across the gap, using the remains of the tank as cover. He creeps forward, inch by inch, until he is close enough to see that it is indeed Franklin. And that he is as dead as a doornail. *In the midst of life we are in death.* He curses: Franklin, like Robinson, was a good and upright man. Surely he deserved to go home. Deserved a life, a family, a future. All Edward can do now is retrieve his body, give him a Christian funeral and break the news as gently as possible to Robinson.

At least this is one fewer body to retrieve from the tank itself. Edward has made it a rule not to allow any of the tank crew to have anything to do with the recovery of bodies. He always does it himself, with Hillman's help. It's an unpleasant job at the best of times: when a tank has been on fire there's sometimes very little to retrieve. Sometimes the remains are welded together. The only sure way to identify body parts is to rake through the bottom of the tank and find the pelvic bones. It is then more or less possible to work out who the people were – commander, gunner, operator, driver or co-driver – by their position in the tank. Edward always emerges thick with soot and sick to his stomach. But it is better, surely it is better, that none of the young men who must enter a tank the next day witnesses the evidence of such a terrible death.

It is a month since D-Day. The Battle for Normandy continues and so does the horror. Bombs fall, anti-aircraft weapons blast, shells explode and tanks crash through the countryside crushing everything in their path. The landscape is scarred beyond belief: houses, farms, churches, entire villages lie in rubble. The smell of cordite and burning flesh is all pervasive. Bodies are still washing up on the shore. These days they are putrefying, grossly swollen, increasingly unrecognizable. They could be male or female, soldiers or civilians, any nationality. Who knows how many Germans Edward has laid to rest.

Daily, the men in his care are wounded, and Edward must comfort them in their dying. Daily, men die, and Edward must bury them. He must write to their families, assuring them of courage shown and a price worth paying. He must sort out their personal effects, removing pornography or anything else that a grieving family would prefer not to see, parcel them up and send them home. He must hold services in the field when he least feels like it, asking God's blessing on this never-ending fight, whether or not he believes the words he speaks. And how can he believe in a benign God? Or any God at all, after having witnessed all he has witnessed? Yet he has no choice. He must do his duty, boost morale. Keep on keeping on.

Several times a day he is overwhelmed by the futility of what he is doing. He clings on to the slender thread of hope that in the face of abomination, his good conduct somehow tips the scales in favour of humanity. He's given up writing to Edith because it is impossible to put his experience into words. Instead he finds himself composing imaginary letters to his father. *Fearful show over here, Papa*, he writes in his head. *Boys are being blasted to bits. Still, mustn't grumble. Here to serve King and country. We'll soon show Jerry who's boss.* Meanwhile he must keep his own demons at bay as he hears of the death of fellow chaplains: young George Parry, who served with the Parachute Regiment, fell on D-Day itself; his colleague, George Kay, the day after. To think how disappointed Edward had been not to make the Paras! No doubt there are others. But no one is safe; only last week he heard that Sanders – a chap he and Evans chummed up with at Church Stowe – died after coming off his motorbike. A wretched motorbike accident. There's even a story doing the rounds that some poor fellow with one of the Scots regiments misjudged his sermon to the troops the day before D-Day, had a strip torn off him by the CO and promptly did away with himself in mortification. Shocking! And from home comes the news that the Deputy Assistant Chaplain-General and 120 members of his congregation were killed when a V-1 flying bomb destroyed the Guards Chapel in London. Of course he knows death is indiscriminate in war, but all this is agonizingly close to home.

This war is relentless, unremitting, and he is exhausted. Numb, in fact, unable to feel any more. Sunday by Sunday he takes services, but he is aware he speaks the words by rote. He has no sense of God's presence; he fears his faith is slipping away like sand through fingers. He thinks, yet again, of Kipling. His father's slender parting gift to him is his constant companion.

> If you can force your heart and nerve and sinew
> To serve your turn long after they are gone,
> And so hold on when there is nothing in you
> Except the Will which says to them: 'Hold on!'

He's not at all sure he can hold on.

The only comfort he has these days is in the few snatched hours he spends with the Duvals. Hélène has finally abandoned her increasingly frustrated attempts to reach her own hospital in Caen; the matron has sent instructions that she should continue her work in the field hospital. Edward wonders if Johnson has pulled strings. Caen meanwhile is under almost constant bombardment. Reports suggest that the Allies are in danger of destroying the very city they are supposed to be liberating. Six thousand people are rumoured to have been killed, and another 6,000 are hiding in tunnels in the Saint-Etienne part of the city. At least three of Hélène's fellow trainee nurses have died. She can hardly bear to talk about it.

Edward's unit is now stationed in a seaside hotel at Lion-sur-Mer, not far from the site of the original FDS. There is sporadic bombing at night, but Lion is out of range of the worst of the shelling. The burial site at Hermanville has now been cleared of mines, so he has no real need to visit the Duval farm. Nonetheless Edward has taken to slipping away whenever he can in the evenings. He is only too glad to avoid the watchful eye of the proprietor, Madame Valentin, who bitterly resents the requisition of her hotel.

Now he picks his way across the farmyard, scattering chickens, averting his eyes from the burnt-out barn and the crater where the outhouse used to stand. The Duvals were lucky: they lost three cows, a couple of hens, the barn and everything in it, but the damage to the farmhouse extended only to shattered window panes and half a dozen broken roof tiles. The kitchen, darkened as it is by the boarded-up windows, offers a reminder of a different life. The room is sparsely furnished, and boasts little more than an enamel-topped table and four mismatched chairs. There is a heartening smell of onions and dried herbs, bunches of which are fastened to the beams. Three large copper pans hang above the range, and an earthenware bowl of eggs sits on the sideboard.

Somehow the Duvals have managed to keep a supply of rough cider and Calvados throughout the War and they are more than happy to share it with him. At Edward's appearance, Hélène's father, Auguste, fetches a bottle from the cellar where they now sleep out of fear of more bombing. In spite of the carnage, Auguste persists in his incomprehensible gratitude: it seems that he views Edward as his personal saviour, bringing rescue to an abandoned people. The three of them sit around the table, making stilted conversation about the weather. Edward is too tired to care; he takes simple comfort from the domestic setting. It is a world away from the horrors outside. With his last sip, Auguste raises a misty-eyed toast, drains his glass and shambles off outside.

When her father leaves, the atmosphere shifts. 'It is a little easier if we can speak English, no?' says Hélène with a shy smile. It emerges that her mother taught English at the lycée in Caen. 'Ma mère would be glad to think I have not altogether forgotten my English language.'

'Your English is very good indeed,' says Edward. 'You must have studied hard. Your mother . . . she's no longer with you?' He is aware he is speaking awkwardly, enunciating his words with care.

'She went to Cherbourg to visit her aunt one day in 1940. Tante Louise had been ill. She lives alone. They were very close, and Maman insisted she must go. It was summer, and she was wearing her favourite blue dress, one my father gave her before the War. She never came home.'

Edward is appalled. While he was kicking his heels in Birmingham, the Germans were intent on crushing France and the Low Countries. He feels a savage, hot anger that he could not have prevented this tragedy. He knows his response is irrational, surrounded as they are by so much death, but Hélène's loss hits him like a blow to the solar plexus. After weeks of dumb horror, it is almost a relief to feel an emotion, even if it is empty rage.

His face must betray something. Hélène shrugs her shoulders. '*C'est la guerre.* That's the war for you.'

'What happened?' he asks after a moment.

Hélène holds herself completely still as she answers. 'We do not know. We know only that the Germans dropped fifteen tonnes of bombs on Cherbourg on the ninth and tenth of June. My aunt lives near the port because her husband used to work at the docks. She tells us Maman never arrived. There was no trace. Nothing.'

'The Fall of France,' says Edward, remembering. 'I'm sorry. So very sorry.'

'It was indeed a great sadness for our family,' says Hélène formally. The words sound rehearsed. 'And a *catastrophe* for our nation,' she adds with more passion. 'France has lost everything. Her sense of identity, her pride, her dignity. Until now, perhaps.'

'Perhaps,' says Edward. 'But I am very much afraid it may yet get worse before it gets better.'

At that moment there is a noise of footsteps, and a door in the corner Edward had imagined was a cupboard opens to reveal a narrow staircase. A young man with tousled black hair and an untucked and dirty shirt appears in the kitchen. He is unshaven and still half asleep. He looks up, startled at the sight of a stranger.

'*Merde!*' he mutters, his eyes darting anxiously around the room.

'*Jacques! C'est bon. C'est un copain.*' A friend. Hélène walks over to her brother, turning her back to Edward as she does so. He hears her murmuring something in a low voice, but can't pick out the words. Jacques fills a glass with water from the pitcher on the sideboard, nods curtly at Edward, and leaves the way he came.

'*Désolée,*' says Hélène. 'My brother, Jacques. He . . . he works at night, so he sleeps at strange times.' She avoids his eye. 'Another drink, perhaps?'

Edward holds out his glass. He does not want to leave. 'He's very like you,' he says. 'The same remarkable eyes. A mirror image – do you know that phrase?'

'*Bien sûr.* Of course.' She refills his glass, pouring a little too fast, so that a few drops of the precious spirit spill over the edge.

'Who is older? Or are you twins, perhaps?'

'Not twins. I am older, by one and a half years. He is seventeen. And now, perhaps . . . if you will excuse me?' She may have refilled his glass, but she wants him to go, Edward realizes. He stands abruptly, so that his chair scrapes noisily on the tiled floor.

'Ah, indeed. You must be tired. I am sorry if I have stayed too long. *Bonne nuit.*'

Edward walks back across the fields to the hotel, navigating by the stars. *The boy*, he thinks. *So young.* It doesn't take much imagination to work out what sort of work is keeping Jacques from his bed at night. The Maquis have been hard at work in Normandy for months. According to Robinson, great efforts are being made to formalize the disparate operational units that make up the Résistance into a single body in order to maximize their effectiveness. The new French Forces of the Interior are on the point of becoming an official part of the French Army.

Before the invasion, it was all about reconnaissance. Now the FFI are playing merry hell with German lines of communication and doing a great deal to hamper Rommel's response to the arrival of the Allies. Presumably Jacques is involved in derailing trains or blowing up ammunition stores. It's highly

202

risky work, and if the reports are to be believed, the Germans have a nasty habit of inflicting reprisals on whichever innocent civilians happen to be nearby. Whole villages have been executed in retaliation, women and children too. He thinks suddenly of his quiverful, of Edith. His family seems a thousand miles away. He struggles to conjure their faces. A blade of fear for them slices into him. He can only hope they are safe. Not true; he can pray, for what it's worth. He will pray they are safe.

Edward's billet is in sight. The night is warm, he notes. Or perhaps that is the Calvados coursing through his veins. He can hear the familiar hiss of shelling in the distance, but the guns are quieter tonight than sometimes. He knows he should watch his step, but by now he is so weary, it is all he can do to put one foot in front of the other.

27
Nell, June 2016

The morning passed entirely pleasurably. 'Left or right?' asked Nell as they left the hotel, determined to prove her spontaneity. 'Your choice.'

'Right,' said George. 'Into the wind this way, and then the way home will be easier if we've had a good lunch.'

'Goodness! How far are you planning to take us?'

'I am not planning at all,' said George. 'We go where the mood takes us.'

Later, they swam. The water was warm and the surf gentle. Nell struck out from the shore with long, slow front-crawl strokes, enjoying the sensation of the waves caressing her. She had no target of lengths to swim or calories to burn. She would not think of soldiers, weighed down by their heavy uniforms, striding through the surf to the shore. She would put aside the killing fields. She simply immersed herself in the joyful physicality of the present moment. One arm after the other, over her head, as she ploughed through the water.

When they decided it was lunchtime, they were in the village of Lion-sur-Mer. The architecture along the seafront was the usual mix of faded grandeur and ridiculously pompous, turreted and timbered holiday homes. There was an odd sort of viewing tower, leading off the promenade. At Nell's insistence, George ran up the steps and posed for a photo. The beach was almost deserted, apart from an immaculately dressed grandmother with a small white dog and a child in a pushchair, and in the distance, a couple of riders on horseback. George spotted an octagonal café, almost on the seafront, with pretty blond wooden tables and pale blue chairs. They took a table outside and ordered moules frites and a carafe of rosé. Nell unloaded her bag on to the table and searched for a comb to run through her salty hair, and George teased her companionably when he discovered that, for all her talk of taking a break, she was still carrying a map, the brochure on the battlefields Camille had given her, and the photographs.

'What else would you expect?' she countered, raising her glass to his. 'I'm prepared for all eventualities. *Santé!*'

It was while they were drinking coffee and contemplating the afternoon ahead that the proprietor shuffled over to their table to make sure they had enjoyed their lunch. He was seventy-ish and almost completely bald, with the weathered skin of a man who had spent his life by the sea. He exuded bonhomie. While he and George exchanged pleasantries about the fine weather, Nell reached into her bag for her purse. *Why not?* She took out the photographs. '*Excusez-moi, monsieur . . .*' she began.

'*Bon dieu!*' The old man gave a startled cry. He picked up the photo of mother and baby. '*C'est ma mère! Comment . . .?*'

Even Nell's French extended this far. She almost jumped out of her seat with excitement. 'Your mother! Hélène's your mother? You're Louis Edouard?'

George put a hand on her arm, but the old man replied, '*Non, non, non! Je suis Pierre. Louis est mon frère.*' My brother.

This was followed by a torrent of questions. Who were they and what were they doing in France? How did they come to have the photograph? The very same one had hung on the salon wall throughout his childhood. Nell more or less followed his drift – she understood more French than she spoke – but her mind was buzzing and she couldn't begin to form a coherent reply.

'George . . .' she implored, and he took control. Speaking slowly, for her benefit, he explained that Nell's grandfather served in Normandy in the War and they were here to trace his movements. They believed Hélène might have been a friend or a colleague. Did Pierre perhaps recognize the man in the other picture? Or the farmhouse?

'*Bien sûr*,' said Pierre, picking up the second photo. Of course! The house was the family home, where his mother grew up. Pierre's own son farmed the land today. It was *à quelques pas*, just a stone's throw, from where they were sitting. He squinted at the picture. The man, as far as he could tell, he had never seen before in his life.

'Louis Edouard . . .' ventured Nell. '*Il est en vie?* Is he alive?'

'*Bien sûr!*' Pierre had seen him only yesterday. He lived in Caen, where he used to run a hardware store, though of course he retired a long time ago. Unlike Pierre, who planned to work till he dropped.

'*Et . . . Hélène? Votre mère?*'

'*Mais oui.*' She lived with Pierre's sister Sandrine, up the road in Luc-sur-Mer.

'Luc-sur-Mer!' said Nell to George in disbelief. 'She's been right there all along! Can you ask him . . . can we meet her?'

George put the request to Pierre. Nell would like to meet anyone who knew her grandfather, he explained. Might it be possible to visit Hélène?

Pierre sucked the air between his teeth. He could ask her, certainly. But they needed to understand that she was very old and a little forgetful. She also suffered from *dégénérescence maculaire*, so had problems with her sight. He'd need to check with his sister, see what she thought. Tomorrow was his day off, so he would put it to her then.

George explained that tomorrow was too late, as they would be on their way back to England. He and Pierre exchanged a few more words, and then Pierre excused himself, took out his phone and stepped a few yards away to make a call.

'We could always stay,' said Nell.

George shook his head. 'I need to get back. It has been a wonderful interlude, but I must be on that boat. I have classes to attend.'

'An interlude?'

'More than that. A precious gift, spending time with you. But look, we have found Hélène! Just when we stopped looking.'

A little bit like love. The thought crept up on Nell. 'If only she'll see us!' she added quickly, as if George might read her mind.

'I am quite hopeful,' said George. 'He was most friendly to us.'

'Well, I'm scared! What if she has a secret she's never told her family? What if she's terribly offended? Or angry with us? Or can't remember? I don't think I could bear it.'

'*Habibti*, let us do away with all these "what ifs". Let us wait and see. Besides, I do not think a mother forgets her baby.'

At that moment Pierre reappeared at their table. '*Tout est arrangé*,' he said. It was all arranged. He had spoken to his sister, and Hélène was having a good day. If they could hang on for an hour or so till he'd finished with lunch, he would take them to meet her himself.

28
Hope, July 1997

Even when Maurice was only halfway down the garden Hope knew that something truly hideous had happened. She was dimly aware that the doorbell had rung, but ignored it because she was busy picking gooseberries. It was always a fight to outwit the birds and much as she wanted to leave them another day or two to swell to the point of bursting, she wasn't going to risk it.

Now what? I suppose he's lost his glasses again, she thought at first when he called her name. The age difference that had been part of the appeal when they'd first met at Greenham – Maurice was a fully fledged grown-up, whereas Per had appeared to have ground to a halt in adolescence – was becoming trying. Seventy seemed much older than sixty. A yoga-trim sixty, that is to say. For all his qualities, dear old Maurice had never been persuaded to take up yoga, more's the pity. Hope had long been convinced that yoga was as good for the brain as it was for the body. But you couldn't teach an old dog new tricks, as they say.

Seconds later, he was in full view and she knew something was seriously wrong. The Tupperware slipped from her hands and the gooseberries cascaded on to the grass as she ran to meet him. *What a waste,* she remembered thinking afterwards. *No jam.*

'Will?' she breathed, and almost fell into Maurice's arms as he confirmed that, yes, it was Will, and no, it wasn't good news. The police were here. They thought they'd found him.

The police, one man, one woman, both ridiculously young, were very kind. They told her that a body of a man matching Will's description had been found on the M1, somewhere

208

north of Luton. The working assumption was that he'd jumped from a bridge. Formal identification was to follow, but he was carrying a driver's licence, an out-of-date bank card and a letter from his sister, so Hope should know that the police regarded it as ninety-nine per cent certain. They didn't advise seeing his body, because it would be distressing. There would be more information after the post-mortem, and then they could start thinking about the funeral arrangements.

She saw that Maurice was taking notes, the reporter's habit of a lifetime. Was he going to file a news report, for heaven's sake? Of course not. He was recording the facts, so that they would have a note for later. It ought, she thought, to be a relief, if it really was Will. He'd been missing for two years, four months and three days now. At least, it was two years, four months and three days since they'd reported his disappearance to the police. And it felt as if she'd been holding her breath for two years, four months and three days. Waiting and wondering, staring out of the window, kidding herself that one day he would walk through the door and everything would be fine. But in the event, relief didn't come into it. Accepting his death meant abandoning the tiny splinter of hope that she'd been clinging on to all that time. It couldn't ever be a relief to know that your son was dead and it might be your fault. That, for at least the last six years of his life, he had been mentally ill, seriously disturbed. Around half that time, he was homeless and destitute. And that you did nothing, absolutely nothing to help. Worse still, that you ignored his wayward behaviour, his volatile mood swings, and refused to believe there was anything wrong. Even though the evidence was right before your eyes.

That's what Buttercup would say, anyway. Not Buttercup. She was Nell, these days, just as Willow was Will. Used to be Will. As she was Mum, when all she'd ever wanted was for her children to call her Hope. To be her friends and equals. Oh God! Someone needed to let Nell know. And she couldn't. Not possibly. Maurice would have to do it. No; she'd ask the police. It was their job.

209

That was a big mistake. Nell was incensed.

'How *could* you?' she stormed, before she was even through the front door. 'How could you leave it to the police to tell me something like that? I had an exam today, you know. Finals. My final final, as it happens. Not that you'd know or care! I came out of the exam hall and there they were, in a squad car, waiting for me. How could you be such a *coward*?'

'Nell, please!' said Maurice. 'Come in, chicken. Let me put the kettle on. Your mother's just as shocked and upset as you are.'

'Shocked' didn't come close. Hope was reeling, giddy from the onslaught of her daughter's rage. The last words Hope had spoken to her father – didn't she call him a coward? – echoed down the years. Her head whirled in such confusion that she thought she was going to pass out. She reached out to steady herself on the newel post at the foot of the stairs.

'Nell, I—'

'You *what*? What are you going to say that could *possibly* make any of this any better, Mum? I told you, didn't I? How many times did I *tell* you that Will was sick? That he needed help? Proper, professional help, not hand-outs of cash when you thought Maurice wasn't looking. Oh, no! You laughed your superior laugh and told me he was just *artistic* and I was too conventional for my own good. I suppose you think it's *boring* to go to the doctor? Is living in a ditch your idea of artistic? No! It's all, "Oh my son, he's so creative he's thrown himself off a motorway bridge!"'

Hope had never seen her daughter so angry. She was shouting, almost spitting with scorn and fury. 'You know something else, Mum? I've been doing some research in the university library. Do you know what they're saying? Doctors are beginning to make a link between cannabis use and mental illness. Schizophrenia, specifically. If you hadn't been so bloody *lax* . . . so *permissive*, do you realize Will would probably be here today?'

Nell's voice cracked at the sound of his name. She took a huge gulp of breath, and now she was sobbing, howling in pain.

'You didn't even notice when he went AWOL, for fuck's sake! It was me who had to alert the police!'

'Darling . . .' Hope ventured out a hand. Nell batted her away as if she was an annoying insect, and stalked upstairs. They heard her crashing about in her old bedroom, then she crossed the landing to Will's. Ten minutes later she appeared with a couple of carrier bags stuffed with belongings. Ignoring her mother, she turned to Maurice.

'I'm off now. You can let me know when the funeral is. Assuming there will be a proper, dignified funeral and not some bloody tree-hugging ceremony. Then that's it. I'm done here. It's over and out.'

29
Nell, June 2016

Nell couldn't sit still. A whole hour to fill! For something to do, she flipped through Camille's booklet and discovered that there was another British cemetery a mile or so inland from the seafront, at Hermanville-sur-Mer. She suggested that they walk there to fill in the time. 'I don't know how it worked, but I'd have thought there's quite a chance that a lot of the men who died on Sword Beach are buried there,' she said. 'Maybe Edward even conducted some of the funerals.'

They told Pierre they would be back later, and made their way to the cemetery. Nothing like as grand as the Bayeux one, it was a field, more or a less, poorly signed and down a narrow little lane. There was a layby with parking for just a couple of cars. Clearly this wasn't on the coach party route. Nonetheless, the explanatory board – in French only, which seemed surprising for a British cemetery – told them that 1,005 soldiers were buried here, most of whom died on D-Day or during the push towards Caen that followed. They wandered among the grave-stones. Again, it was beautifully laid out, immaculately kept.

'Look!' said Nell. 'A padre! THE REVD H. T. WAGG, ROYAL ARMY CHAPLAINS' DEPARTMENT. He was thirty-five – a year younger than Edward. I wonder if they knew each other?'

'It would seem likely.' George read the inscription. 'IN EVERLASTING REMEMBRANCE. GREATER LOVE THAN THIS HATH NO MAN.'

'Ninety-six chaplains died in the Second World War, twenty-one of them in Normandy. All unarmed. They weren't allowed

212

to bear arms. David at the museum told me. There's a memorial to them, somewhere back in the UK. It was unveiled by General Montgomery. And that's just the chaplains! It's the scale of the losses that I can't get my head round. It certainly puts my problems in perspective.'

'I do not think it is a competition, Nell.'

'Maybe not. But still.'

They sat on a bench in silence. 'Do you know? I think I prefer it here,' said Nell. 'I know the Bayeux Cemetery and the Omaha one are very moving, but this is more intimate. It's very peaceful. Spacious. If I'd lost someone I loved, I'd rather think of them buried in a field like this.'

'In my experience, there is rarely any choice about such things,' said George. 'It is a matter of, how do you say, expediency. Especially in the summer time, when bodies decay fast. People just do what is necessary. This is . . . well, this is a different matter.'

'But . . . beautiful, don't you think?'

George paused. 'It is beautiful, yes. Peaceful. And trust me, I am the greatest proponent of all things peaceful. But it would be a shame if this peaceful place caused any misunderstanding to the visitor.'

'What do you mean?'

'Anyone who has lived through armed conflict knows what it is really like. And trust me, it is not about straight lines and rose bushes and neatly mown grass. I am on the, how do you say, horns of a dilemma. I want to celebrate your peace . . . but I do not want anyone to forget the lessons of the past.'

Pierre drove them back to Luc-sur-Mer via the farmhouse, so that Nell could take a photo. She felt self-conscious, but Pierre assured her that his son Luc would be out in the fields, and his daughter-in-law at work in Caen.

After a moment's hesitation she asked George to stand where Edward once stood. She framed the image to replicate the original as closely as possible. Everything looked disconcertingly the same, just brighter. Colour, of course, not black-and-white. The tree was there – just taller and in full leaf. An apple tree. The house was unmistakably the same, although any damage to the roof had long since been repaired. In fact, it looked as if the roof had been retiled in the last couple of years. The pointing in the low wall was fresh, too. Behind the wall she could see a cottage garden of hollyhocks and hydrangeas. The house looked loved and for no reason she could quite put her finger on, this gladdened her.

As a result of the diversion to the farmhouse, they drew into Luc-sur-Mer from an unfamiliar angle. Pierre pulled up outside a stone house with an exterior staircase. His sister, he explained, lived upstairs, while his mother occupied the ground floor. She was *très indépendante*, he said, as he ushered them indoors through the double doors on the ground floor. The room they entered was sparsely furnished: a small table, two upright chairs, and a not particularly comfortable-looking sofa with wooden arms and a garish floral pattern. The floor was tiled, and cool after the sunshine outside.

In the corner, in a high wing-backed armchair, sat a tiny woman with a cloud of white hair. Most definitely an older version of the woman in the pictures. Spread out on a tray on her lap was a set of extra-large dominoes. She looked up from her game and greeted her son with delight. '*Pierre, mon cher! Je suis en train de gagner!*' She cackled with pleasure. Nell had the impression that this was a well-worn joke: Hélène was winning against herself in a game of solitaire.

'*Maman, tu es géniale!*' said Pierre dutifully. You're amazing. He motioned Nell and George to sit on the sofa, and pulled up one of the upright chairs next to his mother. He leaned forward, gently removed the tray to the table, and took her hand. He explained that these were the people he told her about on the phone. '*Tu te souviens?*' You remember?

'*Bien sûr que je me souviens,*' she said, with a touch of irritation. Of course she remembered. Hélène turned her head towards them, and looked them up and down. Nell couldn't tell if she looked suspicious or was simply finding it difficult to make out their faces. She and Pierre had a rapid, murmured conversation, and then she turned back to them.

'Good afternoon,' she said, in only slightly accented English. 'I understand you wish to talk to me about the old days.'

'Oh!' said Nell before she could stop herself. 'You speak English!'

'Indeed,' said Hélène. 'Thanks to my mother and the British Army.'

'They taught you?'

'When I was young, we thought that speaking English was the height of sophistication. The arrival of *les Tommies* gave us the perfect opportunity to practise.'

'And you haven't forgotten, all these years later!'

'So it would seem,' said Hélène. 'Pierre says you have some photographs. May I see?'

Nell fumbled in her bag. She still couldn't quite believe she was here, talking to Hélène. She started with the picture of Hélène with Louis. 'This was the one that Pierre recognized.'

'Ah yes! *Mon chou-chou!* He was such a good baby. Unlike his brother!' she added with a smile. Nell wasn't sure if Pierre was following the conversation. 'Pierre did not like to sleep very much. Nor did Sandrine. But Louis was *très content.*'

'And this is the other one,' said Nell. She watched Hélène's face closely as she handed over the second picture. Hélène squinted at the picture, then reached up for the lamp beside her chair. It had a flexible gooseneck, and a rectangular screen the size of an iPad. '*J'ai besoin de ma loupe,*' she said. I need my magnifier. She fiddled with it, trying to position the magnifying screen precisely over the picture. It was painfully slow to watch, but Pierre shook his head when Nell half stood up in an attempt to help.

'Ah,' she said eventually. '*J'avais oublié cette photo.*' I'd forgotten this picture. She fidgeted with the screen a little longer, and Nell began to suspect she might be playing for time. Finally, she looked up.

'It's *Edouard!*' She pronounced it the French way. 'Edouard is your father?'

'My grandfather.'

'Of course. You are far too young.'

'Pierre . . . took us to the house today. Where the photo was taken. He said it was your home?'

'I lived there until I was married.'

'And from your uniform . . . you were a nurse? How did you meet Edward?'

'I was still learning to be a nurse. But I worked with the doctors at the field hospital, because it was very near our house. I couldn't reach my own hospital in Caen because of the bombing. I was *assistante* to Dr Johnson. He said that our business was the wounded and the padre's business was the dead. But in actual fact, that was not true. Edouard cared for the living, too. He was very brave.'

'How was he brave?'

'He and another person . . . I forget his name. They were . . . *quoi? Brancardiers?*'

'Stretcher-bearers,' said George.

'Thank you. They were stretcher-bearers. Even when the enemy was firing on us. It was a very dangerous thing to do. Edouard is your father?'

'Edward is my grandfather. Was my grandfather. Though I never knew him.'

'*Elle l'a déjà dit,*' said Pierre. She already said that.

Nell felt the conversation slipping away from her. Hélène was getting confused, and Nell hadn't even mentioned the letter yet. She ploughed on. 'So Edward was brave. What else can you tell me about him?' she asked. 'I'd love to know. He looks happy, even though it's wartime. Look, he's laughing!'

'Jacques has made him laugh, *comme d'habitude,*' she said. (As usual.) She looks misty-eyed at the memory.

'Jacques?'

'My little brother. He took the photo. It was his camera. He was only a boy then. Seventeen. But they were thick as thieves, in spite of the age difference. Jacques admired Edouard, and

216

Edouard took an interest in his photography. In later life he became a *photojournaliste*.'

'So . . . there were some happy times, in spite of all the fighting?'

'There are always happy times, especially when you are young,' said Hélène. 'In wartime, life is intense. Every day is a dance with death. There was laughter as well as tears. I was very young, remember. Very romantic. Very idealistic.'

Ah, thought Nell. *Perhaps we're getting somewhere.* 'Madame, Hélène . . . when I found these photos there was a letter, too. You wrote to Edward when he was back in England. And again when Louis was born.'

'Hillman!' said Hélène unexpectedly. Nell was confused. There was a German command post not far from Sword Beach codenamed 'Hillman' by the British, alongside another they called 'Morris'. There was a picture of the concrete blockhouses in Camille's booklet. 'Were you there? Was Edward? At the German strongpoint?'

'*Non, non, non.* The second brancardier. Edouard's friend. His name was Hillman. *Un homme roux*. Red hair.'

'Oh,' said Nell. 'I see.'

'Is Edouard still alive?' Hélène's voice was wistful.

'No. He died a long time ago,' said Nell as kindly as she could. Surely Pierre explained this. 'The year I was born.'

'But he kept my letter and the photos? All that time?' Hélène's eyes were watering.

'Yes,' Nell said gently. 'But I don't think anyone in the family knew anything about them. They were in a locked drawer. I found them by accident a few weeks ago. I think he took good care of them because they were important to him.' Hélène nodded, but said nothing. Tears trickled down her lined cheeks.

'Maman,' said Pierre, and Nell thought he was about to ask them to leave, when all of a sudden Hélène rallied. She asked him to find Sandrine, ask her to make coffee for the visitors. He should take George with him. '*Je vais bien*,' she insisted. I'm fine.

The men left the room, albeit a little reluctantly on Pierre's part. Nell hoped George would reassure him that she meant Hélène no harm. When the door closed, she leaned forward and took Hélène's hands in hers.

'Hélène . . . were you very fond of each other?' This was as direct as she dared to be.

A dreamy expression came over Hélène's face. 'I was entirely in love with him,' she said. 'He was so tall and handsome and brave. And so kind to me! To my father, my family. Not all the soldiers were so *prévenants*. So considerate. I thought he was the perfect English gentleman.' She chuckled. 'I was so young and so naive! I am a little embarrassed to think of that now. But he was my first love.'

'And did he return your feelings?'

'Not in the slightest. Nor did he ever give me false hope. It took me a while to understand that his interest lay elsewhere. Later, much later, I found I had altogether misinterpreted his kindness to my family.'

'So the baby . . . Louis Edouard . . . he was nothing to do with Edward?'

Hélène laughed again, and this time it was a throaty cackle. 'You thought he was Louis' father? No! Antoine had been asking me to marry him for months. When I realized I had no chance with Edouard, I gave in. We married at once. That was not unusual in wartime.'

'Were you happy together?'

'He was a good man,' she said. She didn't meet Nell's eye, but perhaps that was her condition. 'We were blessed with three children. Now I have grandchildren, and great-children too.' She felt the fingers of Nell's left hand in her own. 'No ring? Why have you not married this fine man? My granddaughters are the same with their modern ideas. I tell them, the chance of happiness is too important to squander.'

Nell blushed. 'We hardly know each other. We only met a few weeks ago. But let's talk about you. You named your baby after Edward, and you sent him the photograph.'

Hélène paused for so long that Nell wondered if her attention had wandered again. 'That was my pride,' she said eventually. 'I knew I had been foolish, and I wanted to show him I had a new life. He wrote me a kind letter, and sent his *félicitations* for the future. He said he remembered our family with great affection, and wished us a happy life in peacetime. He was a man of honour. Always the gentleman.'

By the time the men returned – bringing Sandrine, who bustled in with a tray of tiny cups and a jug of coffee – Hélène was asleep in her chair. Sandrine, a heavy-set woman who appeared to lack Pierre's warmth, gave Nell a frosty look, as if she held her responsible for exhausting the old lady. They drank their coffee and made polite, if stilted, conversation. Sandrine gave the impression that, like their landlady, she thought the War was best forgotten. George signalled with his eyebrows that they must not outstay their welcome and stood up to leave. Their time was clearly up. Nell thanked Sandrine for the coffee, and asked her and Pierre to convey their thanks to Hélène when she woke.

Something was nagging at the back of Nell's mind. She only remembered what when it was almost time for dinner. George was in the shower, so she left a note on the bed, dimly aware that if she waited, he might try to dissuade her from a second visit.

Her hopes that she would catch Hélène alone were dashed. '*Madame . . . s'il vous plaît . . . encore un petit moment avec votre mère . . . Seulement un moment,*' she stumbled when Sandrine answered her knock at the door. Could she have just a moment with Sandrine's mother?

Fortunately, Hélène heard her voice, and called out to her daughter to show Nell in. Sandrine stood stiffly aside to allow Nell past, radiating disapproval.

'Madame Hélène . . .' she began. 'Forgive me, but there is one thing I don't understand.'

Hélène cackled again. 'Trust me, *ma petite*, I am a very old woman and there are many things I do not understand. Tell me what is troubling you.'

Nell took the letter from her bag. 'Here, at the end. You wrote, "*Je vous serai éternellement reconnaissante*. I will be eternally grateful to you." Was that . . . I don't know . . . a romantic expression? A way of thanking him for his friendship? Or was there more to it than that?'

Hélène glanced up, in Sandrine's direction, Nell thought. She was hovering in the doorway. 'Edouard . . . performed a great service to my family. He saved my brother's life.'

'What did he do?'

'*Maman! Tais-toi. Tu sais que cela te contrarie.*' Shush. You know that upsets you.

'She is wrong. It does not upset me. I think perhaps it upsets other people in the family. I have always stood by Jacques. But I do not know the answer exactly. The only person who could tell you is Jacques himself.'

During the short walk back to the Hotel de Normandie, Nell racked her brain over what to say to George. She felt her stomach knot with the old anxiety. How would she tell him? She knew he was keen to get back to Oxford, but she couldn't let the trail go cold now.

'It's the final piece of the jigsaw,' she explained, when she'd filled George in on her latest conversation with Hélène. Jacques lived in a *maison de retraite*, a care home, in Rouen. 'I really want to ask Jacques about Edward.'

'And where is this Rouen? How long would it take us to get there?'

'An hour and a half? Maybe a bit more?'

It was clearly impossible. It was almost 8 p.m. now, and they had to check in for their ferry at 7.30 the next morning.

'I have one idea,' said Nell. 'If we travel home via Calais instead of Caen, we could go to Rouen first thing in the morning. Drive on to Calais afterwards. What do you think? It's a lot further on the road, but the crossing's much shorter, so we'd still be home tomorrow night.'

George's face cleared. 'Since you are the driver, that is your decision,' he said. 'But since you mention it, I have an interest in visiting Calais.'

'Oh?'

'Yes. You've heard of the Jungle? The refugee camp? I've been reading about it in my studies. There are children, as you might expect. From war zones. And an inspiring teacher from UK has set up a school, right there in the middle of all the tents. I'd like to see for myself. It would be very excellent for my research. So I say, let's do it. If you're certain Jacques will see us?'

'Hélène promised to phone him. She says he doesn't have many visitors and would be only too pleased to see us. I think there's been some sort of family rift. I don't know why.'

'And there's no, how do you say, dragon guarding his den? No Sandrine?'

'If there is, you can always slay it,' said Nell. The tension in her stomach had dissolved. She felt lightheaded with relief. What had she been afraid of, exactly? 'Thank you so much! Can I use your laptop? I'll go and change the crossing.'

'You're going online? Are you sure?'

'I'm going online.' She was full of confidence. 'I'm fine. I can do it. Give me ten minutes, and then let's go and eat.'

30
Edward, August 1944

Edward drifts in and out of consciousness. He is in excruciating pain, which means he must be alive. From a long way away, he hears a cry, a sound that is almost animal. He realizes that it's his own voice, a primitive howl of agony from somewhere deep inside his very being.

Movement – he's hauled on to a stretcher, roughly a bit – and now he is being carried jerkily and at some speed. The motion makes him feel sick; he fears he will vomit at any moment. Above his head a familiar face swims in and out of focus. Hillman! Dear fellow! His comrade-in-arms! That's the wrong term, but he can't remember why. Hillman seems to be speaking, shouting even, but though Edward can see his lips moving, he can't make out the words. He reaches up his right hand and seizes Hillman's wrist. His arm! That's it; they're not comrades-in-arms, because they are unarmed. More words he cannot hear. A bad dream, perhaps. Edward decides it's too much effort, and closes his eyes.

When he wakes again, he is in a field hospital. The world still feels unnaturally silent, although he can see he is not alone. The ward is busy. Everything hurts, but he finds he can move his hands, his arms. His left leg, too, appears to be fine, but when he tries out the right, he experiences an explosion of pain.

Fairbairn appears at his side and says something. 'Can't hear!' says Edward.

He then moves into Edward's direct line of vision, and indicates that Edward should read his lips.

'No need to shout!' Fairbairn says, or at least that's what Edward guesses. 'You gave us a scare there, Padre! A near miss and no mistake.'

Over the next couple of days, Edward's hearing gradually returns, along with a memory of what happened. In what Monty insists will be the last push needed to defeat the Germans, the Allies have converged on the Falaise-Chambois area to the south of Caen. Edward's unit is fighting alongside the Canadians, forming the northern arm of the noose designed to strangle the enemy. The Yanks are to close in from the south, the theory being that the Germans will be trapped in a pocket. But the Germans are putting up a strong fight. Edward was in the ambulance that went out under fire to rescue his CO, Major John Wickens, and a Canadian soldier, both of whom had been wounded in the fray. On the way back, the vehicle was shelled. Wickens, the Canadian and the driver were all killed outright. Edward, unbelievably, was thrown clear in the blast and although he is badly bruised, he has otherwise escaped with a shattered kneecap, a few fragments of shrapnel in his forehead and temporary deafness.

'Know what saved your life, Padre?' Johnson has stopped by to check on the emergency surgery to Edward's knee.

'No idea,' says Edward shortly. He's deeply sorry about Wickens, and the others. What a bloody waste. And he is fretting; he must get a message to Hélène, make sure that Jacques reached his destination safely. Perhaps he can enlist Hillman's help.

Johnson hands him a small rectangular package. It's his army prayer book, wrapped in what looks like a scrap of his tunic. Embedded deep in its pages is a jagged piece of shrapnel. It looks almost theatrical, a stage prop.

'Just as well you had that in your pocket,' says Johnson. 'That particular splinter was heading straight for your heart. We'd have missed you. But the good Lord looks after his own, eh?'

With a ghost of a smile, Johnson pats Edward's shoulder. 'Brave thing you did out there, by the way. Hope the powers that be take note. But it's Blighty for you now, old man. I've patched you up, done all I can for now. Your ticket home. You'll be missed.'

'Ah. I'm grateful to you,' says Edward. 'Any news?' he adds as an afterthought.

'News?' Johnson looks momentarily blank. 'Ah, the War! That old caper. Yes. Falaise Pocket safely sealed with 50,000 horrible Huns inside. And Paris has fallen. Much rejoicing all round, by all accounts.'

Edward doesn't know whether to laugh or cry. He lets his head fall back on the pillow. He's suddenly exhausted. Bone-achingly tired. It's over, for him at least. England beckons.

31
Nell, June 2016

The Résidence Sainte-Anne was tucked behind Rouen's Gothic cathedral, immediately recognizable from the famous series of paintings by Monet. A historic exterior concealed a modernized and spacious interior. Jacques was hovering in the foyer, clearly expecting them. He was taller than his sister, badly stooped and so thin his clothes hung loose. Nell looked for a family resemblance, and noticed he had the same dark blue eyes. He greeted them warmly in French, and took them to a seating area overlooking a cobbled courtyard, the old man leaning on a walking frame for balance. He pointed out the cathedral spire, just visible over the rooftops.

'He says that your British RAF almost destroyed it during the War. He hopes we come in peace,' said George.

Nell smiled. 'Has Hélène filled him in, do you think?'

She clearly had, because at the mention of his sister's name, Jacques took out a brown paper folder which he opened to reveal a pile of black-and-white photographs. On the top was one taken outside the farmhouse, the same as the one in Nell's possession. There were half a dozen more, all taken from more or less the same spot. In all but one, Edward was posing cheerfully, while Hélène shied away from the camera. One included an older man, presumably Hélène and Jacques' father, shaking Edward's hand. There were several more pictures from the same era. Soldiers drinking from tin mugs, next to tanks. Civilians standing bewildered in the ruins of their homes. In one, a soldier leaned up against a wall in a pile of rubble, his helmet on his knee, with an expression of confused exhaustion on his face. In another, a dead man lay in a ditch. Yet another showed row on row of bodies in bags, presumably awaiting burial. A man was consulting a clipboard and giving directions to two soldiers with rolled-up sleeves, who appeared to be digging graves.

'*Ça, c'est Edouard,*' said Jacques, and looking more closely Nell found she recognized her grandfather's profile. '*Il était très scrupuleux,*' he added. He was meticulous.

Jacques was learning his craft with the camera, he went on to say, although he did not know it at the time. If it hadn't been for the War, he might never have become a *photojournaliste*. But war could be addictive; it was not necessarily good for the soul. His profession took him to Korea, to Algeria, to Vietnam. All round the world. He had experienced some terrible events but met many interesting people along the way. Seen the very worst and the very best the human spirit can offer. Someone had to capture the images, tell the story. And yes, he said in answer to a question from George, he worked in the Middle East, Lebanon mainly, in the 1980s, although he had retired before the First Intifada.

'Ask him about Edward,' said Nell. 'Please.'

Jacques looked at her. 'Of course,' he said in thickly accented English. 'You wish to know about your grandpère. Please know from me, he was a man of honour.' He returned to French, explaining that he was more comfortable in his mother tongue these days. The story came out, morsel by frustrating morsel, as she waited for George to translate. The young Jacques was in the Maquis, it emerged. He was young, hot-headed, drawn in to one of the many tiny guerrilla bands that set out to make life as difficult as possible for the Germans. They were a ragbag of farm workers, shopkeepers, artisans and students, thrown together by a determination to rid France of its hated occupying forces. Jacques signed up after his mother died, recruited by his older cousin Rémy, his father's brother's son. Her death had left him spitting with rage.

At the time of the invasion, there were as many as 3,000 insurgents in Normandy ready to play their part, and it was all a lot more organized than it had been in the early days of the Occupation. In the spring of 1944 they were working to orders from London, armed with weapons parachuted in by British Special Ops. Their task was to lay the ground for the Allied invasion and then, once the Allies had landed, to do everything in their power to hinder the arrival of German reinforcements. Senior operatives were charged with gathering intelligence, creating maps and providing data on German troop movements, but the cell Jacques was part of was concerned with blowing up railway tracks, power lines and telephone cables. Sometimes he worked with Rémy, more often alone. Rémy had his own fish to fry. There were more than a thousand acts of sabotage on or immediately after D-Day, he said with pride. He personally was responsible for the destruction of a whole tranche of phone lines and underground cables. It was part of an operation called Plan Violet. After the War, he heard that this action had tricked the Germans into using their radios for communication, with the result that their conversations were intercepted by the team in Bletchley Park.

It was exciting, but dangerous, said Jacques, made especially difficult because the Germans were ruthless when the civilian population stepped out of line and barbaric in their retribution when any maquisards were unmasked. Jacques' school friend Lucien, an expert clandestine radio operator, was arrested and executed when the Gestapo discovered the crystal radio set he'd built in his father's barn. Like Jacques, he was only seventeen. An only son! His parents were devastated. Jacques and Rémy lost count of similar stories they heard on the network. And there were the reprisals: the hanging of ninety-nine people selected at random in Tulle on 9 June, the annihilation of the town of Oradour-sur-Glane the day after. They found out later that a massacre had taken place right on their doorstep, in Caen. The Gestapo executed at least eighty-seven members of the Résistance, communists and political prisoners, held in the *maison d'arrêt* on D-Day itself. It seemed the Germans became ever more violent as they were forced into retreat.

In the days and weeks after the invasion, Edward visited the farmhouse on a number of occasions. He was courteous to Hélène, and kind to their father, helping him patch up the roof when it was damaged in the bombing. He took a keen interest in the young Jacques, and encouraged his pursuit of photography. Jacques lapped up the attention: his own father was too devastated by the loss of their mother and the daily effort of scratching a living in wartime for such conversations. Jacques confessed to Edward that after Lucien's death, he had almost given up caring. He had got away with his night-time activities so often by now that he had come to the conclusion he was immortal. But Edward had counselled against this attitude, warning him that if he was careless, he risked not only his own life but also the lives of his fellow maquisards, of his sister and father. He begged him to be more careful. And Jacques had listened. He looked up to Edward. He respected him.

Jacques broke off and cleared his throat. '*J'ai soif!*' he said. I'm thirsty. Painfully slowly, he levered himself out of his chair, shambled over to a refrigerated unit in the corner, and returned with three bottles of water, which he offered round. His hands were gnarled. With trembling fingers, he unscrewed the cap of his own bottle and drank deeply. 'Ah!' he sighed. This was harder, much harder than he thought it would be, he told them. It was a long, long time since he'd talked about it. Just once, on a hot night under the stars in Algiers, he had told his lover the story. Otherwise he'd never spoken about it.

After a pause, he cleared his throat a second time and took up the story again. There was a man in his cell – not a local man, a petty criminal, by all accounts – called Marcel. There was nothing you could put your finger on, but Jacques hadn't trusted him. He just couldn't understand how Lucien's radio had been found. It was tiny, small enough to fit in a soup can, yet powerful enough to pick up the coded broadcasts from the BBC. Marcel was one of the few people who had known of its existence. Jacques voiced his concerns to Rémy, but Rémy dismissed them. Told him to wise up. Marcel was an ugly bastard, for sure, but that didn't make him a Judas.

228

Anyway, they had a message one day from Marcel to meet on the northern outskirts of Caen. This was before the Allies had finished the job of taking the city – a far messier, more prolonged process than it was supposed to have been, and the poor bastards who lived in Caen were almost bombed into oblivion before liberation came – and everything was in mayhem. The Germans threw most of their Panzer divisions at the defence of Caen. Everything they had, basically. On the personal orders of the Führer. The rendezvous was a good hour's cycle ride away, perhaps a little more by the lanes. He and Rémy were to travel separately, and arrive in Place de la Croix by 6 p.m. But Jacques couldn't shake off the feeling there was something wrong. They always operated under cover of darkness, and it was summertime and still full daylight at 6 p.m. Besides, the Allies were more or less in control of the north of the city. What was left of it. He'd heard terrible stories about the destruction. Sure, Jacques was only a junior player in all this, but he had it on good authority that most Maquis resources were now focused on supporting the Yanks in their push down the Cotentin Peninsula towards Saint-Lô. It just didn't make sense.

At the last minute his father needed him to help move some cows. Jacques realized he would be late even if he took the main road. Looking back, he hadn't even tried to be on time. He could have argued his father down, but he'd dragged his feet. And all his instincts had been spot on: it was a trap. They'd been betrayed. Someone – Marcel, it had to be Marcel, the *connard* – had given the game away. Late as he was, Jacques was still in time to see Rémy and a couple of other men from the cell being manhandled into the back of a German truck. Jacques turned tail, abandoned his bike, and ran for his life – literally – south, into the city, on the grounds that it would be easier to hide among buildings and shops than out in the open in the bocage. He was counting on the fact that he could weave in and out of streets that were impassable to vehicles thanks to the bomb damage. He was young and fit, and could outpace any soldier he'd ever met, but he was a whisker away from being caught – he

229

could hear the sound of pounding feet behind him, although the sound of his thumping heart was providing competition – when he hurtled round a corner into a scene from hell.

Jacques took another swig of his water. It was terrible, he said. An apocalypse before his eyes. He'd never seen anything like it. The city was supposed to have been evacuated, but of course that hadn't happened. Something like 15,000 inhabitants had remained, many sheltering in tunnels or cellars to escape the bombing. For weeks, without water or sanitation. The city was shrouded in a pall of smoke and dust. In the rubble lay casualties; bodies and parts of bodies. Men, women, children. Cats and dogs. The stink of decomposing flesh was appalling. And there, in the midst of it all, miraculously, was a familiar figure. Edward, and his fellow stretcher-bearer, Hillman. Digging the dead and wounded out of the debris and loading them into an ambulance. Sizing up the situation in seconds, he ordered Jacques to the ground. By the time his pursuers came round the corner, Jacques was in one of the hessian sacks they were using now the body bags had run out.

The last thing Jacques heard was Edward shouting at the German soldiers, 'Can't you see my collar, you stupid buggers?' And then he was summarily bundled into the back of the ambulance on top of a pile of dead bodies, and the doors slammed shut with a thud. The vehicle stuttered into jerky forward movement, and he lay as still as he could, given that he was still gasping for breath from his run and gagging from the stench of death, as the ambulance crawled out of the ruined city. That was the end of the Résistance for him. Anyway, it was all over bar the shouting by then. By the end of the summer, the Germans had collapsed like dominoes. Edward must have put in a word with someone or other because, before he knew it, Jacques was sent away to sit out the rest of the War with cousins of his mother's in Brittany. Probably not necessary, because nothing was ever heard of Marcel after that.

There was a long pause. '*Et votre cousin . . . Rémy?*' asked Nell.

Jacques shook his head sadly. They never even found his body. Worse still, the fact that Jacques had mysteriously missed the rendezvous and was promptly shipped off for the duration meant only one thing as far as the wider family were concerned. What else, other than that Jacques had been the one to betray the cell to the Gestapo?

At a murmur from Nell, George asked him if this was the reason for the rift in the family. Unexpectedly, Jacques smiled and shrugged his shoulders. Maybe, he said. It was all such a long time ago, but memories were long, too. Mind you, most of the people involved were dead now. Those who lived on had grown up knowing simply that Cousin Jacques was a bad lot. He probably hadn't helped himself by spending all but a tiny fraction of his working life overseas. When he retired, he was given to understand that Tariq, the man he'd shared his life with for thirty-four years, would not be welcome at family gatherings, so he stayed away. Once you'd done that for a while, it became ever harder to go home. Hélène had always stayed loyal – they spoke every Sunday on the telephone – but, in truth, he hardly knew the younger generation. Sad, really. He was on his own.

Nell and George had their first proper argument in the bowels of the ferry. It had been an emotional day; first, the meeting with Jacques, and then the flying visit to the Jungle. They'd been pushed for time in the end, once they'd talked their way into the camp, but what they'd seen was simultaneously heart-breaking and inspirational. The camp was a chaotic, muddy sprawl of tents, heaving with people of every nationality, dressed in the shabbiest clothes. In the middle of the squalor, a clutch of primary school-aged children – mainly Iraqi Kurds, they found out later, and all orphans – sat on rickety benches in a shabby scout tent, learning to count in English using their fingers. They sang 'Head, shoulders, knees and toes', pointing to parts of the body, and played games to learn their letters and numbers. The children laughed and smiled, throwing themselves into every-thing on offer.

A rudimentary timetable pinned on the tent showed that the older children studied in the morning, and then did chores in the afternoon while their younger siblings took their place. 'They're all so desperate to learn,' said Charley Shapiro, the teacher from Kent who led the handful of volunteers working in the camp. 'The problem is trying to stop the kids stealing books and pens to take back to their tents, because they want to study. We haven't got enough to go round.' She sighed. 'It breaks your heart. They're just kids! They've witnessed the most terrible things, and here they are, thousands of miles from home. On their own. And our government prefers to turn its back. Treat it as our dirty little secret.'

Charley and George fell into animated discussion about the effects of trauma on learning, and they would have missed the boat had Nell not dragged George away.

'I thought you were the one in a hurry to get back to Oxford!' she said crossly, as she drove up the ramp into the ferry. The doors closed with a clunk behind them.

'I was. I am. But surely you see how very important it was for me to talk to her? That was most interesting. Most interesting! Charley Shapiro is surely a great humanitarian.' George made no effort to conceal his excitement. 'If I can only get another visa, I must go back and stay longer next time. I think I must spend more time with Charley.'

'Lucky old Charley!'

'No, Nell, lucky old you,' he said with passion. 'Lucky you because unlike those refugee children, unlike me, you have not lost everything. You have your country and your home and your job. And you have a family, if only you were not too stubborn to see that.'

'I know I've got a family! I've got Grace. And my cousins. Other people, too!'

'You're happy to spend your time with an aunt who has children and grandchildren of her own, and yet you refuse to see your own mother, who has only you? Life is too short for, how do you say, holding a grudge, Nell. Look at Jacques! Do you

232

want to be like him? All alone at the end of his life, because of a tiff no one can even remember?'

Nell burst into tears. 'You don't understand! It's not a tiff. She isn't . . . It was all . . . You can't imagine! You know, there was one good person in my life, one person I loved more than anyone else in the whole world who made me feel safe and I lost him. I tried and I tried and I tried, but I couldn't save him. And she let it happen! And now, just when I thought I had found someone special, you're going to abandon me, too. I don't think I can bear it . . .'

George looked genuinely shocked. 'Abandon you? What on earth do you mean, abandon you?'

Nell was mortified by her outburst. She sounded like a petulant child. Needy. 'I'm sorry,' she said, as briskly as she could while blowing her nose. 'I just meant I'll miss you when you go home. Horribly. We've had such a . . . a good time together. I can't imagine what it's going to be like when you leave. I'll have to keep myself busy! But I'll be back at school soon. So. All good.'

'Who said anything about leaving?' said George, taking her in his arms. 'If I go back to the Jungle, it will only be for a while. Research for my dissertation. And you could come with me. Maybe you and I could volunteer? Offer ourselves as teachers, like Charley? But trust me, *habibti*. Now I've found you, I have absolutely no intentions to go anywhere. You are my home now.'

32
Hope, July 2016

Hope looked down the garden. It was horribly overgrown and she really should do something about that, but she didn't like the thought of anyone coming in to help. Her neighbour Joan had suggested that she try Land Girls, a garden maintenance company run by a couple of Australians who'd found their way to Newbury. Girls?! From their voices, they were thirty if they were a day. Hope and her friends would never have dreamt of describing themselves as *girls*. They were grown-ups, surely: *women*. Didn't they know that they were colluding with the patriarchy? Give men an inch and they'll take a mile, for heaven's sake!

Still, it was quite a clever name. She remembered Dot-and-Ruby, back in the War. She hadn't given them a thought for decades. One of them – Dot? – married Cousin Fred when he came back from the War, but it hadn't been an easy marriage by all accounts. Fred used to wake up in the night screaming. He didn't find peacetime easy. Any more than her father had, now she thought about it. Not that he'd been a POW, for heaven's sake. Still.

And she had to admit the Land Girls had done a respectable job on Joan's garden. Since they'd trimmed that box hedge and cut back the overgrown evergreens, there was an awful lot more light in the house. And the bedding plants provided a good splash of colour, even if they were frightfully suburban. Heavens, how on earth had Hope ended up in such a respectable corner of a respectable market town? A fucking cul-de-sac, as Will had once put it so colourfully. In Royal bloody Berkshire, no less!

She'd gone to such lengths to plough her own furrow and yet she'd ended up in circumstances about as conventional as you could get.

She was well aware there were advantages. She'd never had a bean to her name, but marriage to Maurice (he wore her down eventually and, especially once her father was dead, it no longer seemed such an important battle to fight) meant financial security in old age. Alongside all the other benefits. Sex. Companionship. Support when the chips were down. All right, love. She really had loved him. The only man in her life who stayed the course. Proved his worth. And she missed him still, God, how she missed him! It had been four years since that awful crash in the bathroom had interrupted her morning Sun Salutation, and she ran upstairs to find he'd had a massive heart attack while reading *The Guardian* on the lavatory. All because he had constipation! Well, not *all* because of the constipation, but it certainly hadn't helped. For all the lentils and organic veg she'd insisted on over the years, he was clearly still straining to go, and one thing led to another. Well, you can lead a horse to water, as the saying went.

Dear old Maurice, he was eighty-five. A good innings by anyone's standards. Although it never sounded like quite such a good innings when you were nearly that age yourself. She'd be eighty next year, which seemed incredible. And it was beginning to feel as if there was no one left. Only herself to blame. She'd always been lazy about keeping in touch, and had let any number of friends trickle away like sand through her fingers. Betty, for example. How did she allow that to happen? She still heard from Nancy from time to time. She wrote when Marsha died, and they'd kept up a sporadic correspondence since. And Daff sent Christmas cards. When Crabapple folded, she went to live with her mother in Kidderminster and set up quite a successful mobile dog-grooming business, of all things. And there were one or two people Hope knew through yoga. Blaze, for example, who used to take Beginners when Hope still had her Advanced class at the community centre. They met most Wednesdays for a camomile tea. No one else, much. The Nut Shop closed decades ago. It was a coffee shop now. One of those chains.

There was Joan, of course. Joan was a friend. And Joan was a good sort. Salt of the earth, and all that, if a bit prone to offering advice. That was teachers for you, retired or not. The Land Girls being a case in point. Joan found them on the line. She was always on that ridiculous iPad of hers. Hope couldn't see what the fuss was about, really. Maurice had tried and failed to teach her how to use email. Now she was just irritated that it was all double-you, double-you, double-you this, that and the other whether you wanted to speak to your bank manager or find out when the bins would be collected. The Maliks, next door on the other side, were friendly enough, too. (Hope's attempts to converse in Hindi when they first arrived were met with blank stares. It turned out they were from Bradford.) She couldn't really complain about the neighbours.

As it happened, Joan had found out one interesting thing on the line. Her inability to distinguish faces had a name. Prosopagnosia. Face blindness. These days it was what Joan's granddaughter Maisie would call a *thing*. A diagnosable condition! Apparently, she wasn't the only person who muddled people up and couldn't remember who was who, unless they had very obvious distinguishing features like Betty and her birthmark. According to Joan, Hope had blanked her in town on several occasions, while being perfectly friendly over the garden fence, which set Joan off on a quest to find out if there was a logical explanation. She liked a good mystery, did Joan. Hope could tell she was bursting with pride at her success.

A disability, then. Not your fault! Hah! It would have been nice if she'd known, growing up, that she wasn't stupid, whatever anyone else said. There didn't seem to be a cure, according to the article, but it might have helped her to know. What about all those films and plays she'd sat through out of politeness, with no clue what was going on because all the characters looked the same? Think of the men she'd slept with in the Sixties because she was never quite sure if she knew them or not, and once the

236

Pill came along it seemed rude not to. Until she worked out a system: Eric's hairy hands, Larry's ponytail, Per's medallion. That frightful fedora hat darling Maurice used to wear as some sort of retro-nod towards the newspapermen of the Thirties. Maybe there was a card you could carry, a Blue Badge for the face blind, so that you wouldn't feel such a fool when you didn't recognize your child's teachers or couldn't tell who was who in the playground. Not that she'd ever been the sort of school-gate type. Easier to stay away. But there you were. You lived and learned.

As for the family . . . well, Prue was long since dead after a distinguished career in the civil service. A CBE, for heaven's sake! It was a shame neither of the parents lived to see that, surely the apogee of their hopes for their children. Although, by their lights, Faith's selfless service in India was pretty impressive, too. How dare her bloody God steal Faith's mind now? Deprive her of a well-earned retirement after all she'd done in his name? Now her letters had stopped, Hope missed her horribly, and phoned the nuns from time to time to check up on her. The answer was always the same: Sister Faith was serene, Hope must not worry. Hah! Grace and Richard and William were all busy with their worthy interests and good works and improving holidays. Their families. Grandchildren. They seemed to have made a better fist of things, somehow. Not that they hadn't had their own crosses to bear: poor William and Ruth lost their daughter to cancer a year or two back.

I might not have been much of a mother, but I bet I'd have been a better grandmother, she thought. *But I'm never going to get the chance to find out.* The loss of her children was a scar that cut deep into Hope's marrow. Over the years, she'd somehow learned to accommodate the yawning hole of their absence, but that didn't take away the pain. Not a day went by without thinking of Will. She tried to marshal her memories around the Crabapple days, when he was happiest, before he was consumed by drugs and illness and despair. Carefree, happy days. Days of laughter. When Will was untamed, a wood sprite, at one with nature.

Will-o'-the-wisp, as free as a bird. Free as she herself had always longed to be free.

As for her daughter, she hadn't seen Nell since the funeral. And that was nineteen years ago. She kept tabs on her through Grace. It pained her to go cap in hand to her sister for snippets of news, but it was better than nothing. And Grace, she had to admit, was kind. She never criticized. So Hope knew that Nell had settled in Oxford and was doing well in her career. A teacher! No surprise there, when you thought about it. Extraordinary, the way she'd always begged to go to school! She knew about Mark, and that it was over. And now, the curious news, relayed by Grace on the phone only yesterday, that Nell had taken it into her head to investigate the Meadows family history.

'Hah! What on earth for?' asked Hope.

'Searching for her roots, I suppose. Isn't that why most people do it?' replied Grace. 'After all, she can't remember her dad. And she never met Father. She probably feels a bit short on male relatives.'

'Not true,' said Hope. 'She did meet him, as it happens. The old sod. He christened her, believe it or not! Gave Nell her name. Too small to remember, of course. But still.'

She sighed and checked her watch. Nearly time to go out. She thought she probably would ask the Land Girls in, after all. To mow the grass for starters, because that was a job she hated and it really was beginning to resemble a jungle out there. Then she could reassess. See if she wanted to take it further. Meanwhile, she had a workshop to attend. She had recently discovered overtone chanting and it was the most extraordinary thing. Once you'd mastered the technique, it was a means of shaping your mouth to produce the most phenomenal harmonics. It was like shooting a beam of light through a prism to create a rainbow of sound. The overall effect was quite glorious, incredibly liberating. Some people claimed it was healing and Hope could well believe it. If she were ten years younger – well, twenty, perhaps – she'd go to Tibet or Mongolia or wherever you went and study it properly. But for now, she'd simply have to make do with Thursday afternoons at St Saviour's. The irony of having found spiritual enlightenment in her local church was one she preferred to ignore.

When Hope came home after her workshop, there was an unfamiliar red Fiat 500 parked in her drive. *Bloody cheek!* she thought, just as the driver's door opened.

'Hello . . . Mum,' said Nell.

'Nell! I . . . Heavens! I wasn't expecting you. Obviously.' Hope was almost speechless with shock. A man got out of the passenger side (beard, nice shoes). 'Goodness. This is a turn-up for the books. How . . . how are you?'

'I'm well, thanks.' Nell was suntanned, and her hair looked glossy. She appeared to be blooming. 'Actually, I haven't been very . . . At all. Long story. But. Well. Much better now, anyhow. Thanks. This is George, by the way.'

'George,' she said, with a nod in his direction. 'Cup of tea?'

Nell held up a box of tea bags. 'Brought my own. In case you still drink that nettle filth.' But she was smiling, trying to make a joke of it.

'Hah! Do you mean you're going to say no to a wholewheat prune slice, too?' ventured Hope. Not that she'd got one to offer. She hadn't baked a cake since she and Betty produced a leaden Victoria sponge in Home Economics at Longbridge Sec. Any cakes ever served in the fucking cul-de-sac were leftovers from the Nut Shop.

'Well,' she said. 'Time and tide wait for no woman. You'd better come inside.'

33
Edward, September 1975

He keeps forgetting he's supposed to be dying. He seems to have been in this bed for ever. Hard to imagine it will come to an end. He's dimly aware that he's floating in some sort of cotton-wool world, hovering between life and death. No-man's-land, perhaps. Like in the War, when no one knew quite where the battle lines lay. Until you heard an explosion or a shout of pain as some poor blighter came under fire.

He can't speak, but every now and again, he hears voices. They come and go. The murmur of one of the nurses, checking his pulse. Edith, saying a few soothing words as she strokes his hand. One of the children, maybe. Not really children. Adults, these days. Adults with their own children. Own lives. Prudence is reading aloud from the Psalms right now. 'The LORD is my shepherd; I shall not want,' he hears. 'He maketh me to lie down in green pastures.' *Ah! It's good to lie down.* He's very, very tired. *What comes next?* 'Still waters. Paths of righteousness.'

Faith is busy doing the Lord's work in India, so hasn't come to say goodbye. It's a shame, because going over to see her had been one of his retirement dreams. He wanted to go to St Thomas's, visit his parents' grave. Ah well. Otherwise, he thinks they've all been at his bedside at one time or another. Apart from Hope, that is. Even the habitual pain of her absence seems slightly subdued today. Blessed morphine. Precious spiky child! Beloved of her earthly father, as well as her heavenly one. All her life, she's fought him tooth and nail but he will not give up on her. There's always Hope, and there's always hope.

All he's ever wanted, all he's ever wanted . . . is . . . what? Impossible to say. Different things as the decades passed. To do his duty to our Lord and His Majesty the King. To keep his head, when all about were losing theirs. To un-see the abominations he had witnessed. Tamp down the memories. To be faithful to his calling. And when that faith hit the buffers . . . well, to do his best. Whatever it took to secure a future for the next generation. Sunday roast and warm beer and cricket on the village green. Peace and stability. 'A new heaven and a new earth.' Order out of chaos. Standards. Dull things, perhaps. Outmoded, certainly. *The world has changed, and left some of us behind. And now I'm leaving the world behind. We're quits.* And love. Like anyone else, he's wanted love and affection.

Now the pain is under control, dying really isn't too disagreeable. 'And God shall wipe away all tears from their eyes; and there shall be no more death, neither sorrow, nor crying, neither shall there be any more pain.'

Edith has been stalwart. Dear Edith! Estimable in all ways. Has he ever told her so? She's had a lot to put up with, one way and another. All those children. The War. Parish life, his high office. Though she enjoyed all that. Marvellous bishop's wife. Not her fault. Not her fault in the slightest that he didn't know how to love a woman. Not that he hadn't given it his best shot. Done his duty by her. Fell in love with an idea, really. Marriage to Edith had offered home and family. An Englishman's home is his castle, and his castle had been pretty much in ruins beforehand. Lonely old childhood, everyone dying like that. And school, he thinks. The dreadful Major! But Uncle Hubert did his best. Aunt Florence, too. Dear, good people.

One can't complain, in any case. He's been fed, watered and housed all his life. 'He restoreth my soul.' Thousands had it worse. A good life, on balance. Worthwhile, he hopes. Done his best with the cards he was dealt. His life saved by his bloody army prayer book, when he'd practically lost all faith out there! God's idea of a joke, presumably. Well, he's kept his side of the bargain, if the Almighty's counting.

'Yea, though I walk through the valley of the shadow of death, I will fear no evil: for thou art with me; thy rod and thy staff they comfort me.' Scripture is a comfort at the end. Familiar words, stretching across the centuries, wrapping themselves around the world. 'Scripture moveth us in sundry places.' In Egypt, Italy, France. Oxford, Birmingham, Walsall. All sundry places. Somewhere else he can't remember. On the battlefield. In the pulpit. On the factory floor. In his hospital bed.

'Thou preparest a table before me in the presence of mine enemies. Thou anointest my head with oil. My cup runneth over.' *Ah! My cup runneth over. Over, and a thousand times over.* What joy he's known! Short-lived, but exquisite. He has no idea if Jacques is alive or dead. He vowed that he would never see him again. Not keep in touch. Though he's prayed for him every single day for thirty-one years. Nor would Edith ever know. Yet Edward can see him now, his perfect youth undimmed by years. So beautiful, sublime in every way. 'My beloved spake, and said unto me, Rise up, my love, my fair one, and come away.'

Someone – Edith? – dabs a sponge on his mouth, a few drops of water on his lips. A kindness he doesn't deserve. Vinegar would be more fitting given that it is not her face but Jacques' that he longs to see as he departs this world. But it was hardly unusual for unsuitable attachments to come about in wartime. Happened all the time, the reasons self-evident. Life on the battlefield was intense, every emotion heightened. You never knew from one moment to the next if you would live or die.

And he's been as good as his word. Stayed true to his marriage vows, even when he fell headlong in love elsewhere. Kept his own bargain with God. *Just keep him safe and I'll walk away.* Heart and soul, but not body. He's been honourable in that, at least.

'Surely goodness and mercy shall follow me all the days of my life: and I will dwell in the house of the LORD for ever.'

Acknowledgements

A number of books have proved invaluable in the research for this novel. These include: *D-Day: The Battle for Normandy* by Antony Beevor (Penguin, 2014), *Voices from D-Day: Eyewitness Accounts of the Battle for Normandy*, edited by Jon E. Lewis (Robinson, 2014), *The Normandy Diary of Marie-Louise Osmont 1940–1944* (Random House, 1994), *By Tank into Normandy* by Stuart Hills (Cassell, 2003), *Chaplains at War: The Role of Clergymen during World War II* by Alan Robinson (I. B. Tauris, revised edn, 2012), *The Man Who Worked On Sundays* by Leslie Skinner (Plus Printing, 1991), *Chaplain at War* by Kenneth Oliver (Angel Press, 1986), *Thank you, Padre: Memories of World War II* edited by Joan Clifford (Chivers, 1992) and *When Daddy Came Home: How War Changed Family Life Forever* by Barry Turner and Tony Rennell (Pimlico, 1996). While I have striven for historical accuracy, this is of course a work of fiction.

I am indebted to David Blake, the curator of the Museum of Army Chaplaincy, who showed me round the museum and answered a great many questions. I'm grateful to him for putting me in touch with Jenni Crane, whose discovery of a leather suitcase in a junk shop in 2014 led her to search for its former owner, the Revd George Parry (1915–1944). Padre Parry served with the Parachute Regiment and died on D-Day aged just twenty-nine (see <http://bit.ly/2wqe2AU>).

Through Jenni, I met Dr Linda Parker, who gave me some valuable pointers. I'm also especially grateful to Jenni for introducing me to Frank Treble, who shared with me his father's unpublished papers. The Revd Harry Treble (1906–2003) was another veteran of D-Day and his adventures in Normandy were such that I very nearly got sidetracked altogether. However, Edward was calling and, while his story is quite different from Harry's, Frank generously allowed me to plunder his father's memoirs for my own purposes. Thank you, Frank.

Readers may like to know, the scholarship that brought George to Oxford does indeed exist. See <www.britishcouncil.ps/en/study-uk/scholarship/gaza-oxford-brookes> for more information.

My thanks to those who kindly read parts or all of my manuscript while it was still in draft and provided invaluable feedback: Nicholas Edwards, Tabitha Gilchrist, Imogen Phillips, John Pritchard and Wendy Robins. Thank you to Aude Pasquier for improving my French; to John Raymond for checking my Italian; to Alison Barr and Amy Carothers at Marylebone House for championing the book; and to readers of *Knowing Anna* who encouraged me to keep writing. As always too, I am indebted to my patient companions on the journey – Ben, Jack and Imogen Phillips.